'If poetry was the supreme literary form of the First World War then, as if in riposte, in the Second World War, the English novel came of age. This wonderful series is an exemplary reminder of that fact. Great novels were written about the Second World War and we should not forget them.'

WILLIAM BOYD

'It's wonderful to see these books given a new lease of life [...] classic novels from the Second World War written by those who were there, experienced the fear, anguish, pain and excitement first-hand and whose writings really do shine an incredibly vivid light onto what it was like to live and fight through that terrible conflict.'

JAMES HOLLAND, Historian, author and TV presenter

'The Imperial War Museum has performed a valuable public service by reissuing these absolutely superb novels.'

ANDREW ROBERTS, author of *Churchill: Walking with Destiny*

'A brilliant, shrewd novel about British soldiers during the phoney war of 1939-40 in France, leading up to the debacle of Dunkirk. Rhodes writes with a wonderfully dry, literate, clear-eyed style — a quietly confident masterwork.'

WILLIAM BOYD

'*Sword of Bone* by Anthony Rhodes is one of the best books to come out of the Second World War. Rhodes is a subtle observer and a superb writer. Focusing on human details and the frequent absurdity of his central character's situation, he presents an honest version of the war missing from any official account. There are no overdramatised heroics here; instead there is sympathy, frustration and dry humour. Readers will laugh out loud as a group of drunk British officers mistake the local doctor's surgery for a brothel. They will wonder how to reply when a woman asks whether she should stay with her husband or flee with their young child as the German army approaches. They will wince as a local man is condemned to almost certain death on the word of a woman with a grudge. But they will recognise the humanity in every situation Rhodes describes. *Sword of Bone* is a rare book; it is easy to read but very difficult to forget.'

JOSHUA LEVINE

SWORD
OF BONE

Anthony Rhodes

IMPERIAL WAR MUSEUMS

First published in Great Britain in 1942

First published in this format in 2021 by
IWM, Lambeth Road, London SE1 6HZ
iwm.org.uk

© The Estate of Anthony Rhodes, 2021

About the Author and Introduction
© The Trustees of the Imperial War Museum, 2021

ISBN 978-1-912423-38-5

A catalogue record for this book is available from the
British Library.

Printed and bound in Great Britain by
CPI Group (UK) Ltd, Croydon

Cover illustration by Bill Bragg
Design by Clare Skeats
Series Editor Madeleine James

About the Author

Anthony Rhodes (1916 – 2004)

ANTHONY RHODES served with the British Army in France during the so-called 'Phoney War', having been a regular army officer before that conflict. Rhodes was evacuated from Dunkirk in May 1940 and based *Sword of Bone* on these experiences. In the latter part of the war Rhodes was sent to Canada as a camouflage officer. After the conflict, he enjoyed a long academic and literary career and wrote on various subjects, including covering the 1956 Hungarian Revolution for the *Daily Telegraph* and producing well-regarded histories of the Vatican. He died in 2004.

Introduction

One of the literary legacies of the First World War was the proliferation of war novels that were published in the late 1920S and 1930s. Erich Maria Remarque's *All Quiet on the Western Front* was a bestseller and was made into a Hollywood film in 1930. In the same year Siegfried Sassoon's *Memoirs of an Infantry Officer* sold 24,000 copies. Generations of school children have grown up on a diet of Wilfred Owen's poetry and the novels of Sassoon.

Anthony Rhodes' *Sword of Bone* (first published in 1942) is very much in this tradition. Rhodes refers to Siegfried Sassoon's poetry and his dislike of staff officers in the novel, where much of the landscape is reminiscent of the earlier war, 'the land of Nevinson's paintings and Wilfred Owen's verse'. In the first few pages of the book, Rhodes notes 'we all had these "Passchendaele" notions about war in those days: it would certainly have shocked Wellington or the Duke of Cambridge or any of the Old Guard if they had been told that one day officers of a British Army at the beginning of a war would be thinking of it more as an affair of mud than of bullets'. Indeed, it could be said that *Sword of Bone* is in the much longer tradition of war literature, when for instance one of the characters, Lieutenant Stimpson, refers to writing an anti-military parody starting with Latin words *'Arma meretricesque cano'* ('I sing of arms and prostitutes') in imitation of Virgil's *Aeneid* which was originally known by its first three words: *'Arma virumque cano'* ('I sing of arms and men').

For many civilians the first year of the Second World War was little different from peacetime, with the essentials of everyday life changing little. It was nicknamed the 'Bore War' at the time, though this phase of relative inactivity (except at sea) became better known by the Americanism the 'Phoney War'. Even for soldiers, little happened apart from deployment to France. Anthony Rhodes was a regular army officer who joined a territorial unit that was part of Major General Montgomery's 3rd Division: 'During the last few days in England, which were spent in Dorset getting our final equipment and vehicles, we came into contact for the first time with the distinguished regular units who were to be our companions in the division'. The officers and soldiers in his unit have opposing views of these regulars, Stimpson commenting on a Guards officer: '"Look at the way he struts – young bantam – he thinks he's no end of a chap. Off to war, off to battle, off to glory and a DSO [Distinguished Service Order] I hope he catches his death of a chill in the trenches," he said unkindly.' Whereas Sergeant Smith 'greatly admire[s] the Brigade of Guards' but 'it was the Scottish and Irish infantry that really took his fancy'.

The majority of the book covers the period when Rhodes' division is in France before the German invasion, describing the author's own experiences in the style of a very lightly fictionalised memoir (character names, for example, are all necessarily fictional as the book was published while the war was still ongoing). Rhodes is in charge of the advance party to France, in order to find quarters for the division. He finds billeting 'an interesting, amusing, and often profitable occupation', the procedure being quite different from Britain as the French 'actually enjoy foreigners' and the 'soldiers were really welcomed in the civilian houses, the people, long accustomed to conscription, thinking of them as part and parcel of their own lives'. On the whole, relations between the French and British are presented as cordial. Rhodes gets on particularly well with his French liaison officer, Georges de Treuil who has previously been a Parisian stockbroker, 'I realised how lucky I was to get such a companion and not a dreary French schoolmaster who could talk about nothing else but *Jane Eyre*'. After billeting, Rhodes' next job is 'to purchase and distribute engineer stores for the division', what he terms the 'stores rag-and-bone man'. Most of these stores were for the important task of constructing pillboxes for the Maginot Line, the main line of defence against a German invasion. Rhodes does not even see the German enemy until after having been in France for six months.

On 9 April 1940 Hitler's armed forces invaded and quickly overwhelmed Denmark, which surrendered within the day. At the same time neutral Norway was attacked. Despite intense British naval actions in the North Sea, and Anglo-French attempts to land troops, by May Norway was largely lost. Prime Minister Neville Chamberlain came under sustained criticism for the Norway failings. Possession of Norway not only gave Germany access to much needed iron ore, it provided new airbases with which the Luftwaffe could threaten Britain.

Worse was to come. On 10 May, Germany launched its westward invasions of the Netherlands, Belgium and France. On the same day, Chamberlain, unable to retain the support of the House of Commons, resigned and Winston Churchill assumed the prime ministership. Within days, it became clear that the fighting on the Continent would be no repeat of the trench warfare of the First World War. By 20 May 1940, German troops had reached the Channel coast, cutting the Allied forces in two. Plans were hastily made to withdraw the British Expeditionary Force. As Rhodes puts it, 'Today we were, one felt, simply competitors in a sporting race to the west. Like greyhounds released as the word for the retreat was given, there was a mad surge for the only two main roads leading to Brussels.'

The latter chapters of the book detail this retreat, culminating in Rhodes' experiences at Dunkirk. By 24 May, things 'were hourly becoming what the French insisted on telling everyone they were *not* – catastrophic'. The Belgian, British armies and some French divisions were now 'crowded into a small pocket in the north of France'.

On 27 May, the colonel returns from a conference with the general to announce that a mass evacuation will take place: 'We are going to attempt something essentially British; I venture to say that only the British would dare to attempt such a hare-brained scheme. Let us only hope that it will be as successful as it was last practised – by Sir John Moore at Corunna.'

The 'miracle of Dunkirk' from 27 May to 4 June was a brilliantly improvised naval operation that extracted more than 338,000 men – 118,000 of whom were French – from the Dunkirk beaches and brought them safely back to England. Some 850 vessels, including channel steamers and fishing boats, took part in this, Operation

'Dynamo'. Rhodes' text depicts both the approach to Dunkirk ('the Grand Queue') and the evacuation from the beaches itself. He anticipates the evacuation to be a simple and orderly affair, but this is not quite borne out by events:

> *I asked them how successfully the evacuation had gone on the previous day.*
>
> *'The British ships came in to the docks but they got bombed to hell,' one of them replied. 'They all had to go out and wait till dark. I shouldn't think they'll come in at all today.'*
>
> *This was a nasty shock to those of us who had hoped to get a bath and breakfast in the town and catch a boat after it at about ten o'clock. I mentioned this to the Frenchman.*
>
> *'Breakfast,' he guffawed. 'You make me laugh. Do you really think that there are any hoteliers or tradespeople left in the town? Listen to me,' he said confidentially. 'I have just come from near Boulogne. The Germans are there. This port, Dunkirk, is the only one left in British hands, the only one from which your army can get away, do you see? Do you think the Boche is going to leave it alone? Believe me, he isn't. He's going to blast it into a ruin. And don't these people know it?' He pointed at the long line of civilians passing us on the road; they were coming away from Dunkirk. We had become so accustomed to refugees that no-one had given a thought to the direction in which they were going.*

The final pages of *Sword of Bone* outline Rhodes' experiences of the chaos of the evacuation, scenes which are depicted in vivid detail – a marked difference from the earlier stages of the book, where the main concerns are finding billets and building supplies, all rendered rather matter-of-factly:

> *'Burning mighty pretty,' said one of the men to me suddenly; he was looking south towards Dunkirk. The centre of the town was on fire; yellow flames, twice as high as the houses, licked up into the cloud above – a combination of yellow and*

black that seemed to throw off a rainbow effect, as if other colours were generated by it. Along the dunes behind us the yellow flames sometimes gave place to a dull, glowing red, where a pile of embers now marked the site of a house.

In the excitement of the queue we had ignored these fascinating colours. It was only now that I noticed the effects they produced on the sand. Looking northwards along the beaches, the sand, like a white dress in a variety show, reproduced whatever colour shone upon it. Near the burning houses it flickered red and yellow; where incendiary bombs had fallen it glowed green; and in the light of a parachute flare it had turned violet.

* * *

Both sides interpreted Dunkirk as a victory, though Churchill felt obliged to point out to the British public that 'wars are not won by evacuations'. The 'Dunkirk spirit' is often evoked at times of national crisis and the fascination of the memory of the evacuation continues to the present day, most recently in the 2017 film *Dunkirk*.

Rhodes was invalided out of the Army in 1947 having served for twelve years. He went on to write fiction, biography, and history including a well-regarded three volume history of Vatican diplomacy in the twentieth century. The novelist LP Hartley described *Sword of Bone* as 'the best and most vivid description of Dunkirk that will ever be written'. Similarly, Elizabeth Bowen thought the novel had a 'quality which differentiates literature from reporting'. This welcome reprint will bring this literary classic to the attention of another generation of readers.

Alan Jeffreys
2021

Then with what trivial weapon came to hand,
The jaw of a dead ass, his sword of bone,
A thousand foreskins fell, the flower of Palestine.

John Milton, *Samson Agonistes*

CHAPTER ONE
Soldiers of Misfortune

'THREE OF OUR officers have just got married,' said the officer who welcomed me at the mess. 'Seems like war, doesn't it?'

It was the 3rd of September 1939 and it seemed even more like war two days later when a general visited us and addressed the troops for a quarter of an hour.

'Officers and men,' he said. 'The test has come and we are at war. The enemy is strong and cunning but we can defeat him. You fellows are now going to put all your knowledge – and all your courage – and all your training to the test, the acid test – the test of war,' he said sternly. 'I know you will not fail, you are all Englishmen.'

There were two Welshmen in my section who were very offended by this, and out of the two hundred and fifty men in the company only a very small proportion had been to more than two Territorial camps, so that it was hardly fair to talk about 'all our training'; but it appeared that in spite of this we were destined to go abroad very shortly as part of a regular division. The general who had addressed us that morning was fortunately not going to command us in the field, he was merely touring the area making encouraging valedictory speeches. Our own divisional general certainly had no illusions about us or the state of our training; he ordered our major to make us work like n——.

I had arrived at St. Helens in Lancashire at ten o'clock on the morning of September the 3rd where I had been immediately ordered to change into uniform; and when war was declared an hour later I was having what I supposed would be my last drink in civilian clothes in a pub. I had travelled up from London overnight and any bitterness I felt about the war and its sordidness was intensified when I saw my new surroundings. It was drizzling when I arrived in St. Helens; beneath a dirty grey sky I found dirty grey cobbled streets and factory fog, industrial buildings and industrial people, a town enclosed by a solid wall of grimy chimneys and mountainous piles of rubble. It all seemed a very suitable comment on my future life.

Inside the mess that afternoon I met a newly joined subaltern called Stimpson.

'Cervantes did it,' I heard him say to someone.

'Did what?'

'Spent ten years as a slave in an Algerian galley and then wrote a masterpiece,' he replied.

He told me that he had been learning to paint in Paris when the war had called him away. He seemed very sad; perhaps this was not surprising, because like myself he was going to purchase stores for the British Army.

'The only difference of course is that the galley slaves were at least sitting down,' he said, 'they didn't have to stand up to their necks in mud.'

We all had these 'Passchendaele' notions about war in those days; it would certainly have shocked Wellington or the Duke of Cambridge or any of the Old Guard if they had been told that one day officers of a British Army at the beginning of a war would be thinking of it more as an affair of mud than of bullets. The prospect of living for years in a dreary ditch was repulsive and it was perhaps hardly surprising that we put undue optimism and credence in our reading of the newspaper reports.

One of these reports stated that a fleet of English aircraft had flown over Germany scattering six million propaganda pamphlets in passing; it was pointed out that there had been no opposition and that many German peasants had waved to our airmen, the writer characteristically concluding that the German A.A. gunners had disobeyed the order to open fire, and that the country was therefore bordering on a state of revolt. And then there were the equally misleading reports of interviews with enemy soldiers who had deserted across the frontier complaining that the Siegfried Line was flooded and far too wet to stay in. 'Out of this nettle danger,' although already a year out of date, was still uppermost in our minds; the equally Shakespearian notion of imitating the action of the tiger had less appeal in spite of the warnings of the more realist and, to our minds, more barbaric, politicians and journalists who were forecasting a three-year war.

When we heard of the RAF pamphlet raid most of us were certainly very hopeful about its outcome; the wishful even began thinking.

'There'll be peace in a week,' said the Quartermaster, whose name was Heddon, a man who had had 'four years in the trenches in the last war' and who had no wish to repeat it.

'There'll be no such thing,' said the Major, the youngest field-officer in the British Army, a man who was said to be on the look-out for still further promotion. 'We're going to finish the Boche off this time – good and proper too. There's nothing about your pamphlet raid reported here,' he said, tapping his copy of *The Times*. 'You shouldn't believe what you read in the gutter press.'

'Well, sir,' said Heddon whom I afterwards found to be a 'communist intellectual' of the highest order, a man of remarkable candour, 'I was born in the gutter and what's good enough for my mother is good enough for me.'

The Major, who from his birth had been a keen hunter and shooter, could find no reply to this shameful but disarming confession of plebeian birth. The Major was really our only firebrand worth speaking of. In intensity he quite easily compensated for Heddon and Stimpson who appeared only lukewarm about the war; he was not very kind to Stimpson who he knew was a painter.

'You'll go to Paris. Never fear,' he said. 'But not to paint. But never mind. You'll be able to have your Café de la Paix all right.'

To a painter with *fin de siécle*, Château Rouge notions of life, this reference to a popular café was wormwood, but Stimpson, unlike Heddon, if he had the gift had not the courage of his own repartee. Heddon was undoubtedly the chief antagonist of the Major in all political matters. He held advanced and not always limpid views; for instance he thought that by declaring war on Germany we were declaring war on Russia and, *ipso facto*, declaring war on 'progress'. He produced a copy of the *Daily Worker* to prove that all wars were imperialistic and therefore not worth fighting.

'Fancy saying that,' said Stimpson, 'and you an old soldier too.'

'That's just why I say it,' replied Heddon. We learnt later that he had left the Army in 1934 at the request of the Indian Government for founding a communist cell in Bangalore, so that his remarks, apparently inconsistent with his vocation, had some foundation in fact. Of course he held extreme views, but I found the beginning of the war chiefly notable for the variety of views and opinions it produced among the soldiers who were going to suffer from it; some even thought they were going to profit by it, and the Major told us one evening at dinner that it would enrich our experience of life and broaden our minds.

'Of course he read that in some trashy magazine,' said Stimpson to me afterwards. 'You know what war really is, don't you? – what Anatole France said it is? He said that, whatever the gazettes may say, it simply consists of stealing pigs and chickens from the peasants. When soldiers are on campaign that is all they think about.'

This pronouncement about war had an evocative effect on Heddon. 'War,' he said wearily, in the character of an old man repeating the same thing for the hundredth time, 'is the composite evil, the whole gamut ranging from the Satanic to the venial is contained in war. It is in fact,' he went on definitively, 'so wrong and so evil as to transcend all ordinary bounds of jurisdiction. It exists in a world of its own, a festering, all-befouling, all-contaminating plague-spot for which no medicine is discoverable. It is a sort of counterpart to the panacea, its obverse. It is also,' he went on, getting into his stride and becoming metaphysical, 'the obverse of the philosopher's stone – every metal which it touches, from gold to lead, reacts in the same way – to a mouldering mass and then finally to the last state – ashes.' He paused for breath. 'I quote,' he said, 'from Orensky's *The Doing and the Undoing*. It is at present banned in this country but if either of you are interested I can obtain a foreign unexpurgated edition.'

'Yes, you're quite right,' said Stimpson. 'But I should put it more briefly and more constructively than that. When the last politician has been strangled with the entrails of the last general, then, and only then, shall we have peace.'

The other opinionated member of the mess was the Padre, a man whose views on the treatment of Indians did more credit to Kipling than to his cloth. I heard that he had served in India for several years and by way of polite conversational gambit at lunch, I introduced the topic of the Frontier; it seemed a good, sound, apposite subject, but unfortunately Heddon blundered in with a question about the bombardment of native tribes. There was a Calcutta look in the Padre's eye as he turned to Heddon and answered him.

'If the natives misbehave they are punished,' he said ferociously. 'And by gad they deserve it.'

I saw there was going to be trouble.

'Oh yes, I'm sure they deserve it,' I said hastily. 'What Mr Heddon meant, I'm sure, was – are aeroplanes used much in carrying out the punishment? Are bombs dropped? A purely scientific point.'

'We drop fewer bombs than the Germans would if they were in our shoes,' said the Padre sturdily, still evading the question and adopting the celebrated 'Versailles-was-an-unfair-treaty-but-just-think-how-much-unfairer-the-Germans-would-have-made-it' line of argument.

'Ah, Padre, I quite agree,' said Stimpson. 'But if on the other hand the Hottentots were in our shoes, think – just think – how cold they would be.'

I heard the Padre talking to the Major afterwards. 'A very silly young man,' he was saying. 'I can't think why they gave him an emergency commission.'

'Well, he's one of these specialists – one of these linguists,' said the Major. 'And he knows Europe very well. He's only attached to us for the time – to see what sort of stores engineer units will require so that he can take his place on the purchasing commission if and when we go abroad.'

We thought quite a lot about going abroad during those first three weeks of the war. My corporal told me he thought it would be absurd to go to France again, he said Roumania would be far better; he seemed to expect something more imaginative and enterprising from the Government than a mere repetition of 1914. I had never been to Roumania and it seemed most improbable that a member of a purchasing commission would visit a country he did not know; but I left him his illusions.

'But I suppose they'll do the same old thing,' he said pessimistically. 'Old Neville Chamberlain – he won't startle us with anything new. Good chap and all that, but no good in a war. What we want is a man like Hitler. A dirty dog. You can't fight a war any other way.'

'I see they've brought Churchill in,' I said.

'Yes, that's something,' he agreed.

The men certainly worked hard those three weeks trying to turn themselves into proper soldiers. They were mostly sturdy northerners who had spent their lives in the factories and mines of St. Helens, working in an atmosphere of perpetual gloom and putrefying fog, so that all the dreariness and misery of the war seemed to come more easily and naturally to them than to the foreigners from the south. One day I accompanied a party of these men to the ranges fifteen miles north of St. Helens, a place of surprising green fields and unforgettable odd occasional patches of blue sky, so pastoral after St. Helens that we all fell in love with it. We were under the control of an inoffensive little sergeant called Smith, a man with a round ingenuous cherubim face and periwinkle blue eyes; he looked completely guileless and I was surprised to hear later that he was a Bren-gun fanatic. He approached me fondling one of these weapons, patting its parts.

'Them's like babies to me, sir,' he said. He was a deadly shot with the thing and I shuddered when I reflected, such was my humanity in those days, that some good German *hausfrau*, like the mother in Sassoon's poem, would sit eternally knitting and 'dreaming by the fire' for a son whose face was being hourly 'trodden deeper in the mire' as a result of the handiwork of this simple, patriotic, and obviously kindly sergeant.

Heddon with his *démodé* pacifism was particularly annoyed about Smith and his Bren gun when I told him what Smith had said.

'Poor miserable wretch,' he said. 'Do you really believe that man wants to go about perpetually killing, slaying, and knocking things down? Of course he doesn't. He's just another of the credulous myrmidons of the capitalists, another crashing half-wit. He's being made to kill – so are we all, all being made to kill. Why don't the people revolt? Why don't they liquidate the governing classes? Why don't the poor throw the leaders out?' he asked rhetorically, throwing his hands in the air.

'Because the poor don't like Hitler any more than the leaders do,' said the Padre who had overheard him.

'It's all very well for you to say that,' said Heddon turning on the Padre. 'You think Hitler's Anti-Christ. You treat him religiously and he becomes a nice easy symbol you can revile – just as the Fathers of the Church did in such a vulgar fashion in Byzantium.'

'Yes,' said Stimpson, joining Heddon's side. 'You completely forget about all the non-Christians. Just think of all those poor Russians who don't believe in God. Hitler is a flesh-and-blood reality to them. He doesn't just cancel out like an easy simple algebraical fraction, they can't turn him into a nice straightforward Anti-Christ who has simply appeared in order that the prophecies may be fulfilled.'

I could not quite follow the argument which was becoming too mathematical for me, but the Padre had a very ready and glib reply.

'All the more reason,' he said, 'why those heathen Russians should recant and stop being idolators and rationalists and become good Christians again – in double-quick time too. Anyway,' he said drily, 'they aren't fighting the Germans.'

This ought to have been the knock-out blow but Heddon was indefatigable.

'Your remark about the Russians recanting is, if I may say so,' he said, 'a case of special pleading. It is so much poppycock. Now just consider the Russian point of view. According to them, religion is all right so long as it doesn't interfere too much with a man's public life...'

'According to Lord Melbourne,' cut in Stimpson unable to resist the opportunity, 'religion is all right so long as it doesn't interfere too much with a man's *private* life.'

'I refuse to argue on these lines,' said the Padre getting up and going out. 'If you really want the view of the Established Church on the subject I refer you to the latest utterance of His Grace the Archbishop of Canterbury.'

'Of course I know the speech he means,' said Heddon after he had gone out. 'Although it was only made a month ago it's already ten years out of date. They're all out of date, these people. What's wanted is more propaganda, not more preaching; more films by Charlie Chaplin about Hit and Miss, not cheese-paring chatter about right and wrong. There's very little substantial difference between Archbishops and Bren guns really,' he finished strangely.

The Bren-gun worshipper, Sergeant Smith, would certainly have been shocked if he had heard this; not to mention insulted at being described as a 'poor miserable wretch'; so far, in fact, from being miserable, he was highly elated at the prospect of getting on to a battlefield, not so much, he told me, because he particularly disliked the Germans, but because he just liked the idea of fighting; it appealed to him. Although he had spent every day of his working life in a St. Helens glass-tube factory, he was really the lineal descendant of the great medieval soldiers of fortune.

'It's a man's life,' he told me. 'Why, these fine young fellows,' he said, proudly surveying our section drawn up in front of us, a forlorn, grimy, rather smelly set of Lancashire workmen, 'these young fellows will love it. Give me these men in the field for a month and they'll all be soldiers, good fighting soldiers – every one of 'em.'

Like Corporal Jackson who had wanted to go to Roumania I found that few of the men really relished the idea of fighting alongside the French, although their reasons were various. The driver of my car could not stand the French; he was a football pro.

'I once played for the United against a team of Froggies,' he said. 'Dirty set of brutes.'

'Yes, but they are fine chaps to have as allies,' I pointed out. 'Remember what they did in the last war.'

But he was not to be convinced so easily.

'Pack of pansies,' he said. 'They bite – and kick – and scratch if they're losing. Why – I once even saw some of them crying.'

'You'll find they aren't too bad when you get there,' I said. 'You'll enjoy the food and drink anyway.'

'Huh,' he said scathingly. 'They drink *wines*.'

He should not have been quite so caustic, because he was a 'driver'. And being a 'driver' was, I soon realised from the amount of applications that came in for it, one of the softer jobs; because, in order to preserve all their acumen for keeping their vehicles on the road, drivers were forbidden to help with the digging, dynamiting, or any other work on which their fellows might be engaged, a regulation which they scrupulously observed.

We spent most of the three weeks' preliminary training in St. Helens on these digging and dynamiting operations; and then on September the 19th the whole company moved south to Dorset. It was perhaps wise that we left St. Helens when we did because, as the men became more and more familiar with the dynamite, they increased the size of the practice charges, until, during the last week in St. Helens we were breaking between forty and fifty panes of glass a day in local civilian houses.

During the last few days in England, which were spent in Dorset getting our final equipment and vehicles, we came into contact for the first time with the distinguished regular units who were to be our companions in the division. There was a Brigade of Guards to which Stimpson took a peculiar and unreasoning dislike. They were quartered in our village and one day as we passed two of their officers in the street, he told me why he disliked them.

'People who glory in war are the most detestable class alive,' he said.

'I don't suppose for a moment that they glory in it,' I said. 'I expect that war is the last thing in the world that they want; in fact they probably hate it more than anything else. Just think of all the polo they're missing.'

'Yes, but they're all going to be heroes and they would much rather be that than be polo players,' he replied. 'Look at that one with the moustache and the silly face,' he said pointing rudely. 'Look at the way he struts – young bantam – he thinks he's no end of a chap. Off to war, off to battle, off to glory and a D.S.O. I hope he catches his death of a chill in the trenches,' he said unkindly.

Sergeant Smith of course took a different view. All his previous military service had been spent in the glass-works contingent of the Territorial Army at St. Helens; and now, for the first time, he actually had an opportunity of meeting the famous regiments he had read about so often. Although he greatly admired the Brigade of Guards it was the Scottish and Irish infantry that really took his fancy.

'The King's Own Scottish are the chaps who never used to take prisoners in the last war,' he admiringly told the corporal and myself as we watched some of them marching down the street. The corporal was always rather insubordinate to Smith.

'Go on,' he said. 'And I suppose the Ulster Rifles always castrated theirs with bowie knives.'

'That's just what they did do I believe, Corporal Jackson,' said Sergeant Smith in all seriousness. 'That's just what they did do in the last war.'

After a week in Crewkerne I was summoned by the Colonel.

'I am putting you in charge of the advance party, Rhodes. I don't know where you are going but these maps will tell you,' he said, handing me a large roll of sealed maps. 'You are not to open them until you receive orders to do so. You are to leave tomorrow. Your job will be to find quarters and prepare a reception generally for the main body of the division which will follow a few days behind you. In order that the men may not suspect that you are leaving I want you to pretend that you are merely going on a preliminary training exercise in England. Tell them that, in order to make the thing realistic, you have to take full battle order with you.'

I was allowed to go home for the last time that evening but only after promising on no account to mention what was happening the following day. My mother was living on a farm near Ilchester at the time and when I arrived I found the family helping the farmer get in his corn.

I must have acted pretty badly because I have since been told that although I gave nothing away verbally, most of the family suspected that it was a leave-taking visit. I should perhaps have appreciated this at the time because when I left my mother was more than normally concerned to see that I took my woollen vests back with me.

At three o'clock the next day on a brilliant warm autumn afternoon a long crocodile of drab Army vehicles pulled out of Crewkerne bound for a sort of melancholy Erewhon; that at least was how I felt about it but the leader of the convoy was a little better informed. He had been given 'sealed order' which, when opened, instructed him to report at Blandford 'forthwith'. We accordingly set our radiators to the east and at Blandford another sealed envelope was handed to our leader by an officer who suddenly sprang out from behind a hedge just outside the town. This envelope contained the name of another destination, which in turn yielded yet another concealed officer and yet another sealed envelope; and so it went on throughout the afternoon and evening like a treasure hunt.

The country we passed through that evening looked at its finest. Even if one is in an Army convoy, motoring can be very enjoyable among the close Dorsetshire hedges and groups of spinneys gradually fading into darkness under the dull evening light. Except for an occasional labourer collecting the hay in a field, the long train of Army vehicles stretching out for miles on the road ahead was the only sign of life that evening. And it seemed to me that one's appreciation of the English countryside was heightened to the extent of being almost painful by the sure knowledge that it was a last view.

There were thirty other vehicles in the divisional advance party, each containing an officer, a driver, and a batman, and each representing a unit in the division. My batman was called Cooper; he was a reservist who had rejoined the Army only the day before we left. Being an old soldier he was not deceived by my story about an 'exercise somewhere in England'.

'I suppose it'll be France,' he said gloomily at one of these halts as we sat by the roadside smoking cigarettes. 'Blast it.'

'What if it is?' I said. 'What's the trouble?'

'Well, sir,' he said, 'I've been out of the service six years all bar three weeks. Another bleeding three weeks and I'd have done my reserve time and they couldn't have called me up. Just my luck, of course. It's that attestation form they get you with,' he said sourly.

I sympathised. It certainly was bad luck to have to leave your wife and family just because you had signed a small piece of paper fourteen years before.

'How often do you shave, sir?' he inquired suddenly.

'Every morning,' I said surprised. 'Why?'

'Just wanted to know, sir,' he replied. 'When I was in the Army before I had an officer to do for who used to shave twice a day – regular. Of course I've had all sorts,' he said obviously confident that he could cope with any eccentricity that I might show.

'Have you always been a batman?' I asked.

'Yes, sir. Best job in the Army,' he replied smartly.

I got an inkling then into the workings of the Army mind. I have realised many times since then, that unlike civilian life where most people have an ambition of some kind, there is a large section in the Army who have none, who seek only a niche, a safe quiet place withdrawn from the hurly-burly where they may rest in seclusion and honourable obscurity. Cooper told me that he asked only one thing of the Army, that he might remain a batman for the rest of his military career.

His colleague, my nineteen-year-old driver, was as naive about the Army as Cooper was sophisticated about it. I liked him, but I was sorry that he had replaced the Francophobe football pro, because it seemed almost certain that we were going to France, and in view of what the pro had said about French wines I longed to hear him when his first carafe of *vin ordinaire* was put in front of him. As we neared Southampton and the barrage balloons appeared above the harbour, the driver realised, as Cooper had done some hours before, that it was WAR we were bound for and not simply a dreary exercise 'somewhere in England'. He was delighted.

'I told them when I joined that I wanted to go abroad,' he said gratefully.

'Well, if you get killed,' said Cooper, 'don't say I didn't tell you.'

Now that we were in Southampton there was no longer any need for secrecy and I gave them the official instruction not to post letters, and for the first time I had to use my official authority – to stop a soldier posting a letter. The poor fellow was probably only sending love and kisses to his best girl, but as he posted it under my nose in full view of a group of soldiers whom I had just expressly forbidden to do such a thing, I had little alternative but to report him to his officer – whom I found later in a 'phone box.

Southampton was crowded with troops that night. All sleeping accommodation was soon taken and the huge remnant had to make the best of it on the roads; it reminded me of Coronation night in Hyde Park. Only a few of the troops belonged to advance parties, drawn like ourselves from other divisions; most of them were members of larger formations, signifying amongst other things that we were not the first division to go abroad. When we arrived it was already dark and we were told by a military policeman to sleep in the 'Rest Camp', so called because it was an assorted conglomeration of tents, huts, and barns just outside the city, sited near a factory which made 'rest' impossible. I was fortunate enough to find a place in one of the tents, but most of the others had to sleep in their vehicles or in the wood under the trees. I woke up the next morning to find Cooper standing near me with a cup of tea; he was scratching himself.

'These 'orse flies,' he said. 'They don't 'arf suck your blood.' It was immediately obvious where he had slept. He had also brought some boiling shaving water in a little mug and a beautiful white towel which I was sure did not belong to him.

'However did you manage to get that?' I asked.

'You don't 'ave to ask, sir,' said Cooper winking. 'Told you I'd been in the Army for seven years.'

It was the first time I had ever had a batman and I was delighted; it seemed most profitable.

Later in the morning I managed to get a bath in a hotel; I lay in it for longer than usual relishing the warmth of every drop with sensual satisfaction and prolonging the pleasure until the manageress knocked on the bathroom door and then, finding that it had no effect, finally turned off the hot water supply. All very much after the fashion of the Victorian music hall celebrity making his last appearance on the boards, who refused to quit the stage until the manager, having rung down the curtain once and found that the comedian merely came out and continued in front of the footlights, was finally obliged to turn off the electricity. I was determined that the bath, together with the last view of Dorset fields and the last pint of English beer, was to stand as a symbol for all that I had left behind when I found myself in the inevitable ditch, an exquisite memory when I was sleeping upside down in the rain with my head in a puddle of mud.

At three o'clock that afternoon we embarked on a miserable grimy little cross-channel boat called the *Duchess of Atholl*, which had been painted a dirty grey and which, except for what appeared to be an inexplicable pair of blue knickers drying on the bridge, had little enough connection with her eponymous aristocrat.

The last man had to be aboard by three-thirty that afternoon, but nothing further happened until ten-thirty when suddenly, with feverish vibrations, the ship's engines started up and the vessel jerked forward into motion like a motorcar. We supposed that this was done for secrecy, a quick getaway to ensure that no enemy aeroplanes should see us depart. After that we quickly moved out into the Southampton roads where we stopped again to wait for the other members of our convoy, five companion ships and a destroyer. I stood on the bridge peering at the land until it was too dark to see any more of England and then went below.

The lounge had been turned into an officers' mess; it contained people from every type of Army unit, Infantry, Artillery, Engineers, Guards, and Signals, all evincing that particular brand of forced humour that tells of uneasy minds. They were having tea and I thought it a little unfair that one should have to pay half-a-crown for a kipper and some weak sugarless tea so early on in the war.

'The profiteers have got going already,' said the man sitting next to me, a captain with a subtle face; he told me that he had been called up from the seclusion of writing *A History of the Foundations of Eton College* and, as he seemed so sad and miserable, I assumed that he was distressed at being separated from what was presumably his life-work. I sympathised with him.

'You'll probably find time to continue your writing in the Army,' I said.

'Good God,' he said. 'I don't want to continue writing.' He went on eating moodily, hating his kipper. He turned to me suddenly.

'Has it ever occurred to you,' he said despairingly, 'what the rates and taxes are going to be like after this war?'

Then I realised that, like the man in the Scriptures, he was very sad for he had great possessions.

After tea I went on deck again; it was a warm evening, one of those fragrant autumn nights when one should be sleeping in the upstair room of a Dorset cottage, the windows flung wide open on to an orchard. When I visited the deck again later in the night I found the men all asleep, huddled side by side, giving off that subtle military smell at once so characteristic, so indefinable, and so obnoxious. They had ceased their talking and singing towards midnight and, apart from that peculiar muffled clanking which ships' engines always make, a silence had settled down over the whole ship; the officers in the lounge dossed down on their sofas and improvised bunks, the lights were turned down, and beneath the small unwinking blue lamp in the ceiling above my head I tried to sleep. It was difficult in a lifebelt, but somewhere towards two o'clock I must have succeeded because, apart from strange dreams about Hitler and vast limitless inanes of mud, I was conscious of nothing until I heard someone saying, 'Yes, it must be Cherbourg'.

CHAPTER TWO
Carnival Journey

I LAY ON my bunk for a minute or two still half-conscious but stimulated, even faintly encouraged, by this piece of news. Yesterday had been a day of regret, of parting – 'partir, c'est mourir un peu' as Ulysses had said to Polyphemus – it was inevitable. But the following morning, with the realisation that we had arrived in France, at once the most sordid and the most subtle country of all, I felt a strange new sense of enjoyment; it seemed that in spite of all the traditional dreariness and misery of army life, a new and interesting experience lay ahead simply because we were in France. I dressed quickly and went on deck to find that we lay at anchor in the harbour of Cherbourg. It was a brilliant warm morning with the early mists still half-hiding the land; encircling the harbour were the familiar little white and dove-grey houses of Brittany, and on the quay stood the massive Municipal buildings erected in that questionable taste more often associated with the Département du Nord than de la Manche. It was six o'clock and the town was not yet awake, but on the other ships in the bay we could just discern the movement and excitement of soldiers crowding the rails, all eager like ourselves to get a first glimpse of the new surroundings.

I went below to pack and found the officer who had slept in the bunk beneath me quietly being sick into a brown-paper bag; this, together with the military stench given off from the hold where many of the troops had spent the night herded together like cattle, and the litter of cigarette packets, half-finished sandwiches, and chocolate wrappings that now strewed the decks of the *Duchess of Atholl*, seemed a prophetic and very suitable commentary on the French provincial streets in which we soon found ourselves. My young driver, something of a puritan I later found out, was disgusted by them; an extremely tidy and sanitary person, he was particularly offended by a public urinal which, although adequately screened against the wall of the Municipal buildings, was drained into the street. I told him later that Cherbourg was the 'Falmouth of France'. He mistook my meaning.

'I never wanted to go to Cornwall anyway,' he said.

We had our first drink on French soil at nine-thirty that morning, a Vermouth cassis sipped on the pavement of the principal street; it was like a hot July day and we were able to sit out at a marble-topped table beneath a brilliant red-and-white striped awning bearing the comfortable words '*Du bon – Dubonnet*'. The General Staff obviously expected some trouble in the matter of alcohol because they had given great publicity on the ship to their first order, forbidding all troops (as distinct from officers) to drink spirits, aperitifs, or wines; the men, it enacted, were to confine themselves to beer. The officer who read this order to the men incorrectly told them that beer was the same word in French as in English, an unfortunate mistake because a popular aperitif called Byrrh, a sort of sweet Vermouth of high alcoholic content, is pronounced in French just like our own word 'beer', the French equivalent for our beer being of course *biére* with a distinguishing accent on the last syllable. This aperitif Byrrh is on sale in almost every bistro in the north of France, and it is recorded that a drunken English soldier who was taken into custody that evening, on being smelt was very properly accused of having taken the forbidden aperitif and of having broken the first commandment of the General Staff. Although the soldier had little to say for himself at the time, the defending officer at the subsequent court martial made such pretty play with the phonetics of the case that it was dismissed.

By ten o'clock that morning all the troops had been disembarked and only the vehicles remained in the hold. The two cranes on the quay were unable to handle all the transport in one day, and because most of the vehicles of our advance guard would be dealt with last, we were told to spend the day and night in Cherbourg. My own vehicle by some fortunate freak of unloading was among the first to appear on the quay and I was able to use it throughout the day for taxiing people about the town.

Accommodation for the night was arranged by the mayor; he had formed a pool of guides in the town hall to direct us to our billets. The guide whom I was allotted was a tall well-built man who looked as if he ought to have been in the Maginot Line; and on my inquiring how it was that he had been given such a soft job he told me that he had been graded C3; he could see no objection to the job personally he said.

To my surprise the billet to which he escorted me was the Grand Séminaire de Notre Dame, a large building in one of the side streets, which was well equipped with high railings and iron-studded doors, forming a sufficient preventative to any handsome Manon who might think of entering and persuading the young things to renounce their vows.

'*C'est certainement un séminaire,*' the guide said when I asked him if he had not made a mistake in bringing me to such a place, '*mais la Mére est une Belge qui a beaucoup de confiance en les Anglais – elle est un peu fou-fou,*' he added, tapping his head and spoiling the compliment.

This seemed a broad but unlikely view for a Mother Superior to hold, and I was most surprised when I met the Mother herself to find her eyes full of tears, and an expression of the utmost delight and sympathy on her face as she warmly shook my hand. She told me that during the German advance in 1914 her house had been set on fire and her father, one of the local aristocrats, taken as hostage. She herself had escaped to some relations in France but only through the help of the English; it was this that made her ready to do anything for us in return. I thanked her and, thinking that she might be able to recommend a friend who would take some of the others, told her that I was hoping to find accommodation for fourteen officers.

'But that is easy,' she said. 'They shall have a dormitory.'

When I explained that we did not want to inconvenience the people who normally slept in the dormitory she would not hear of it. '*Les soeurs doivent se débrouiller,*' she said, and I had visions of the unfortunate sisters sleeping on the floor of the cellar. It was a very hospitable introduction to France but, as one of the older officers who had fought in the last war pointed out, it was necessary to remember that the Mother Superior was Belgian and not French.

After leaving our luggage at the Séminaire I returned to the town to do some shopping with a friend, a London doctor called Allerton, whom I had accidentally met while leaving the boat early that morning. He was searching for a French dictionary from which he proposed to learn the language; he said that the war in France, whatever happened in the gazettes, was not going to be a wasted war for him. After some searching we found what he wanted, a bijou dictionary which would easily fit into his pocket. I thought it far too small but he disagreed, saying that it would be sufficient for his life henceforth, which was to be far simpler, confined mainly to eating, drinking, and what he called the 'carnal verities'. Like many older men who have had to work hard in civilian life the war had come as a relief to Allerton; he pointed out how it simplified everything, how agreeable it was going to be to have one's life regulated, one's food and lodging assured, even one's salary paid in advance. He behaved that morning rather like the comic English businessman who goes for the weekend to 'gay Paree'; he had only one French phrase which he used generally in conjunction with some ironic statement about French morals. It was '*marquez mes mots*' and it was not until he had used it to a waitress who obviously thought he meant something quite different and who therefore refused to bring us our drinks, that I was able to persuade him to give it up.

There was not a great deal to do that day. After ambling round the dirty streets of the undistinguished French port, examining the significant Bofor guns on the quay and talking to the half-shaven poilus who manned them, as they stood around the guns, their hands in their pockets, all smoking offensively powerful cigarettes and smirking at the foreigners, it only remained to go to the bistros where they had, of course, no licensing hours; there were hundreds of these in Cherbourg. Any loss that the bistro and restaurant proprietors may have experienced through the General Staff's regulation about the troops drinking was easily counterbalanced by the officers. Allerton insisted on having two bottles of champagne at lunch because, as he said, 'My dear fellow, it's perfectly ridiculous at fifteen francs a bottle'; as if he thought it was being offered at sale price. There were three fairly drunken majors in the restaurant by four o'clock that afternoon and two subalterns in a somewhat worse condition. The climax came when a sergeant entered the restaurant a little later with a message for one of the majors; he fell down when halfway across the floor, whereupon he was greeted by the drunkards with a chorus of jeers, cheers, and catcalls.

The British military police who had taken complete police control of the town were kept busy that night incarcerating or at least discouraging drunks.

The advance guard of our division was commanded by a very charming Horse Guards colonel who called his officers together for a conference at six-thirty that evening in order to explain our future movements.

'Gentlemen,' he said, 'I can at last give you some idea of what is going to happen and where we are likely to go. You may now open your maps. As soon as we can get away from Cherbourg we are going on towards Laval.' Laval was a provincial town about fifty miles north of Tours. Our maps, I noticed, included large tracts of the Belgian frontier so that it was surprising to hear that we were going to move south. 'When we arrive there,' he continued, 'you will arrange billets and all facilities for your units in the main body which is following two or three days behind, I don't know how long we shall stay there or where we shall go afterwards. The maps, you will observe, contain the whole French frontier from the coast to as far south as Strasbourg, which gives one some indication; on the other hand there is a rumour that Roumania may be attacked by Germany at any moment, in which case it is much more likely that we shall go to Marseilles. We leave, gentlemen, tomorrow at nine o'clock.'

This last order at least was encouraging, because all moves normally take place in the British Army at dawn. It meant that one could sleep easily without the disquieting subconscious knowledge that one was going to have to get up early. In any case sleeping on the nuns' beds was not easy. They were hard beds, obviously spartan in intention, the surface of each shaped like a dish cover, demanding great poise if one was to stay on them all night; they were the complete reverse of the traditional French bed which is voluptuous and pleasure-loving.

At about two o'clock in the morning Allerton told me he gave up all attempts at balancing on his bed and transferred to the floor. This put him in a very bad temper, and when his electric razor would not work the next morning on the seminary voltage, he made some alteration within the machine so that when he tried to restart it, all the lights in the building were fused. It was a poor form of thanks to our hostesses but not, I think, intentional.

Our awakening the next morning seemed to me unorthodox. On the other hand it may be quite usual for Mothers Superior to walk round the nuns' dormitories touching them on the shoulder in order to wake them. And it would have been quite a pardonable mistake under the circumstances to forget that we were visitors; after all forgetful husbands are frequently said to treat their visitors in the early morning as if they were their wives. But Allerton would not agree with me, saying that the Mother was a lewd woman; he was very widely read in Boccaccio and he reminded us that there was a story about a Mother Superior and a dumb gardener. At eight o'clock that morning I had felt myself being rubbed on the shoulder and, on opening my eyes, I saw the Mother Superior bending over me, a look of great piety on her face. I could not believe that she did it out of any motive other than charity, but Allerton who is rather good-looking said that he was rubbed with great familiarity.

At nine o'clock precisely we left Cherbourg. An Army regulation decrees that there shall be a halt of five minutes in every hour; we arranged that these halts should be made in the villages, so that we could talk to the bystanders who had turned out in large numbers to welcome us and who bombarded us with apples. They also garlanded the vehicles with flowers so that when we entered the village of St. Lo, where we were to spend the night, we looked more like a carnival procession at a harvest festival than a line of armoured fighters. And in those days we really supposed that we were armoured fighters; even the French admitted that, if nothing else, we were at least *fort mechanisé*. We thought of the German panzer divisions as an imitation of the British model, superior perhaps in number but not in quality. Because there were no tanks to be seen in the opening months of the war one did not immediately conclude that they did not exist; one assumed, in the words of a contemporary French cliché, that they were being used '*dans un secteur plus important*'.

The journey through Brittany was memorable for the charming hospitality of the peasants and for the end-of-summer heat and haze that still hung over the fields. At certain times of the year it is said the atmosphere of the south invades Brittany. The clear air of Aix 'where a man can paint all day and all night' creeps northward and then for a few weeks you feel the fat prosperous noonday heat of ripening vineyards, the heat that sent all the inhabitants of Clochemerle into a drunken stupor after lunch although they had drunk nothing. A romantic and ingenious German writer has divided up the west coast of France into three climatic regions each of which he says is symbolised by some human activity.

In the south, he says, the Mediterranean winds are warm and caressing and the people are beautiful; even if they are not in love with one another they obviously ought to be. Sex, he says, is everywhere; it is on the railway station when you arrive, in the cypress and olive groves when you go outside; if you avoid it in the taxicab it crops up again when you are having your bath. Even the little waiters at dinner who appear to most people to be an assortment of insignificant Polish, Armenian, and Bulgarian Jews he regards as the last descendants of the great and mysterious cult of Egyptian phallicism. He accordingly identifies this part of France with 'sex'.

Of the other parts he has less to say. He identifies the second region, the area bounded by Tours in the north and Aix in the south where the air is warm yet clear, with paint, painters, and vineyards ; and to the third category, the northern part where the Atlantic winds bring a harder, harsher climate, he gives the double symbol of fish and Englishmen.

I explained these categories to Allerton during the journey, remarking that although we were in the extreme north we were experiencing the atmosphere of the vineyards and painters, that the second type of climate seemed to have invaded the domain of the third.

'Well, it's high time we had the first up here,' he said; and with that thought we travelled wishfully on to St. Lo.

The village of St. Lo where we arrived that evening provided us all with excellent billets and charming hosts. I found myself that evening over a rickety fifteenth-century shop near the church, chiefly notable for its overhanging stories; from the top window one could quite easily lean out and shake hands with someone in the house on the opposite side of the street; it seemed to have come out of a Dumas novel. Although a small village, St. Lo had the usual church of almost cathedral proportions, a vast affair fit to house any English bishop. Its incumbent, a modest little curé with whom I spoke inside the church, contrasted very favourably with his English counterpart, although, as Allerton said, there must be *some* English deans who are nice.

The mayor, corporation, and band turned out to meet us in the Grande Place of St. Lo, and a ceremonial greeting took place between them and our representative – the colonel. The mayor did something I had always understood was confined, in its practice in France, to the President of the Republic and the public executioner: he wore a top hat. It was perhaps a shade too big, the brim just touched the tops of his ears, but he made up for it by the excellent stance he adopted, as if posing for an early daguerre photograph. Perhaps he had special permission from the President to wear it, at all events he did full justice to it. Our colonel, on the other hand, had had his hat blown off while crossing a bridge and he looked much less imposing.

The mayor immediately offered the colonel for his personal use the hospitality of his own private house – a fish shop. For one awful moment it looked as though the colonel was going to refuse, but then all the inbred gallantry of the Horse Guards came out and he graciously accepted in elegant, somewhat Ollendorfian French, pronounced with a strong English accent:

'*Mais je serais ravi, Monsieur le Maire...*'

And so it was settled to the satisfaction of both parties, the mayor delighted at having a colonel under his roof, and the colonel delighted at having done his duty. The rest of the party was dealt with in much the same way, citizens stepping forward at intervals and offering to take us, as at a Roman market. Allerton said we should have presented ourselves in turn on the rostrum in the bandstand, with the colonel acting as fugleman:

'Now who'll take this fine young fellow? Useful, tidy, clean habits about the house, etc., etc...'

It was all very well for Allerton to say this because he was handsome and many of the bidders were buxom young grass-widows; it was perhaps fitting that he fell to a Derby and Joan couple who only gave him a hot-water bottle in bed that night.

I was knocked down to a charming person who took me back to her curiosity shop; it was here, from the top story window, that I attempted to touch hands with someone in the house on the opposite side of the street. It was a delightful warm autumn evening, the whole atmosphere of the house one of quietness and peace, and I praised my good fortune; but it was not to last. She was preparing a fabulous meal for me in the kitchen, while I sat warming myself in front of the fire and describing the langouste I had had for lunch to her, when an English major with a black moustache made his way into the house and told me, or rather ordered me, to go to the hotel in the next street; he said that the colonel had instructed him to billet in the curiosity shop in place of me. It is vain to argue with a major; I thanked my hostess and went to the hotel where I found I was to share a bedroom with a horrible Scot called McDougal.

Not knowing anything about him I agreed to have dinner with McDougal and some of his friends that evening in the hotel. Six of us sat down to dinner and six bottles of wine were placed in front of us on the table. I don't object to drunken people and I don't object to argumentative people, but I detest drunken and argumentative people; these people were both before the fish had arrived. There was one peculiarly sinister member of the party, an officer belonging to one of the most expensive regiments, with a Mongolian face, high wooden cheekbones, and expressionless eyes. I learned later that he was a Russian émigré. He began the evening noisily enough, swearing fluently and bilingually in Russian and French; but as time went on he became quieter, intenser, and much more drunken – behaving, in fact, just like the popular Russian. I expected him at any moment to scramble to his feet and grind his glass into the face of his nearest friend. Instead he gradually slipped further and further off his chair until he finally disappeared completely from view beneath the table where he spent the remainder of the evening.

The rest of us were meanwhile arguing fiercely about blood feuds, a conversation started by the Scotsman. McDougal said that the blood feud was the greatest, the noblest, and the most holy undertaking with which a man could be entrusted, a sacred duty to his ancestors. The Russian, before he slipped from view, agreed wholeheartedly with this; he was for killing all Poles, Germans, and Finns. McDougal merely wanted to do away with all the members of a Scottish tribe called the Campbells.

'Never,' he said, thumping the table, 'never will I sit down at the same table with a Campbell. Never will I fight alongside a Campbell. I hate and detest them. We McDougals,' he said proudly, 'hate and detest all Campbells – the loathsome, creeping, crawling toads.'

'But a Campbell's a man for a'that,' I said, trying to take an intelligent part in the conversation.

'A Campbell's a heel,' he said, suddenly breaking into the language of the cinema, 'a heel, a low-down rotten scum.'

Another member of the party pointed out to him that although the Russians and Scots might think that revenge was the noblest thing on earth, all thinking Frenchmen and Italians, the majority of thinking Scandinavians and Englishmen, and a handful of philosophic Germans, wanted only peace, security, and quiet.

'Only their bourgeoisie,' said McDougal scornfully.

This confession, that wars were run for and on snob values, was too charming for words, at once so true and so preposterous that I burst out laughing.

'Huh – you drunkard,' said McDougal, averting his eyes from me in disgust.

The discussion became more and more heated, McDougal finally proving himself a 'Pax Britannica' man; his solution to all world problems was ideal. He wanted to make everyone British and Christian, the whole lot, yellow men, black men, brown men, and white men all worshipping the same symbol. The argument finally lost cogency and they all staggered off to look for a brothel.

Meanwhile I went along to the men's quarters to see how my batman Cooper was getting on. Although the officers were well provided for in St. Lo, the men, proportionate to their rank, had a harder time. They had been allotted the Cavalry Barracks. These barracks dated from before Vauban and apart from the stables were in ruins and uninhabitable. When I arrived I found Cooper lying in some straw and grousing about the number of fleas it contained. He blamed this on the French. The only consolation I could give was to remind him how lucky he was not to be the football pro I had had as driver in St. Helens, a man who really hated the French; Cooper replied that it only needed a few more fleas for him to have the same outlook himself.

The cavalry barracks were on the far side of the town and on the way back to the hotel I passed a cinema which was showing *Les Misérables*. I accordingly paid three francs and was admitted to a seat in the pit. The film had just reached one of its most thrilling moments, the chief of police and Valjean had just met for the second time, when it was stopped and a notice was inserted on the screen, 'Do not miss the next mighty instalment of the gripping film'. Everyone went out quite happily and I was left wondering what would happen in an English village if Metro-Goldwyn-Mayer behaved in such a fashion. Governments have been known to fall for far less. A little thing, for instance, like the injudicious siting of a public urinal against a church in Clochemerle caused the French Government to topple. But in England it is the cinema and the Press that have the power to stimulate public feeling in this way; the chain of Gaumont cinemas is one of the main arteries of the country; a curtailment of the supply of American films into the country would rock the whole of Parliament.

After leaving the cinema I fell in quite by chance on the way home with McDougal and my other dinner companions. They were also returning to the hotel. They seemed very depressed and I assumed that their adventure had not been successful, that they had not found what they were looking for. I was only partly right. The adventure had not been successful although they had certainly found what they were looking for. McDougal had been robbed; he had had his wallet stolen and they wanted me to come back with them and remonstrate with the lady who owned the establishment. They said they had not succeeded in making her understand that they were going to report her to the police. I agreed to help.

Beneath a dull red light in a little side street was an uninviting door firmly bolted and barred. After some shouting a woman in a nightcap appeared at one of the windows with a candle. I explained the situation to her. The line of argument she took was disarming; instead of behaving as I expected, like the usual virago of her class she was scrupulously polite.

'What is it, monsieur? What is the trouble?'

'These officers here, madame. They have just come from your place. They are worried about a small matter.'

'Oh yes – what is that? They are charming. So English. It was so nice to be able to entertain them.'

'Yes, madame, but they fear they have lost a wallet while they were with you.'

'A wallet. I have seen no wallet. Wait – I will come down.' She appeared at the door in a dressing-gown and conducted the conversation with great fluency.

'We have found no wallet,' she said mystified. I felt that the time had now come for straight words. Quite a band of interested and amused spectators had collected and I wanted to get away.

'They think it was stolen,' I said.

'Stolen! In my house! But that is impossible.'

I determined not to mince matters.

'The officer thinks it was stolen from his coat while he was with one of the girls,' I said.

At this she too threw off the cloak of politeness.

'Ah, Dieu Seigneur,' she said turning to the bystanders. 'With one of the girls? What in heaven's name does he mean? These officers evidently do not know hospitality when they see it. What happens? My husband and I see them an hour or two ago walking down the street. They are foreigners. They know no-one in the town. We invite them in for a drink. We give them drinks and they behave in a strange incomprehensible fashion with two of my daughters. We do not know what to do but we decide to ignore it. We put it down to their strange English customs. And then,' she said with great indignation, 'and then – what do they do? They return and say we have robbed them. Robbed them? I – who am the daughter of a town clerk. Why – it is an outrage.' She turned to me coldly.

'Monsieur,' she said, 'since you do not seem to know what polite behaviour and gratitude are I can only ask you to leave this house at once. If you do not do so immediately I shall send for the police.'

I turned to McDougal to tell him that the matter of who reported who to the police had now become questionable. He was leaning up against a lamp-post roaring with laughter.

'I'm frightfully sorry, old boy,' he said, raising his hands and guffawing loudly, 'but we must have brought you to the wrong house. This is the doctor's house. We had a drink in here earlier in the evening. The place we went to after is in another street. It looks awfully like this – but, old boy,' he said, tears of laughter in his eyes, 'you were doing so well that we just couldn't bear to stop you.'

It was then that I remembered that in certain parts of France doctors' houses have red lights above the door too. The only consolation I had afterwards was that McDougal never got his wallet back.

I had to spend the next eight hours after that in McDougal's company – in the same bedroom. He turned out to be more drunk than I had imagined so that it was very unpleasant. Cooper woke me the next morning with a copy of *Figaro* and a cup of tea.

'Good news this morning, sir,' he said, pointing at a headline. 'The Padre says it means that one of the Jerry generals is dead – bumped off at Hitler's orders he thinks.'

It was good news. Von Fritsch had been killed at the Polish front. I could remember him walking in the Ludendorff funeral procession in Munich in 1938 looking like a death's head as he stalked along clasping his baton, his eyes fixed on the back of the little figure in the mackintosh in front. I did not believe the 'foul play' story. But I always refuse on principle to believe the stories and fables of padres; they are the lowest form of quidnuncs.

After a French, and therefore totally inadequate breakfast in the hotel we set out for the town of Laval, still sixty miles away. Before I left the proprietor made the interesting observation to me that there was a politician of the same name as our destination, a man whom he execrated. He made the nice point that the name spelt equally well either way.

It was another perfect day; once again Brittany stewed beneath the heat of the south. Against the perfect pattern of thickly wooded slopes and spinneys and Corot-like glades, the line of tin Army vehicles all emitting their stupid tinny sounds seemed an impertinence. And I thought of Oscar Wilde's excellent aphorism that 'all art is useless' and of applying its inverse to these grossly utilitarian buses and trucks, lorries and charabancs with their assorted contents of tin hats and tin whistles, tin cans and tin heads, the constituents of a modern army.

We stopped for lunch at Mayenne where the river runs Spanish fashion in a deep gorge and where there are still traces of the East, the cathedral standing high above the gorge like a sort of miniature Santa Sophia with an assortment of civilian dwellings clustering about its base; it made me realise just how far the Moors had penetrated when they had overrun the Iberian peninsula in the great barbaric ages (a fact that now seemed even topical). I had lunch on a terrace overlooking the river at the table of the colonel and his chief of staff; the colonel had seen me searching for somewhere to sit and, all the other tables being occupied, he had very kindly asked me to sit with him. The manager of the restaurant with that quick appreciation of what is important, so characteristic of his race, immediately realised the eminence of our table and treated it accordingly. He bowed unctuously to '*Monsieur le Colonel*' and said he hoped we would condescend to eat a meal which he had specially prepared for us, a '*repas qui vous fait merveilles,*' a meal transcending all others. The colonel, who was no epicure, told me that he would just as soon have had a pint of beer and some steak and chips but that he felt, just as he had in the fish shop of the mayor at St. Lo, that he owed it to the advance guard to accept these embarrassing and unwanted favours. This characteristic devotion to duty, practised in another sphere, earned him the D.S.O. eight months later.

We were then given, in quick succession, caviar, sole Meunière à la Reine Pédauque, langouste au gratin et fines herbes, and a crêpe de volaille that melted in your mouth, the whole washed down with three bottles of delicious iced Sauterne. When it was all over and we lay back panting in our chairs the manager, a fat little Alsacien, appeared again and inquired if the colonel '*était satisfait de nos frugales orgies,*' to which the colonel replied with equal gallantry in his fulsome French, culled, he told me later, almost entirely from the pages of Bovary. I imagined him in peacetime, during the dreary hours of waiting to change the guard at Buckingham Palace as sitting in a long, draughty anteroom unceasingly turning the pages of Flaubert. After the meal I was absolutely sincere when I thanked him '*du fond de mon estomac*' for his kindness in inviting me to sit at his table. The people at the other tables had, relatively speaking, poor fare that day.

After lunch the colonel called all the officers together to say that he had received more specific orders about our destination; the divisional engineers were to go to Evron, a small village about ten miles from Laval. He stressed that under no circumstances was anyone to visit Laval itself; it was to be the seat of the Corps Headquarters. The reason for this was not clear to me until I remembered what Heddon had told me about the organisation of the Army when I was in St. Helens. An army, he had explained, consists mainly of 'divisions', each division containing about twenty thousand men; these divisions are usually grouped together in twos and threes constituting a 'corps'. A corps headquarters is therefore obviously an important place, a sort of nerve centre. He told me that the great thing to do, the aim of every officer, was to 'get on to Corps', by which he meant to become a member of the staff at corps headquarters; it was the pick job of the Army. As an occupation he said it had been consistently reviled and lampooned by Siegfried Sassoon and others throughout the last war, but it had nevertheless very positive merits. I asked him how one set about 'getting on to Corps', and he said that the qualifications varied from place to place. In Singapore it depended largely upon being able to play squash rackets; in India he believed it was more a question of having a liking for bush country. He could not say what it would be like in France this time. I accordingly determined to visit Laval at the first opportunity to see for myself.

We arrived at the sleepy little village of Evron at six-thirty that evening, and I began my real war work – finding houses for other people to live in. It seemed an infamy to have to wake up a little village which had obviously been asleep for a thousand years, which had in fact I suppose never really been awake. Evron had the peace which passeth all understanding on it when we arrived; even the bistro proprietor was sleeping quietly in the evening sun at a little table outside his establishment when we drove into the village. When we left ten days later the place had been transformed. Telephone wires and cables everywhere, priceless fifteenth-century gateways shattered where Army lorries, like elephants, had tried to ram them, all the private houses in an uproar and clamouring for their billet money, the mayor's hat stolen by a practical joker, and even targets hung on the church wall for practice.

Billeting was an interesting, amusing, and often profitable occupation; being concerned very largely with other people's charity it can be very cold. To the civilian who offers to take in a soldier billeting is, quite frankly, a gamble. It is like a horserace; the soldier may completely ruin the house and eat the pigs and chickens; on the other hand he may bring in a regular quota of free government petrol. Like the quality of mercy, billeting is twice blessed, it blesses equally both him who gives and him who receives. The job as always is to get the giver to see this.

I found the billeting procedure in France quite different from its English counterpart. The French actually enjoy foreigners whereas we, as a country, enjoy only the exotic; for instance, if given the choice, we would far rather have a Renoir than Renoir. In France I found too that soldiers were really welcomed in the civilian houses, the people, long accustomed to conscription, thinking of them as part and parcel of their own lives. In England, in 1939 at any rate, a soldier was still a thing apart, requiring an annual Act of Parliament for his existence; to our people, a marionette with about as much life as a toy soldier in a child's Christmas present.

In France I found that, unlike in England where every man is king of his own back garden, and where every man has an inalienable right by law not to have soldiers billeted in it, there is a universal desire actually to get soldiers to come and sleep in it. The French in fact liked and desired our company – at a price. Being a non-hypocritical people they welcomed me in Evron with open arms when they saw me take a five-hundred-franc note from my case and buy an eiderdown. Although, as my purchase showed, I am full of bourgeois tastes and instincts, they thought I was an English lord.

'*Mais c'est un élégant,*' I heard a shopkeeper's wife say to a friend as I staggered out with my purchase.

After that it was easy, billeting was simplified, and I was welcomed wherever I went by kind people all beseeching me to come and stay with them. Finally I chose the house of the notaire, an admirable little man with a charming daughter. And I made arrangements the next day to billet Heddon, when he arrived, with the curé, the major with a notorious pacifist called Lègume, and Stimpson with Colonel de la Haute Barbebiche who ran the local branch of the old soldiers' league, a militant organisation said to be connected with the Fascists.

CHAPTER THREE

M. Octavo Busch; and the Nice Conduct of a Clouded Cane

THE NOTAIRE'S NAME was Octavo Busch and his daughter was called Geneviève. She was nineteen years old and she had just passed one of the many Baccalauréat exams which so confuse the foreigner trying to understand the French educational system. I was invited to dinner with them three days after my arrival in order to celebrate her success. She was apparently a great one for exams, because the walls of the spare room in which I slept were covered with the framed certificates, diplomas, orders of merit, awards for saintliness, and other good conduct medals which she had gained during her school days. There were also innumerable school groups of girls in mortarboards and gowns, the equivalent presumably of our own girls' hockey groups; and over my bed was an enormous doxology done in blue and gilt with lovesick turtledoves at the corners announcing inappropriately: 'My peace I give unto you. My peace I leave with you.' There was also the inevitable crucifix over the mantelpiece, of harrowing, Greco-like reality but this I found less offensive, possibly because it was generally in the shadow.

Octavo Busch himself was, as he told me almost immediately I met him, a self-made man. He apparently took a liking to me because he confided all sorts of secrets with a Rousseau-like candour that was almost embarrassing; he told me all about his early life, how he had worked in a railway engine factory in Bordeaux where his employer had tried to get off with his wife, how he had cheated the railway company out of three hundred francs in order to pay for his law examination, and how he had worked at night by candle in order to pass it. I generally used to listen to him in the evening after returning from supper in the local bistro; he would get out a bottle of *fine* and we would sit by the fire drinking it while his ham-fisted wife beat out Chopin nocturnes and waltzes at the piano.

They had a son, Léon, who was at the front, and poor Madame Busch could never restrain a tear when his name was mentioned. He was the pride of the family, an even more formidable exam-passer than his sister it appeared, and as his father loved to talk of him Madame Busch was seldom dry-eyed.

M. Busch who had fought from 1914 to 1918 in Alsace was not very enthusiastic about the war, but like all old soldiers his army days seemed pleasanter in retrospect and he often used to say how much harder it was for Madame Busch and himself than for little Léon in the Maginot. I learnt later from a friend of the family that little Léon was no longer in the Maginot; he was in a detention barracks near Paris. But I was advised not to say anything about this to the family because little Léon, when he thought fit, was going to inform his parents himself. In any case it would never do to disparage Léon before his family; he stood slightly dazed and bewildered in an oval photograph above the fireplace, wearing a uniform a shade too big, a household god long before his time.

I met M. Busch quite by chance on the evening we arrived in Evron. He was coming out of the church as I was entering it. The church at Evron, like that at St. Lo, was typical of most Brittany churches, as large as English cathedrals and sometimes more imposing because the villages from which they rise are often so small and inadequate by comparison. M. Busch was, I think, particularly impressed at finding an Englishman (and a soldier at that) making straight for the nearest church as soon as he arrived in a village. He congratulated me on this and I told him that I could never resist entering a church if I was passing it (especially in the evening). He accordingly offered to show me the Brussels tapestries and the splendid reredos, made like our own Gothic mouldings from the finest crumbling yet enduring chalk, of which his village was so justly proud. These magnificent embellishments, together with the steady drone of the penitents and confessors closeted together in their little cells, and the musty smell of walls impregnated with centuries of Sunday incense and immemorial dirt, gave to the place the true atmosphere of Romanism, an atmosphere which M. Busch, a devout Catholic, was at some pains to point out to me as such a vast improvement on the drab Protestant variety. In his Alsace days when he was young, he said, he had come much into contact with that dreary faith; he said he had found it a poor religion, a bastard form of Christianity, a cross between

Catholicism and nothing. He said that the sense of the power of tradition in these Catholic churches was greater than one could find anywhere else or in any other sphere of life. I agreed that, by contrast, our English conception of birth and aristocracy as the true symbols of tradition seemed almost jejune. I told him that to give him some notion of these English conceptions, I would like to introduce him to one of the officers in the advance guard, an aristocratic youth who delighted in his only asset, a pair of exclusive purple trousers which, worn with a khaki jacket, distinguished him from everyone else as a cavalry officer, at once a figure of pride, a figure of tradition, and a figure of fun. M. Busch said that nothing would delight him more than to meet a British officer in purple trousers.

Finding that we had so much in common M. Busch kindly invited me to stay at his house. I was doubtful about accepting this invitation when I met him outside the church; much as I liked him, the extreme simplicity of his dress (he had only a collar band with a stud in it for neckwear) made me suspicious about his 'house'; I suspected it might be a barn. This dress, together with the great interest he showed for tapestries and Gothic mouldings made me put him down as a needy intellectual, at the best a bookseller who had gone bankrupt, a man of more value in conversation and as a companion than as the provider of a comfortable bed and a dry hearth. He fulfilled all that Herrick has to say on the subject:

> A careless shoestring in whose tie
> I see a wild civility.

But in any case I was not prepared to live in a civil wilderness. He seemed to understand why I did not accept immediately.

'I am, you know, the notaire,' he said, drawing himself up, 'and as for these clothes – I have just been taking a nap in my garden. It adjoins the church. You must come and see it some time.'

The house of a notaire is always bound to be habitable, so I accepted his invitation immediately. Three days later, when I went to dinner with him, our conversation was more topical; we talked of nothing but the war and the atrocity stories which, after three weeks of fighting, were just beginning to appear in the French Press. M. Busch had heard many of these stories in the last war and he said he refused to believe any of them.

'The Germans,' he said, 'are just the same as you and I. They would just as soon be sitting in a beer garden.'

'But,' I said, 'when I lived in Belgium I often used to meet people who swore that they had actually seen the Boche in the last war committing some barbarity – machine-gunning children up against a wall or cutting off their arms.'

'In Belgium,' said M. Busch, 'people will swear anything. I can only tell you my own personal experience. It happened in a disused railway carriage near Metz. This carriage stood alone in a siding; it had been there for many months and we soldiers used to take a night off occasionally to sleep in it. It was so much more comfortable than the Army quarters; we had fitted it out with a bed and some chairs and a lavabo. We thought it the last word in comfort I can tell you. Well – one day the Boche made a surprise raid into our territory. He didn't go very far and he was soon driven back so that we didn't think much of it at the time. But two days later towards evening I managed to get away from the trenches unseen and I made straight for the railway carriage. It stood all alone in a waste piece of ground that had been much devastated by enemy fire,' said M. Busch, pausing to give effect to the scene he had depicted. He wiped his hand over his forehead and poured himself out some more wine. His wife, who had presumably heard the story hundreds of times before, went on with her knitting in front of the fire, smiling indulgently.

'You can imagine what it was like,' he said. 'Night was falling and I had had a hard day. I was very tired. I had spent the whole day chopping up bits of wood. I was looking forward to a quiet and peaceful night. There was food in the carriage too, I knew. We French soldiers who used the carriage always used to keep a little food in a cupboard. We relied on one another to be honest about it. We had quite a brotherhood in those days,' he sighed such was his nostalgia, and then continued more intently. 'Imagine my surprise when I entered the carriage to find a Boche lying sound asleep on my bed! I knew he was a Boche by the cleanness of his uniform;

our men used to be very dirty, you know, but the Boche was a great one for washing and spit and polish. He was lying quite quietly on the bed, breathing very deeply. I didn't know quite what to do. At first I thought of shooting him; but I couldn't do that, could I? – not while he was asleep. But then I looked at him more closely and I saw that from time to time he smiled in his sleep. And then I noticed some plates on the table; and then, worst of all, the cupboard doors flung wide open and all the food gone. I was very angry at this and I determined to hand him over to the police immediately. So I moved towards the bed with my bayonet in front of me.' At this point M. Busch picked up his table-knife and holding it in a defensive attitude in front of him, stealthily advanced his arm towards a sausage lying on a plate in the middle of the table.

'Suddenly,' he said, 'I stumbled and made a noise. It woke him up and when I had recovered my balance he was looking at me, his eyes wide open. I thought he was going to jump at me so I rushed forward and placed my bayonet against his chest. And then what do you think he did?' said M. Busch, laying down the knife as if implying that hostilities were over. 'He talked French. Quite good French too.

'"Monsieur," he said, "I am an Alsatian. I was born near Metz. Please do not kill me near my home town."

'I did not know what to do. What would you have done? I stood and looked at him for some moments. I did not dare to speak. It seemed so strange to talk French to a German. I waited a little and then I said

'"Why have you eaten all my food?"

'At this he smiled.

'"Mais, mon ami," he said, "I have not eaten all your food. It is in my pocket here," and with that he tapped the pocket of his tunic.

'"Let us eat it together," he said.

'"But," I said, "I shall get into hot water if I am found eating with a German."

'"Do not worry about that," he said. "I am really no more German than French. It was only because my father was pursued by the French police that he was forced to run away to the other side of the frontier in 1860, and that I was born a German. Do not let us worry about a little thing like that. See – I have a bottle of wine here and together with your sausages and bread we can have a proper meal. When we have eaten I will return to my regiment and then you will be able to have the bed."

'I was so delighted at finding that the food was still there,' said M. Busch helping himself to the sausage he had been menacing only a few moments before, 'that I agreed to share it with him if he would give me some of his wine. He was a good fellow and hated the army as much as I did.'

'What happened then?' I asked.

'The Boche was as good as his word. He left after we had eaten. But I saw him again the next day. He had been captured and he was in a line of marching prisoners. He recognised me and called out. He seemed quite happy.'

'He was lucky to be able to make the best of two worlds, wasn't he?' I said. 'The French and the German.'

'Yes – I can't say I should have been happy to have been a prisoner,' said M. Busch. 'But ever since that evening I've never believed that the Germans are really any different from us.'

After dinner some friends came in for a glass of brandy and we spent the rest of the evening round the piano singing polite and patriotic songs. Geneviève was a charming singer; she sang in the old style, with her vocal chords and not with her legs after the fashion of so many modern singers. And Madame Busch, who gave a piano recital afterwards showed that although obviously a Chopin lover, she could turn her hand to other things as well; she alternated the 'Alabama Blues' type of music with Brahms' Hungarian dances. The instrument she was playing lacked some of the piano wires of various notes, but she played these silent notes all the same, singing them vocally to make up for their absence. This gave a most curious effect to one of Beethoven's sonatas. But altogether it was a very enjoyable evening.

My work in Evron during those first days was confined almost entirely to arranging billets for the main body. It seemed a simple enough task at first, but I soon realised that it was more complex. Apart from arranging the great leisure occupations of an army, eating and sleeping, there were many other domestic matters to attend to; the provision for example of baths, lavatories, offices, vehicle parks, stores dumps, coal dumps, refuse dumps, all of which often call for as much persuasive power and forthright method as the more primary things. Dumps, in fact, are far and away the most characteristic part of a modern army, far more characteristic than the soldiers. This type of work was new to me and I was glad to have the help of a French liaison officer.

Before we left Mayenne the colonel of the advance guard had told us about these liaison officers; he had impressed upon us all the importance of being polite to the civil population and as I had no notion of how the French would react to foreign soldiers in their houses, I was particularly pleased to find when I arrived at Evron that I had been provided with this French officer. All the other units had been similarly equipped, the liaison officer in each case being a permanent attachment, as much a part of the unit as its British members. The French had formed a pool of these English-speaking Frenchmen, but by some mischance several of them were Dutch interpreters who could not speak a word of English and who had therefore to communicate with their English companions by means of signs. Much confusion was caused and time wasted before they were replaced, the French authorities stupidly maintaining that a man was either an 'interpreter' or he was not, regardless of what foreign language he spoke.

The functions of the liaison officer were, in active operations, as the title describes, to form a link between the British Army and the various French civil and military authorities we might become connected with; in non-active conditions he was to help us placate the civilians, both tasks calling for low cunning and duplicity, both well-suited to a Frenchman.

I had been instructed to meet my liaison officer, who was called de Treuil, in the Mairie at ten o'clock on the day after I arrived at Evron. In this way I met the man who was to be one of my closest companions for the next eight months. I found him standing with his back to me in the Grande Salle – hatless, whistling gently, and looking up at one of the great skylights where a pigeon was vainly trying to escape. His hands were in his breeches pockets as he balanced back upon his heels; he was dressed in a beautiful brand-new uniform, of the quality worn only by the elegants of the French Army. In spite of this I knew he was no soldier; a little too fat, his cheeks a little too flushed, his eyes too glassy and too bulgy, the eyes of a luxurious moth that has breakfasted too well and too regularly upon only the richest and most exclusive of tapestries. He had the air of having lived permanently at Pruniers, and of having drunk more cocktails than were good for him; all the signs, in fact, of a civilised man. He could not be a soldier.

He had evidently been told to expect me for he knew my name, and when I said questioningly, 'de Treuil?' he turned and shook my hand like an American.

'Rhodes? Well – this *is* a pleasure.'

He had a personality which could only be described as 'terrific'. He overpowered you; after talking to him for a few moments you felt bruised. Yet instinctively I liked him and throughout our acquaintance I never went back on this first impression. As soon as he had shaken hands with me he characteristically took command. His English was flawless; it was American.

'Come on,' he said. 'It's cold here. Let's go some place where we can get a drink.'

We found a bistro near the church where we sat out on the pavement sipping our cassis and telling one another our life stories.

Georges de Treuil was thirty-five years old and he had done everything. He was by profession a Parisian stockbroker who had opened up a branch office for his firm in the United States. He had soon filled his pockets and his alert, penetrating mind must have quickly brought him recognition; I was not surprised to learn later from another source that he was one of the most successful stockbrokers in Paris and his firm one of the most prosperous. Not only had he done everything but he knew or appeared to know everybody. Although a Frenchman by birth he was a cosmopolitan in everything else. Educated at an English luxury school, tempered at the Sorbonne, polished in Paris, and finally case-hardened in New York, he was a liberal, like Terence, who was prepared to interest himself in any human activity – whatever it might be. Liberal notions of this type generally tend to make people vague, uncertain, and unpractical; appreciating all sides of an argument or question, they can make up their minds about none. They become aesthetic or at the very least, in Dickens' phrase, dangerously intellectual. Georges had successfully avoided these pitfalls. He was still convinced, like all New York businessmen, that time is money, although he admitted readily enough that Socrates had once said that it was made for fools.

As we sat on the pavement that morning I realised how lucky I was to get such a companion and not a dreary French schoolmaster who could talk about nothing else but *Jane Eyre*.

Georges, like our forefathers, went to war accompanied by his wife – and also his Bugatti; but he was doubtful how near the front line his wife would be allowed to go. She was a charming young American called Alsacia, as discreet as Georges was rampant, full of the same vivacious spirit as her husband, but possessing the quiet formal charm which nice Americans so often display in front of the Old World and Old Masters. When the war began she had just given Georges a son in a Dinard nursing home, but by the time Georges arrived in Evron she was fit to travel and one day he slipped away in the Bugatti to collect her. It was against all the rules for anyone to leave Evron, but Georges, with typical ingenuity, had obtained permission to make the trip from a stray colonel we had picked up in a bistro, a man who had no jurisdiction over him whatsoever. We were having dinner with this man, a boisterous fellow whom we had found sitting at an adjacent table, when Georges asked for the permission. The colonel was a member of the British advance guard it is true, but he belonged to another unit and he had no power to authorise any of Georges' actions or movements, I found it very interesting to watch Georges' technique. At exactly the right moment, when the colonel, fascinated and dazzled by Georges' conversation, had had exactly the right amount of drink, Georges said casually:

'I'm thinking of collecting my car tomorrow, sir. I suppose it'll be all right?'

'Good gracious – yes,' said the colonel, helping himself to another drink. 'What make is it?'

After that Georges steadily steered the conversation away from the subject of the Bugatti; but it was neatly done. If Georges had been subsequently arrested and court-martialled for going to Dinard the colonel would have regretted the drinks he had had that evening.

Georges returned the following day with his wife and I immediately fell for her. She was much younger than Georges, twenty-two against his thirty-five, with a prim Botticelli face and beautiful golden locks hanging weightily about her neck like flax from a distaff. I learnt later that she was Georges' second wife, but whether his first had divorced him or whether she had merely been worn out by his energy I could never find out.

Being young and pretty Alsacia soon had trouble with the British soldiery. While walking in Evron one morning three soldiers fell in behind her and dogged her all round the village with an audible running commentary. Thinking of course that she was French they spoke freely.

'Coo. Not bad, eh?'

'Nice legs these little Frenchies have.'

'Bit hoity-toity, ain't she?'

'Let's get her in a café. Give her something to drink. That'll liven her up.'

'How do we start?' etc., etc.

After some discussion among themselves the most courageous of the soldiers ran up to her and attempted to introduce himself, holding a Hugo's phrasebook in his hand from which he read some polite formula. Alsacia thought it would be a pity to spoil the fun so, avoiding smiling, she turned and answered haughtily, as if an improper suggestion had been made:

'*Mais ça – c'est dégoûtant*,' and then turned with dignity and went on her way, ignoring her followers.

The British soldier retired to a safe distance with his companions and, still following her, produced a pocket dictionary in which he looked up the word 'dégoûtant'.

'"Dégoûtant" means disgusting,' he said indignantly to his friends. 'She says we're disgusting.'

'Blimey, these French hussies!' said one of his companions. 'What the hell! You ain't suggested nothing, did you? What's up with her?' and with that they all started abusing her in unlovely English. After a minute or two of this Alsacia felt that she was learning more than was good for her so she turned and said in English:

'Please do not continue. I can understand everything you say.'

When she turned round again, she said, the soldiers had disappeared; they had dived into the nearest bistro to hide their heads.

One of the difficulties caused by the presence of Alsacia was the new allotment of billets. Georges and Alsacia were billeted on the grocer, the richest man in the village. His house had a bathroom with hot and cold water and a proper w.c.; it was the luxury billet. And it seemed only fair to me, believing in the old-fashioned theory of unmarried couples fending for themselves, that married couples should have accommodation provided for them – and the best accommodation at that. But what troubled us was the problem of housing the engineer colonel when he turned up; he would presumably want a bath occasionally and Georges now had the only one in the village. In fact the whole question of Georges and his wife and the colonel's probable attitude to it was a constant source of worry to us. We could not make up our minds how best to inform him that one of his officers proposed to remain actively married throughout the war. We considered various methods of approach. Should Georges, for instance, do it in a hearty manner on the station when the colonel alighted from the train?

'Hello, sir. Pleased to meet you. Meet my wife,' etc., etc. Georges was in favour of this method himself but I believed in a more indirect approach. I thought that he should do it progressively, at first concealing his wife and then gradually making her presence felt by easy stages; first as an acquaintance, then as a girlfriend, then as his mistress, and finally, when the colonel had got thoroughly used to her, announcing that they were man and wife; very much after the manner of the Grand Guignol in which a chambermaid in the household of a rich man becomes successively his parlourmaid, cook, housekeeper, mistress, and finally his wife; but of course avoiding anything suggestive of the anti-climax in the play in which she comes out in front of the curtain when it is all over and says '*Mais quand même – c'est toujours moi qui vide le vase de nuit*'.

We finally decided on the first course, except that the meeting was not to take place on the railway station; it would take place in a restaurant – with Georges as host. Even then the question of the colonel's billet still remained. The communal baths I had visited on my first morning would certainly not be suitable. They had reminded me of some pithead baths in Alaska I had once read about: 'There was little water in the district, so that great economy had to be maintained in the use of baths; all water had to be strained, reheated, and then re-used.' The straining arrangements in Evron were evidently wretched.

Before the colonel arrived I took the opportunity of visiting the forbidden city, Laval. Georges, who had eighteenth-century standards of dandiness, fancied himself greatly in his uniform and wanted to buy a malacca cane and a snuff-box. We went into Laval, not, as is normally the case in the Army under similar circumstances, in a three-ton lorry, but in Georges' Bugatti; he drove it like a racing driver. He told me he was determined to take this car with him wherever he went in the Army. He had certainly used it to good purpose during the first three weeks of the war when, as an ordinary French soldier, he had had the job of Army postman. He had been given a bicycle with which to make his day's rounds; the Bugatti had enabled him to knock off his day's work at about eleven o'clock each morning.

I was pleased to hear when I arrived home in England nine months later that he had succeeded in taking the Bugatti everywhere with him after he left our unit; he even took it into the Maginot Line where he used it during the fighting in May and June of 1940. When the great retreat started it appears that he managed to get back to Bordeaux with it, just in time to ship it on the last boat sailing for America.

Laval was a dreary little town, newly smarting under its selection as a British military headquarters. It was full of British staff officers with coloured armbands, grimly stalking about as if the battle of Waterloo was just about to start; it made me understand Byron's romantic nature; he could never have consulted any responsible eyewitness about the Duchess of Richmond's ball. These people in Laval were presumably the descendants of her guests; but, even allowing for the departure of the age of chivalry, they seemed grossly unromantic.

We visited one or two bookshops full of the latest nonsensical propaganda, with such titles as *Pourquoi Hitler ne peut pas gagner…* or, as some humourist has entitled them, full of *I Was Himmler's Aunt* books; then there were the familiar astrological almanacks of native Old Moores forecasting that Hitler would die of a gallstone on the Ides of March because Aries and the Plough had precessed while his father was being confirmed. One suddenly became conscious of a Great Truth, the gigantic platitude that people were really the same the whole world over.

Georges gave me an excellent lunch, after which he bought his baubles and then visited his liaison chief. Georges had only been under Army discipline once before; he had been just old enough to take part in the Rhineland Army of Occupation in 1919, and any little sense of discipline and Army procedure that he had gained during it had now entirely disappeared. It amused me to see him in conversation with his chief, a captain in the French regular Army, a soldier of the old school with a Foch-like face and a stern unbending bearing. Georges seemed uncertain how to behave with him. At first he instinctively treated him as a fellow stockbroker, saluting as if it were a rather shameful and uncivilised action. But after a little the iciness of the captain and his office seemed to penetrate even Georges, and before long he had become quite self-conscious, doing his best not to slouch in his chair and answering questions in an unnaturally servile manner, some achievement for a man who, I liked to suppose, was accustomed to spending the day in a New York skyscraper, signing cheques and making and breaking fortunes by the hour.

This captain, who later followed us up to Lille, was the only person, as far as I know, who had ever subdued Georges. Most people always accepted Georges' opinion after he had spoken to them for a minute or two. The mayor of Evron, a timid little man called Rossignol, he soon bullied into complete submission. The mayor had refused permission for some of my men to sleep in the grande salle of his mairie, a reasonable enough refusal because, after all, the mairie was his own office and the civic centre of the town. I had been unable to find any other place and it was Georges who had encouraged me to make the request. I told Georges that the mayor had very rightly refused. Georges dealt with him summarily.

'Why cannot these men sleep in the grande salle?' he asked the mayor.

'Monsieur, but it is my mairie. It is my only place. It is the centre of the life of our town. It would never do to...'

'Do you realise what you are doing by refusing in this manner?'

'No,' said the mayor unwisely.

'Well – I will tell you. You are hindering the war effort of the nation. This officer here' – he indicated me – 'has come specially to fight against the Germans – against our enemy. He has come to protect Evron, to protect you – yes – you,' and he jabbed the mayor with his finger.

'But, monsieur, the Town Hall – it has never been...'

'Yes – you are impeding the war effort. You are being rude to our brave allies. You are no patriot. You are a helper of the enemy. You are a...' – but there was no word for fifth columnist in those days.

In the end, after a short and heroic struggle, the mayor gave in. It is in such circumstances as these that a liaison officer is invaluable. The only person to argue with a Frenchman is a Frenchman.

In this way, and by subtler methods, we had made all arrangements for the reception of the main body by the end of September and, drinking more Vermouth in the bistros than was good for us, we waited patiently in Evron for it to arrive.

CHAPTER FOUR
Army Hierarchy

THE MAIN BODY of the division arrived early one morning in the first week of October; they came as unexpectedly and as frostily as the first day of winter. To Georges, Alsacia, and myself, still sunning ourselves in front of the bistros or lying and chatting in the warm fields outside the village, their arrival meant the end of autumn. Indeed, in retrospect, it meant the end of a charming and memorable interlude, a sort of autumn idyll in which '*les jours caniculaires*', uncertain how long they could decently remain with us, had struggled and tilted against the uncertainty and instability of the Hitlerian moment. Of course they were bound to lose the struggle but they had at least gained their point; they had acted as a buffer between peace and war, easing the transition and making war seem for the time as fantastic and preposterous as peace was fantastic and impossible.

To this idyll came an Army division full of strange oaths and Bren guns; the idyll collapsed violently and the colonel ordered us to do gas drill daily. He was renowned for his 'drive'.

Evron railway station did its best to welcome the division that morning. The three of us rose at 6 a.m. and stood on the platform in the company of the mayor and the man who did duty as stationmaster, signal-master, and porter. We had our handkerchiefs ready but the flags which had celebrated the signing of the Triple Entente, struck when Edward VII was last in France, had unfortunately been mislaid. It grieved the stationmaster greatly; he had always used them at public functions of this kind.

The train arrived and the colonel got out first. He was hot, tired, and dirty; he shook hands cordially with Georges, appeared slightly bewildered by Alsacia, and asked me where he could get a bath. Thanks to M. Rossignol I was able to reply immediately. In spite of Georges' bullying (or, according to Georges – as a result of it) M. Rossignol had behaved with extraordinary magnanimity; knowing our difficulty, he had suddenly offered one day to billet and *bath* the colonel. It was the bath that had surprised us most, and, seeing that we were sceptical, he said that he was prepared to divulge his secret in the public interest – he had had a bath in his house for more than three years! He hoped the colonel would honour him by using it.

Among those present on the station I noted Stimpson and Heddon both looking deathly pale; like everyone else they had had an appalling journey without any sleep. Stimpson had crossed in a destroyer and he was regretting it.

'The Navy,' he said categorically, 'is worse than the Army; it has all the faults of the Army except that you go up and down as well. It is a sort of Army afloat. Never, never again. I shall take all my leaves in Paris if they decide to ferry us back in those Navy boats again.'

We escorted them to their various billets where they proposed to sleep and wash. Georges said he hoped that all the officers would consider themselves as his guests at dinner that night; he had ordered a special dinner at the bistro. It was a wise step because the colonel who had appeared so crusty and irritable on the station in the early morning turned out to be a dear, kind old man when he had had a bath and had got a bottle of wine inside him. He was quite charming and gallant to Alsacia at dinner, setting all our fears at rest. This admittedly was probably due to Georges, whose conversation and obvious social gifts had their usual effect; it was, as I had expected, not long before the colonel was eyeing him with that blend of interest and deference called by most people admiration, but by the uncharitable, class-consciousness. Georges had the unusual knack of appearing What he was – a wealthy Franco-American patrician, as cultivated as he was worth cultivating. To such charms we are all susceptible; all the world loves a lord. The colonel certainly did.

The conversation, as conversations will under the influence of good food, good wine, and a man like Georges, soon became elegant and indelicate. After the usual banalities about the superiority of French cooking and the British Navy, and the stupidity of the police of both countries, Georges deftly conducted the conversation as he willed; it lighted for a moment upon the orgies of Babylon, touched upon the infidelities of the Duchesse de Maintenon, steered into a more navigable channel on the subject of Adolf Hitler and Leni

Riefenstahl and then finished, surprisingly and prosaically, on our War Aims. Someone thereupon mentioned the British Empire, but he was immediately squashed, whether for committing blasphemy or for being merely surpassingly stupid I could not tell. Georges characteristically said that we were fighting to prevent the Old World from destroying a culture that had such good market value in the New.

'Pierpoint Morgan would be just wild if he knew what was going on in the Warsaw picture galleries,' he said.

The adjutant, a widely travelled man, had visited lands where people did unspeakable things. He knew what we were fighting for, but he wondered if he ought to say it. The party had become sufficiently convivial to permit candour, so he lowered his head and, glancing in the direction of Alsacia who was talking to Heddon, said slowly, weighing every word:

'I can tell you what we are fighting for. We are fighting to prevent our womenfolk from being raped by inhuman savages. I was in Belgium in the last war. I know.'

Without thinking, I said, 'You must meet Monsieur Busch, my landlord. He has a good story about a German,' but fortunately no-one was listening to me. They were all looking very grave when Stimpson said absently, 'I am fighting for Pergolesi's Stabat Mater and a few lines of Sappho.'

No-one know what he meant; they all thought he was drunk. He explained what he meant.

'You can hear a bit of old music or poetry anywhere or any time,' said the adjutant.

'Exactly,' said the padre, who loathed Stimpson.

'You are a young decadent,' said the adjutant.

'Well,' said Stimpson turning to the padre, 'which would you rather be, Padre – young and decadent – or old and virile?'

'Old and virile,' said the padre manfully, without thinking.

'Exactly,' said Stimpson, and no-one seemed to understand why he smiled.

Heddon and Alsacia de Treuil were meanwhile having an argument on the same subject but on more political lines. They were arguing about democracy and communism. It was interesting to hear so many and so varied opinions from all these people who were leaving their money-making to make war instead.

'I know all that stuff about democracy,' Heddon was saying. 'Democracy means all men are equal, doesn't it ? – all men, that is, who wear bowler hats. Now, in the case of true socialism you can wear what you like because of the communist method of...'

'Liquidation,' cut in Alsacia who had lived in Southern Carolinian luxury all her life. 'I know all that stuff too. Liquidation makes people equal, doesn't it? It brings them all to water level, to the lowest level, doesn't it? That's why I'm fighting for capitalism.'

The conversation would probably have become quite heated had not Georges suddenly entered it.

'I don't know what you're all arguing about,' he said, becoming serious and abandoning his previous view. 'We're really all fighting because we've got to, because there's a thing called conscription. We haven't any choice.'

This summing-up so delighted the colonel that he immediately went off to bed, reminding us as he went that we were to be on parade in good time the next day. His order seemed very effectively to underline Georges' last statement.

The next few days saw the arrival of the remainder of the division, so that by the end of the first week of November everyone was ready for the next move. The High Command were said to be pondering it; we expected it to be north towards the Belgian frontier, but we hoped it would be south towards Nice. My principal job had been explained to me by the colonel as soon as he arrived at Evron; it would be 'to purchase and distribute engineer stores for the division'. He could make it no more explicit than that; he said that without knowing exactly where we were going he could not forecast what sort of work the engineers would be called upon to do. The engineer section of a division is under the command of a lieutenant-colonel who acts as adviser to the divisional commander. It is therefore essential that his staff shall be in the closest touch with divisional headquarters; wherever the general is, there must the engineer colonel be. Having left the field company I was attached to at St. Helens, it was in this way, as a member of the engineer staff, that I found myself throughout my time in France always in the closest theoretical touch with the general; although I only once had the good fortune to meet him personally. He was a dynamic little man of obvious compressed energy, charming and genial in manner, something of a small prehistoric bird in the jerkiness and rapidity of his speech and gesture, and a hater of unnecessary formality and letter writers. If one said, in short, that he fulfilled as nearly as any general I can call to mind, the conditions and qualifications laid down for good generalship by our great daily newspapers, one would do him no injustice. Indeed it would be great praise, for of few public men can it finally be said 'he satisfied the Press'; as an epitaph it is unsurpassable and unknown. He was immensely popular with the troops and he was once described to me somewhat ominously by one of his staff officers as 'a glutton for punishment'; I took this to mean that if there was any fighting to be done, his men would be in the thick of it.

In this way, having fulfilled my first mission as divisional harbinger, I found myself in Evron on the 1st of October 1939 as a member of both a divisional staff and an engineer mess. The various regimental constituents of the divisional staff, although they work together, live their own domestic lives in their respective messes – and the establishing of a proper engineer mess, a compact body consisting of seven British officers and Georges (Alsacia was not mentioned by the colonel much to everyone else's distress) was one of the first cares of the colonel when he arrived. He was particularly anxious that no foreign elements should creep into it because the Royal Engineers, like all other regiments of the British Army, take great pride in their own regimental flags, tunes, customs, and legends. There are for instance two polite legends which they frequently repeat about themselves, one of which says that Royal Engineer officers are 'the Brains of the Army'; while the other maintains that they are all either 'mad, married, or Methodist'. The second of these legends, as a compliment has always seemed to me the more skilfully turned; there can be no doubt that each of the three conditions of man referred to in it is at least blissful. Yet the engineer officers themselves, I found, did not regard it so; they treated the second legend as a jest, a mere piece of amiable buffoonery, while the first they modestly acknowledged as profoundly true.

In time I found that I was able to classify regiments according to their own opinion of themselves; I am a great believer in always taking the best opinion. Generalisations are so much out of favour nowadays that one is almost bound to make them. Thus one sums up units in the following manner. The cavalry – here all who are not cavalry are vulgarians. The engineers – here they think that everyone else is brainless. And the gunners – here they are convinced that all other men are teetotal. These are only a few cases but the principle holds good throughout the Army. The result is that you know exactly where you are. If you are invited out to dinner at a cavalry mess you expect to be treated as an amiable outcast, at an R.E. mess as a necessary cretin, and at a gunner mess as a sort of potential Toby Belch. There is a very great deal to say for it: this attitude which characterises the officers of the whole Army is an admirable one, one of those simplifications which our modern civilian life is so often seeking and so seldom finding; a return to those straight-forward feudal sets of values which existed before people like Bright and Mills came forward prating about equality and incidentally putting every self-respecting citizen into a maze of self-doubt while trying to be socially equal with everyone else – an obvious impossibility. It is this simplification in which eating, drinking, and sleeping are the main functions and not climbing or equalising that must be the secret of the attraction of the Army to older men; otherwise, how can one account for the enthusiasm for it which one finds on every side?

As buyer, distributor, and journeyman to the Royal Engineers I naturally counted myself a member of the cognoscenti, of the Royal Engineers. I found that everyone in the Army was prepared to recognise this except the Royal Engineers. I think some of them thought I was a low fellow but whatever they may have thought, they treated me throughout our association with the utmost consideration and courtesy, so that it was not long before I was as proud and as zealous of the regimental traditions as they were themselves.

Nevertheless, in spite of every tradition, innovation was doing its best to intrude even into the Army; and one of the most interesting conversations I have ever had, took place three weeks later in Paris with a cavalry officer who revealed to me just how far it had succeeded. This officer was, it is true, only a renegade cavalry officer, a man who after six years' service had left the regular army in 1926 in order, as he put it, to embrace 'la vie bohême'; he had embraced it in Paris until war was declared in September 1939, when he had been recalled to his regiment. But his views, even if they were not therefore strictly representative of a cavalry officer, were at least candid. He told me of the changes that had confronted him on his return. The change that troubled his colleagues most, he said, concerned their club in London; it had been thrown open to the officers of the Royal Tank Corps. I asked him what was wrong with the officers of the Royal Tank Corps.

'They are nearly all mechanics,' he said simply. He confessed that it did not worry him much; he had lived for many years among the disciples of Amadeo Modigliani and was accordingly above such pettiness.

'But – the cavalry officers,' he said sympathetically, 'you can imagine what it means to them – born and bred into a four-legged world – why, almost transformed into it, almost a part of it themselves;' he spoke with deep emotion.

'Time,' I said soothingly, as the waiter brought us our brandies, 'marches on. It waits for no man. We must learn to take the good with the bad, the rough with the smooth, the motorcar with the machine-gun, Mr. Bernard Shaw with the Industrial Revolution, the Defence of the Realm with Mr. Churchill, the...'

'But not, surely not,' he said, 'the Tank Corps with the Cavalry.'

CHAPTER FIVE
Of Castles, Food, and Champagne Magnates

ORDERS FOR OUR next move came on October the 4th, while we were still in Evron. Georges and I were instructed by the colonel to 'proceed immediately in the direction of the Belgian frontier'. Further orders he said, would be issued when we arrived there; our task, as at Evron, would be to find billets for the main body. We would move in the company of other vehicles each representing another unit of the main body; and on no account were we to go through Paris. Georges was particularly keen to visit Paris because he had various domestic affairs to arrange at his *appartement* in the rue de Rivoli, and we accordingly tried to devise some means of detaching ourselves from our companions in order to visit the city. It must be borne in mind that all these deliberate violations of rules, although at first sight undoubtedly wrong and reprehensible, were dictated very largely by one's ideas about the future. The prospect before us of months, perhaps years, of obscene trench warfare, of oceans of mud and countless lice, of a life in fact which, according to first-hand reports of the last war, was about the lowest and meanest to which man has ever been ordered to sink, was enough to make one snatch from the welter of unpleasant wartime experience ahead any odd straws of pleasant experience that it might unintentionally offer. Because, throughout the following eight months of inactivity on the Belgian frontier, we were constantly expecting to pass through the last week of civilised living, I was determined to make the best of that week; which is merely another way of saying that in the long run I made the best of every week, an expensive and exhausting process when carried out over a period of eight months.

When I deliberately broke the rules and visited Laval some days before, I did it partly because it meant a pleasant ride across a charming landscape and partly because it was another head to add, American-like, to my collection of places visited, places seen – in this case of even sweeter memory because it had been done at Government expense.

I had little doubt that my service would take me to many foreign towns and that I would see much of the world in this way. But whereas Laval was visited in the light of a quiet warm autumn evening, in a pre-eminently civilised fashion, most of the places I visited later would, I imagined, be in ruins, or on fire and full of mouldering corpses.

As a matter of fact all Georges' carefully laid plans for going to Paris failed to mature, because, when we reached the Seine, things moved too quickly for us to put the scheme into effect; he had proposed the same methods as he had adopted with such success for his visit to Dinard earlier in the week; to obtain permission from a duped, alien, and irresponsible staff officer. We realised later how fortunate it was that we had been unable to carry out this scheme because our own colonel, unknown to us, was following close behind to see how we were getting on; and he would have caught us.

Unobserved, we slipped away from Evron in the early morning of October the 5th. There was a suspicion of frost on the brass handle of the great mairie door as we passed it; the winter had come, but I had at least enjoyed my autumn days in Evron with M. Rossignol and the Buschs, and I was mortified at having to leave without being allowed even to say goodbye. I left a note for the Buschs in my bedroom saying how I hoped to see them again one day, and giving them my address in England. And I was charmed later to receive a long letter from Monsieur Busch at Christmas telling me all about little Léon's visit from the Maginot Line *en permission*.

We had no specific orders about our final destination; our instructions simply told us to meet a certain staff officer in Rouen. It was certainly a great stroke of fortune to have to wait in Rouen because, as an English guidebook explains, it possesses not only one of the most perfect restaurants in the world, where you can get an unparalleled sole Marguerite but also a cathedral of magnificent proportions, 'much admired by painters and others for its western front'. Georges promised to introduce everyone to the famous restaurant in the place Jeanne d'Arc, and one of the other interpreters offered to take a party round the cathedral after lunch. He said that in civil life he was much interested in cathedrals.

The journey to Rouen took longer than we expected owing to a breakdown outside Evron in the early morning; it fortunately occurred at a small village called Ste Suzanne, and while the vehicle was being repaired we were able to inspect one of the most interesting remains in Brittany. Ste Suzanne, a village as charming as its name, appears to the traveller inspecting it from afar as if, in a more romantic age, it might have inspired Grimm to write a fairy-tale about a princess in a castle on a hill. Standing high and alone, it dominates the plain around it, a sort of dry-land Mont St Michel; in the distance a maze of turrets and crenellations, at near view a heap of rough-cut medieval stone; wherever you stand it is the focus of your vision, compelling you as Ely does across the plains of Cambridge. It would be hard at any time to pass such a place without stopping to ask some fellow on the cobbles something about its past; yet we were preparing to do so and I was deploring the inexorability of an Army convoy when one of our vehicles let out a cloud of steam from beneath its bonnet and, protesting for me, would go no further. This happened at the foot of the hill that leads to the village, and while mechanics busied themselves with spanners, Georges and I climbed the hill into the village of Ste Suzanne, and from one of the turrets we looked out towards the south, over the hot early mists of the plain, and saw, or thought we saw, the valley of the Loire gleaming forty miles away.

A self-appointed guide with a goitre on his neck and a skin so unhealthy that he might have been one of Leonardo's diseased men, hobbled up to us and told us without preamble that the village was 'impregnable', a quality that we had scarcely associated with it; he obviously thought that in the eyes of military men a place can know no greater praise. At Georges' expression of polite surprise he offered to conduct us personally round the walls, saying that he would tell us all about the great historic sieges withstood since the beginning of recorded time by the village on the hill.

'Not even the English could capture Ste Suzanne,' he said to me waggishly.

'My English friend would much rather look at it,' said Georges.

'Ha-ha,' said the old man. 'But his king – *celui du coeur d'un lion* – he didn't want to look at it. After three years over on the other side of the valley there, he got tired of looking and went away. Here – look,' he said pointing to a moss-covered hole in one of the walls, 'this is what he left behind – a cannonball. There are hundreds of them all round the walls. But,' he said proudly, 'cannons can do nothing to such walls. You could fire all day at them without even disturbing a sparrow's nest. Look – see how thick they are. And here you see is another of your cannonballs – it is still in there. If you bend down you can see it glinting.'

'Yes,' said Georges, putting his eye to the hole in the wall, 'it's there sure enough – just as it came out of the British armament works.'

The old man rambled on, talking partly in French and partly in the English he had picked up from tourists. The village had been a fortress of inestimable strength, he said, sometime associated with William the Conqueror, Henry of Navarre, and many other military titles unknown to me. In spite of its name and quiet charm, it had lived like a man.

Later, when the mists had cleared we motored on to Rouen in the freshness of the October morning, almost unconscious of the war in the indescribable calm and serenity of the fields and spinneys and meadows, conscious only of the peace of the moment or, to use a much abused phrase in its proper connotation, the peace which passeth all understanding. The proprietor of the famous restaurant in Rouen, an old friend of Georges, was delighted to see him, particularly as he brought with him thirty hungry officers. He insisted on our sitting at a magnificent oak table, his *table Edouard sept*' as he proudly called it, not as one might at first suppose a piece of period furniture, but so called because Edward VII had once eaten a calf's head at it while on his way to Paris in 1906. We were given an equally excellent Edwardian meal, during which Georges instructed us in the French habit of filling one's mouth with choice cheeses and then swilling them with a draught of Beaujolais before swallowing, a practice which he asserted enhances the flavour of both wine and cheese.

After lunch we received the expected orders; we were to continue as far as Auxi le Château, a small village near Amiens where we were to spend the night. Other British divisions, our military informant told us, were also converging on Amiens; I regretted that we could not have passed the night at Rouen, because any village near Amiens was by now certain to be full, as Heine once complained of England, of coal-dust and Englishmen. But before getting into our ugly little trucks we took the opportunity of admiring the beautiful west front of the cathedral and inspecting the repellent memorial to Joan of Arc. By three o'clock we were climbing the hill that overlooks the city from the south and following a road that bends as it rises, giving intermittent and ever more distant glimpses of the cathedral beneath, with the Seine at its side twisting its way through the city to the sea. With the last bend and the last view of Rouen we seemed to leave the beautiful country and pass into the waste land of the last war, the land of Nevinson's paintings and Wilfred Owen's verse; ahead was a country still bearing the scars of 1914 while preparing anew to accept those of the future.

The first indications of war were given as we neared Auxi le Château, not so much by the countryside itself, as by its inhabitants who were all carrying gas masks, and who faithfully put up their black outs when it became dark, two practices quite unknown in Evron; M. Rossignol had replied to my inquiries about them by saying that if the Germans got as near to his village as all that 'it would be a bad day for France'. It was an answer that had amused us at the time, but it had a dramatic irony that now seems pathetic.

Auxi le Château was, as I had expected, chiefly notable for its grime, a characteristic which it shares with all that part of northern France. In fact, if a line be drawn from Paris to Amiens and another from Paris to Douai it will form a rectangle containing all that is grimy in France – grimy, that is, in an industrial sense, for such places as Marseilles and Lyon have an obvious individual griminess of their own; theirs is a sweaty, rather Neapolitan variety, more redolent of people sitting about in the sun and being too lazy to wash, than of the earnest Mancunian grime of the Nord, which is obviously the product of coal-dust and business men.

After crossing the Seine at Rouen one senses this industrial flavour, but the metamorphosis is not really complete until the area of Lens, Harnes, and Hénin-Liètard is reached. But then one is truly in the black country, the air thick with factory fog, the earth piled high with factory excrement; here is Lancashire at its grubbiest. Even the private houses are grey and drab – transitory things, one feels, built only to shelter one or two generations; they wait patiently, after the manner of all frontier districts, for the inevitable attack and destruction which, since the days when the ancient Germans first began meting out *Sterbensraum* to their unfortunate neighbours, have been a regular feature of their history.

We arrived at Auxi as night was falling, and while the usual haggling for billets was going on at the mairie, Georges and I had our hair cut in a dirty little tobacconist's shop. The proprietor was evidently a man with some knowledge of human nature, because when we were completely concealed, except for our heads, beneath the usual white drape, he called in his wife and asked her to guess which of us was English; he said that he was mightily impressed by an apparent anomaly. His wife, after gazing intently at us from all angles for some moments at last did what was expected of her.

'*Mais le jeune n'est pas anglaise,*' she said emphatically, almost touching my head with her finger, '*ça c'est la vraie tête française tandis que ça,*' pointing at Georges' nose, '*ça c'est le nez aristocratique anglais.*'

They formed an ingenious pair of exotic compliments which, after the fashion of such things, delighted both Georges and myself; they also ensured a liberal tip to the proprietor when we left for having such a clever wife.

Of the town of Auxi le Château the less said the better; the noonday heat and laziness of Evron had departed as far as I was concerned, and we were once more back again in the gloomy St. Helens atmosphere, among a race of people who looked as if they had been bearing fardels all their lives, grimly sad, weary, and steadfast. They treated us politely but without enthusiasm; most of them remembered us from the last war so that our most marketable quality, the novelty that had endeared us to Evron, was no longer a compensation.

At Auxi, after being given our final instructions the next morning, we separated from the other members of the advance guard in order to make our way independently to our various destinations; Georges and I, representing the divisional headquarters, were to go to the 'Lille area'. This seemed a piece of the greatest good fortune because Lille is one of the few places in the north-eastern pocket of France where ordinary life has not been entirely submerged by the mines, factories, and goods-yards. Admittedly enormous sums of money are made from these sources, one-fifth of the wealthy people of France are said to reside in the département du Nord; but the class that makes it there fortunately spends it there as well, so that theatres, cinemas, American bars, and all the other great features of civilisation are to be found among the slag-heaps and chimneys. Lille was undoubtedly the best place to be quartered in, and Georges and I immediately set about making it our headquarters. But, as is so often the case in the Army, no amount of ingenuity on one's own part can counter the ordinances of the General Staff; the General Staff had decided that our headquarters was to be *outside* Lille and our instructions about 'Lille area' had been deliberately vague with this in view. In short, we could not make our headquarters where we wanted. But before we left the city for the village allotted us, we had enjoyed ourselves to the extent of some hundreds of francs.

Extravagant as this sounds, it is not simply the case of a stores officer giving himself the airs of a cavalry officer, but simply the behaviour of two people who still thought they were living in an Indian summer; even as we drove into Lille that evening the newsvendors with their 'P'ris-Soirs' were announcing that Hitler, his Polish campaign completed, was already massing troops on the Belgian frontier. There seemed every reason for eating and drinking well, not only because of this, but also because we were accompanied by another French interpreter, a friend of Georges, with the enviable name of Chandon-Moët.

Charles Chandon-Moët, who had eyes rather like Leslie Henson, was unusual in that he had a passion for the product of his own firm. This, I believe, is not customary. After years of living and working for the same thing one should be nauseated by it, but Chandon-Moët, immediately he arrived in the city, telephoned to his local agent and ordered a cask, with which he presented us. Georges called him Champagne Charlie.

When we arrived in Lille that evening we could not make up our minds whether to go to the Huîtrière restaurant and eat oysters and drink Moët et Chandon champagne with our friend, or to go to the Théâtre where the Comédie Française were playing *Cyrano*. Thinking that in any case French plays would continue indefinitely, we finally decided in favour of Champagne Charlie, an unfortunate choice because, whereas champagne is always procurable if you can afford it in France, the Comédie Française is not. And the Théâtre very soon gave itself over almost entirely to the laudable and necessary evil of ENSA.

The Royal Huîtrière where we dined derives the first part of its title from a prince of the blood who is said to have fed there; whether a German, French, or English prince I could never accurately ascertain; it appeared to vary according to the soldiery occupying Lille at the time. The main part of the name, however, is simple enough; it is taken from the custom of the place which permits you to choose your own oysters alive from the glass tanks which stand on either side of the vestibule as you enter. Here, in the tanks, are not only oysters but controllable fishes of all kinds; plaice, sole, and eel all glare at you as they glide constricted in their last aquarium.

It was unlike Georges not to know the maître of the Huîtrière but he made up for it by behaving as if he did; and we were straightway conducted to the table where the maître in person attended to the wants of his patrons. I pointed out to Georges that this treatment was, for once, due to me and my strange uniform, and not to his familiar manner, a point he gracefully conceded; but later, when Champagne Charlie arrived and sat with us, it was immediately obvious that the main interest of the management centred around him. And I later observed from the corner of my eye that the unfortunate and affable young waiter who had unthinkingly offered us a Heidsieck '29 was being soundly rated for his lack of tact.

We spent our first night in Lille at a small and disreputable hotel in the rue de Seclin, all the larger hotels being full; Georges said this was due to the sudden influx of Parisian business men all hoping to open up credit accounts with British officers; it was a reasonable explanation because, as I learnt later, most Frenchmen thought that British officers were very highly paid.

The hotel was kept by a slatternly creature whom we had great difficulty in rousing when we arrived back from the Huîtrière after midnight. She grumpily let us in at a side door, saying in a most curious fashion that we had behaved improperly towards her and threatening to turn us out if we were late again. Georges said she flattered herself.

In this way we came to Lille, not knowing that it was to be our home for the next eight months and not knowing, until after we had left the following morning, that I was to be cleverly swindled out of forty francs by one of its hotelkeepers on my first visit.

CHAPTER SIX
Pillbox Land

LESQUIN, THE VILLAGE chosen for our divisional headquarters, is four miles to the south of Lille on the main Douai road. We had no difficulty in finding it the next morning because the highway to Douai is a wide cobbled thoroughfare, easily identifiable by the almost Roman precision of some of its straighter stretches. Lesquin itself stands back about half a mile from this road and, as a village, is about as typical of its kind as any in the district. It has a population of a few thousand peasants who do little more than cultivate their own gardens; it is not dignified enough to have a mayor of its own and accordingly shares one with another village. It is rated in the guidebooks as notable for its antiquity, a characteristic invariably attributed to places notable for nothing else.

If you stand by the bistro at the crossroads on the Douai road and look eastwards across the flat interminable agricultural plains, you will see Lesquin as a cluster of dirty chimney pots and jerry built houses, with here and there an architectural extravagance in bastard Baroque where some retired businessman has attempted to distinguish himself from his neighbours. The house in which we finally established our headquarters was a particularly good example of this latter variety. It stood alone on the Douai road, a perfect manifestation of the mind of its owner and creator. We chose it because it was sturdily built, had an excellent hot water system, and appeared to be dry; but M. Dufy, its wealthy owner, would have been most offended if he had known this. I don't know what he called it, but Georges, who had lived some years in Bavaria, called it Hohendufy. The best thing about it, in fact, was its height, one of the turrets leaping like a castle on the Rhine to at least sixty feet and providing an unparalleled spectacle of the countryside stretching from Lille to Douai. The worst thing about it (also said by Georges) was that it had about as much coherence and uniformity as a surrealist painting seen in a hashish dream. In the severe setting of strict geometrically shaped fields and simple cottages, it was about as appropriate as a gargoyle on a classical pediment. Georges said that M. Dufy must have been to *Snow White and the Seven Dwarfs* before he designed it. Elizabethan casements, Flemish gables, medieval turrets, Norman crenellations, and Palladian columns all jostled one another in bright red brick. The phantasy was visible from Lille; M. Dufy if he had done nothing else, had succeeded in leaving his mark on the countryside, such a mark as only the destructive Germans would be able to put out.

We found him to be a charming and agreeable retired businessman who at once said he would be delighted to have a British colonel billeted in his house. When he saw us ringing the bell on the marble steps he opened the door himself and asked us to come in and have a glass of port; he and his wife, he said, were just about to have dinner. His wife curtsied to us, and unless I was badly mistaken, was quite bashful.

'I hope you will excuse my husband in his slippers,' she said. 'On Thursdays we always have dinner in the kitchen.'

We drank our port in the kitchen and then M. Dufy offered to show us round 'his place'.

'We built the château ourselves,' he said as we went up the stairs, 'with the help of my wife's brother who is an architect. What do you think of it?'

'I find it very striking,' said Georges truthfully.

'Yes – I think so too,' said M. Dufy. 'Of course some people don't like it but that is because they don't understand it. Architecture has always been my hobby you see. It is only people who are really interested in architecture who can appreciate such things.'

We spent a half-hour in this way while M. Dufy showed us all over his château, omitting nothing, not even hesitating at the steepest and most winding turret staircase, a climb which taxed his own powers considerably; and finally taking us to the garages which he ingenuously said were built '*en même style*'. He had one of the kindest and most generous natures that I met during my stay in France and later, when the main body arrived, no trouble ever seemed too great for him to take, if by so doing he could be of service to us; his grandmotherly cordiality remains one of the pleasantest memories I have of Lesquin. In addition to billeting the colonel and the adjutant he put a complete set of his outhouses at our disposal for use as offices, and he said that we could always use the telephone which he had just had installed in the château. We knew quite well that the Army would never leave us long without its own telephone system, but we accepted his kind offer all the same. Judging by our old office in Evron where it had been almost impossible to get out of the front door without tripping over a wire of some sort, one felt certain that there would be no lack of telephones; telephone wires would come into the office from all quarters of the compass, hung, Japanese-lantern-like, from all the trees in the garden. M. Dufy, I felt certain, would hate the sight of a telephone after we had been with him a week.

'Thank you so much,' said Georges tactfully. 'We shall certainly make use of it for ringing up the other units.'

If M. Dufy's hospitality was, in a material sense, the most generous we received in Lesquin, it was, in spirit, no different from that of the other inhabitants; they were just as helpful and ever ready to do what they could for us. Thanks to their kind co-operation we were soon able to arrange the billets, finish our work, and consider Georges' suggestion for a quick trip to Paris before the main body arrived. The project seemed quite feasible, because the staff officer who had given us our instructions at Auxi le Château, had said that the main body would be following at least seven days behind; and as our billeting only took two days, we felt we would easily be able to spend a day or two in Paris and be back in time to welcome the colonel at the château.

'If you've got to wait for people you might just as well do it in Paris as Lille,' Georges argued.

Georges had a lot of friends in Paris whom he promised to introduce to me. Paris, he said, would by now have got over the first pangs of the war and would be settling down to civilised life again. There would be plenty to do, he assured me; I needed no encouragement.

Thus it was that we were actually on our way to the railway station in Lille when I noticed a familiar motor-bicycle leaning up against the pavement. Further inspection proved that it was being used by one of the divisional engineer officers; we found him in a nearby shop. We immediately asked him what he meant by coming to Lille before he was due there. He replied that the colonel and all his retinue had come on in advance and were following close behind – that they were expected to arrive at any minute; he said they were hoping to find us in Lesquin ready to receive them. It was an unpleasant but extremely fortunate surprise; another five minutes and we should have missed the bicycling officer and have been on our way to Paris. All our schemes shattered, we returned to Lesquin as fast as the tram could carry us. We were only just in time, because the colonel and the adjutant who were in the leading car arrived ten minutes later. We welcomed them and escorted them to their respective billets.

Alsacia, I was sorry to see, was no longer with them. I asked Georges about this and he told me that, after much consideration, she had decided that we would all be better without her and had accordingly returned to Dinard with the Bugatti. It was a pity, because if she had stayed she would probably have given a little of the oil of harmony to our Lesquin days, something that by the end of eight months of one another's company we were all badly needing.

There was, however, one newcomer who in a sense replaced her – the doctor. A divisional headquarters must always be equipped with a doctor and the question which the staff had been debating was to whom he should be attached. Finally, after much discussion (for everyone wants a free doctor), the lot fell upon the engineers and we found ourselves saddled with a delightful but eccentric young London gynaecologist. Quite why the authorities had seen fit to attach him to an active division no-one could say, least of all the doctor himself; he possessed not even the most rudimentary notions of soldiering. He arrived at dinner time, shortly after we had installed ourselves at Lesquin, smelling strongly of chloroform.

'I have just been delivering a French peasant,' he explained.

He said it was really rather pointless to expect him to look after men, when all his interests lay with women. He told us that he had only been in the Army three weeks, having volunteered on September the 6th in a fit of pique against Hitler after having failed to get a taxi in the blackout.

'But I had absolutely no intention of coming out here,' he said sadly. 'When I joined up I thought I would be sent to a base hospital in England.'

It had obviously been a great shock to him, and when we got to know him better we supposed that it must have been his youth and fine physique that had sent him out to France, for he had no other military qualifications. Throughout his eight months in France he was undoubtedly of great value – not to the English soldiers but to the French female peasants.

With the arrival of the colonel, the doctor, and the main body, we settled down in Lesquin to wait and see what Hitler had in store for us; it seemed from the very start that we had nothing particular in store for him. All our work was immediately concerned with *defending* the Belgian frontier and not with *attacking* it, as the German propaganda mischievously tried to make out. Lesquin is only about four miles from the frontier so that we had almost reached the limit of our movement; another step would have taken us into neutral country. And one of my first tasks was to inspect the frontier line itself.

At the yellow and black barriers that mark the dividing line, I found a Belgian frontier sentry; I had the curious sensation of standing on belligerent ground and talking to someone a few feet away who was still at peace. I pointed out the peculiarity of this to him.

'As far as I'm concerned,' he said dolefully, 'we might just as well be at war.'

The European land frontier, a geographical feature rather difficult perhaps for us islanders to appreciate, seems to possess a peculiar sort of feng-shui or spirit of its own. You feel it even in peacetime; crossing the frontier from Liège to Aachen has a sinister significance even if you are only going to Garmisch to frolic in the snow. Perhaps it is merely the remains of Mr. John Buchan's magic over us as small boys, but, whatever it is, an undeniable frontier spirit exists; it is as perceptible as it is eerie. If it is sinister in peacetime, it is almost diabolical in war, and this particular bit of Belgian frontier, on a bleak windy October afternoon, with great tracts of flat featureless country stretching for miles in every direction around me, seemed to stand for everything that I was not fighting for; it possessed a sort of Hardyesque ruggedness and mystery combined with a dim feeling of Celtic Twilight and Inscrutable Decree – the sort of things the Irish are always said to be fighting for, although in actual fact they are only really arguing about them. I have little love for such things.

On the other hand, later in the afternoon two episodes did take place on the frontier, whose homeliness an imaginative daily newspaper might well make out to be my own personal War Aims. I had finished my frontier work, a simple task in the circumstances – it merely entailed counting the number of existing French pillboxes between Lille and Douai (I did it on the fingers of one hand) – and I had decided to have a drink of coffee in the solitary little bistro near the frontier gates.

The bistro was warm and cheerful, a pleasant contrast after the sweeping east wind that had chilled me to the marrow while I promenaded the line of the frontier. I was delighted to find a crowd of French soldiers inside all having lunch, very much after the fashion in which one would expect French soldiers to have lunch – boisterously, greedily, and actively. They were typical poilus, short, dark, smiling, and laughing, all equally dirty and scruffy, all obviously enjoying their food. They had brought their food with them and the patron of the bistro was doing the cooking. They were evidently stationed near and were regular customers because she seemed to know them well and called them all by their Christian names.

As I entered, a young girl, perhaps the daughter of the patron, was handing out the plates amid the chatter and pleasantries of the soldiers who flirted with her, patted her on the back and (the more daring of them) pinched her cheeks as she came to their tables. She answered all this with naïve little smiles and blushes; but when one of them, more daring or more drunken than the rest, caught hold of her as she passed, and asked her to sit on his knee and kiss him, she drew herself away and frowned so hard at him that everyone laughed. The soldier pulled a wry face and took a long draught from his glass. She was evidently annoyed because she smiled no more, and her blush turned to the dull deep red of anger. The whole episode seemed a page out of a Gounod opera, marvellously come to life.

My entry caused a mild sensation. It was only the second day after the arrival of the British Army in the district, and my uniform still evoked curiosity and interest. I was given a table near the fire which I was told belonged to their officer who would be returning shortly. While waiting for my coffee we discussed the great topic that in wartime takes the place of the weather as a conversational hare – the War. Everybody seemed to take part in the discussion, which soon degenerated into one of War Aims. Germany, someone said, must be cut up into little bits: the Boche, they said, was always the same: it would take time to beat him of course; two, perhaps three years: but the Allies could afford to wait, the Boche was admittedly a good fighter but he had to eat to fight and the blocus would see that he didn't eat for long (*le blocus* was a great word in those days): we would starve him out; that would teach him to go round making such a damned nuisance of himself, upsetting everybody.

I asked them what they thought of their leaders.

'Gamelin – he's a fine fellow,' said one of them. 'He won't waste lives unnecessarily like that old ass General Cambon at Verdun in the last war. Oh – we'll win all right.'

'*Mais pourquoi parler de la guerre?*' said someone else laughing and suddenly realising that we were being serious: '*Mangeons, mes vieux.*'

At this point the officer entered with his senior NCOs and sat with me at the same table, where we all drank black coffee together. It was interesting to note that although his men individually treated him with proper respect, they behaved quite naturally among themselves after he arrived, laughing, joking, spitting, and eating as before. I learned later that small French units, when detached from their parent body, always behave in this democratic manner. The officer ignored them completely, so that our table with its serious-faced members seemed quite apart from the other inmates of the bistro. He was an elderly little lieutenant with pince-nez. He did all the talking while his subordinates listened, occasionally nodding their heads in agreement with him. He was immensely self-confident in his own speech, while he paid an almost critical attention to everything that I said, as if trying to floor me linguistically. When he spoke he used a minimum of words, rapping them out sharply as if giving an order. In this manner he told me quite categorically that the British Army was certain to be on the frontier for the whole winter and that the Germans would never attack Belgium or Holland. I said I was sure he was right.

The other homely incident occurred after leaving the bistro, when I was visiting some of the frontier farms to inquire about the cutting of woods for timber. Most of these farms take what advantage they can from the sparsely scattered woods and spinneys in order to protect themselves from the wind and rain that drive so violently across the open plains; and I generally found them hidden among little clumps of trees, forming an incongruous scar on the plain patchwork pattern of the flat agricultural spaces, standing out forlornly against the grey sky of the background.

Most of the men had been conscripted. There was something pathetic in the dry-eyed women as they stood at their farm doors or worked in the fields, carrying on the work of the land as best they could with the help of old men and boys. They were strong, sturdy women with the sallow complexions of the district and, as I saw them, they appeared grave and humourless, too conscious of their responsibility and loss to smile. They came to the doors or stopped their work in the farmyard at my appearance, and while I talked to the mother or the head of the house, they watched us, interested perhaps to see what kind of person an Englishman was.

'I cannot give you permission to cut down the trees without first asking my husband,' one woman replied, 'and he is in Alsace so that it will take time.'

It was the same everywhere. People, when given the option of having their property destroyed or not, will naturally decline. After a little experience of trying to obtain concessions from them in this manner, I became more subtle and invariably introduced a note of command into my request. But of course the only really effective method in wartime is the Teutonic one of knocking down everything and everybody and then beheading anyone who squeals. One of the peculiar features of allied warfare was this failure to recognise the platitude that, because war is a barbaric affair, it is necessary to wage it barbarously. Ideally, the frontier should have been completely cleared of civilians and handed over to the Army.

The *douaniers* and guards at the barriers had a difficult task not only because the frontier zone was full of these civilians who could slip from one side to the other in a matter of seconds, but also because each day hundreds of Belgians had to be admitted to work in the industries of Lille.

'It is impossible to keep a check on all of them,' I was told by one of the frontier guards at Baisieux as I watched him examining their passes. 'They come over early in the morning, they go to the factories, and then they return through here again in the evening.'

It seemed astounding. I asked him why it was necessary to use Belgians in French industries.

'Because the factories would stop,' he replied, 'if we did not make use of these Belgians. You see, there is a labour shortage. And all these men have been working in the factories for so long now that they know the work, and it would be uneconomical to turn them away.'

It seemed to me uneconomical *not* to turn them away; every one of them was a potential spy; it was perhaps hardly surprising that the Germans, when they attacked eight months later, were said to have complete information about our defences. The *douanier* complained that his men could not take on the work of examining all these Belgians single-handed; he hoped that the British would help them, he said. His request was answered within a week of our arriving at Lesquin, because the division supplied a member of its Field Security Police section to help at each barrier.

It was in this way, on a chance visit to the frontier, that I met one of my oldest and best friends who, unknown to me, had joined the Army in a patriotic fit and had become a corporal in the Field Security Police. The meeting could not have been more opportune, because I was just beginning to regret the loss of all my old friends. He was wearing one of those horrible Army motorcycle helmets when I met him, a close-fitting affair, as supplied to dirt-track riders and Egyptian priests, and it made him look ghastly. I thought his voice vaguely familiar as he examined the credentials of a Belgian workman, but it was some time before I recognised him, whereupon we embraced in a manner which, I was told later by a bystander, while enthusiastic was unseemly – ill befitting an officer and a gentleman. I had forgotten;

Jasper was an NCO. But this did not prevent us from going into the bistro together and congratulating ourselves on being in the same division. I learnt later from the frontier guards how popular Jasper was with them.

'Monsieur Jaspaire,' said the old *douanier* to me as we sat down at his table in the bistro, '*c'est un beau garcon. En croyez-moi. Mais*,' he said admiringly raising his hands in mock horror, '*il boit, mon Dieu, il boit comme – comme*,' he searched for a criterion, '*comme un Polonais.*'

This is the most alcoholic thing you can say about anyone in France, and I asked Jasper what he had been doing to get himself such a reputation; he had not been a great drinker in the old days.

'My first night here,' he explained in English while the old *douanier* grinned amiably at us across the top of his glass as if he knew perfectly well that we were talking about him, 'I stood them all drinks, and, to impress them, I pretended to drink an enormous quantity myself. There is nothing they admire more. As a matter of fact I threw most of it away.'

It was certainly a good idea because all the customs officials appeared to worship Jasper; they seemed willing to do anything for him. It was certainly not only the drinking episode that had made him popular; being one of the most likeable and agreeable persons in the world he would never have had difficulty in making friends anywhere; and to find him, not only in France, but in my own division, seemed an unbelievable piece of good fortune. We agreed to have supper together once a week at the Baisieux frontier bistro; and these regular meetings, which soon became a feature of my life in France, had a particular value and attraction, because they enabled both of us to keep touch with the life we had known in England before the war. The prospect of a long war, with its attendant danger of loss of contact with England, came prominently into one's mind again, and made the meetings seem all the more important.

The patron of the frontier bistro expected us every Tuesday evening, whatever the weather; she always prepared a simple but special meal with free cheroots at the end. I have since often wondered if I did Jasper as much good as he did me on these occasions. His self-confidence and his peculiar belief in the present I found stimulating, and, in a man who had less cant than anyone I know, rather surprising. I never quite found out what he really thought about the war; he seemed to treat it as a necessary joke. When I once rather stupidly asked him if he was sorry for his German friends he replied pointedly, grinning at me over his glass:

'I am sorry for all my friends – particularly my best ones.'

He certainly enjoyed his life in France, treating it with a peculiar blend of intentness and levity which baffled his superiors, but which must have been an admirable quality for the work on which he was engaged.

The *douaniers* always had something to tell me about him when I arrived at the barrier every Tuesday evening, while I was waiting for him to return. How 'Monsieur Jaspaire' had, for example, listened for an hour to the conversation of a suspect Pole in a bistro only to find that the Pole was a French detective; how he had waited the whole night outside a house to catch a spy (and had then finally got his man); they were full of praise and admiration for him.

Jasper was awarded the Military Medal on the retreat in May 1940 and it was one of the ironies and, to me, tragedies, of later events that he should have been killed while leaving Dunkirk on the same day that I was there. During our serious moments together I often used to bring up the subject, saying that I could not make up my mind whether, when the war started, it would be better to be bumped off straight away or to live for years in a ditch; and he, who never gave death a second thought, dismissed my doubts by saying that some people would be much better dead than alive.

CHAPTER SEVEN
Work

OUR MESS IN Lesquin had ten members, which meant that it was just small enough for everyone to hate everyone else. Indeed, considering this, together with the length of our stay and the conflict of interest among its members, it is really most surprising that, except for the time when the doctor threw some tubes of chloroform on the floor and stamped on them, we managed to avoid behaving like the Gunners. I am told that they always pull the shirts off one another's backs after dinner each evening. Admittedly there was plenty of ill-feeling, ill-will, suspicion, scorn, scandal, and gossip, but we always managed, like women, to conceal them cleverly by smiling and detesting one another in secret.

In the mess the literary approach to life was represented by Stimpson; the pleasure-loving by Georges, the doctor, and sometimes Heddon, who still kept his old soldier's love of a French brothel. The military side was represented by the colonel, the adjutant, the padre, and their hangers-on, although they occasionally took a night off in Lille and tried to emulate the pleasure-lovers; but no-one ever tried to emulate Stimpson. The colonel in fact did his best to get rid of him. I never quite made up my mind which of these parties I should join, although I was on the point of joining the third when the Germans invaded Holland; it had seemed so much more practical. Stimpson used to entreat me to join in the war against the Philistines.

'You really must help us to stop that old padre from talking about his farm in Scotland,' he said one night after dinner. 'It's so monotonous. You are a beast to encourage him.'

The doctor, as we got to know him better, revealed himself to be such a good caterer that he was soon put in charge of the officers' mess. Every morning he would go into Lille at ten o'clock and stay there till lunchtime, bringing back with him the choicest things, only to return again after lunch to continue buying food for the rest of the day. He really led the best life of us all, although there was little enough in my own life to complain about. The work took me anywhere between Lille and Paris in search of engineer stores, and I quickly took advantage of such good fortune. The stores had great variety, ranging from train-loads of pneumatic drills to buckets of whitewash.

By the end of my time in France I had handled, I used to claim, every form of engineer store that existed. It was therefore hardly surprising that my name was put forward as the person best qualified to rewrite the R.E. stores inventory, published in three volumes and much in need of re-editing. Electric light switches, elephant shelters, plugs, concrete mixers, and road rubble; everything seemed to come my way. And while I was in Lesquin I hired three steam-rollers.

Most of the stores bought during the early months were needed for our first and most important task, the construction of pillboxes. The newspapers were telling everyone in England that the British Army was spending the winter 'strengthening the Maginot Line,' a clever half-truth which concealed what the British Army was really doing – *constructing* the Maginot Line. When we arrived on the Belgian frontier in October there was no Maginot Line; there were a handful of pillboxes fifty miles apart, a few French soldiers equipped with 1914 rifles, and a strand or two of wire to keep French cattle from straying over into Belgium. But nobody really worried. If we were short of weapons, they said, how much shorter must the Germans be!

'You see they lost the last war,' a French soldier in a bistro earnestly told me. 'They can't *possibly* be as strong as we are.'

The merchants from whom I bought my stores had the same outlook. Having been told by the newspapers and politicians that they could not lose this war because they had won the last they very naturally thought that patriotism was not enough, and accordingly sold concrete as if they were selling their souls – to get rich quick. While setting up a Maginot Line they thought they might as well set themselves up; anyone in their position would have done the same. The only lesson one learned from it all was that the newspapers, except for one or two advertisements, are so much rubbish. The German Army, the Allied newspapers argued, had only been started in 1932, whereas the French Army had been going ever since 1918; the Maginot Line, they said, was the genuine article, while the thing on the other bank of the Rhine was a hasty makeshift; '*C'est pas comme quatorze*' was the cry of the hour. If ever winning one war lost another this was the time.

The businessmen with whom I dealt treated the whole thing therefore as an inevitable but not wholly unnecessary evil, selling everything they could lay their hands on. And they would undoubtedly have made their fortunes had we not abruptly left France in June 1940 without paying them – making them bankrupt instead.

The materials in greatest demand were of course those used for making Pillboxes – concrete and steel. Concrete is made from small stones, cement, and sand; and the businessmen with whom I came into contact were chiefly purveyors of these commodities. Although I had many contracts to make personally, all the larger ones were contracted by Army headquarters; there was one particular merchant who had ambitiously contracted in this manner to supply small stones to the whole British Army, to supply every division regardless of where it might be – a prospect so lucrative that he had evidently waived all practical difficulties. When you are daily supplying thousands of tons of material to widely scattered railway termini it is not easy to ensure that the right quantities always arrive at the right places; and it was not long before the regularity and the amounts of small stones arriving daily at the little frontier railway station of Ascq, our divisional unloading point, began to fluctuate in an alarming manner.

We had been allotted a normal quota of five trucks each day, a manageable quantity which our unloading parties were able to deal with quickly and effectively. Then suddenly, without warning, we started receiving twenty-five trucks daily. This continued for four days and then mounted to thirty-five daily, at which figure it remained, so that the station of Ascq rapidly became a sort of quarry for trucks of small stones. The stationmaster was desperate. It was evident that the mechanism of distribution had slipped and that we were receiving most of the trucks intended for the rest of the Army, because other divisions were complaining that their men were standing idle, deprived of small stones. I immediately visited the offices of the firm in Lille.

In anticipation of quick returns the firm had opened a branch office, luxuriously furnished in the American style, and their representative, a little man called Bèle with a Charlie Chaplin moustache, had sprung up overnight to become a branch manager; his enemies told me that he was really only a small-timer.

'Tut-tut,' he said when I told him of our difficulties. 'We must see about this.'

And he immediately turned the pages of a huge ledger in front of him on the desk. After a while he found an entry which appeared relevant; he examined it for some moments, then shut the book with a bang and began putting on his overcoat. The matter was evidently closed.

'At any rate,' he said naïvely, 'it is much better for you to have the extra stones than for the other divisions to have them.'

'Yes,' I said, 'but that's not the point. Do you realise that we are receiving thirty-five trucks each day in Ascq and that we cannot possibly unload them all? There are so many in the station now that the stationmaster is afraid that the sidings will get full and that many of the trucks will be left out on the main line, and that then there will be an accident. Besides there's the demurrage charge.'

'Do not worry,' said M. Bèle, putting on his hat, 'I will see to it.'

He did see to it. And then for a month we received no trucks at all. The work in our division was held up and the colonel began blaming me. I complained to M. Bèle again.

'You shall have your small stones,' he said. 'It is the railway companies' fault. I will settle them.'

And then we had an alternating service, some days ten trucks arriving, some days only one or two; anything but the orderly sequence of five that we had ordered. And so it remained for the rest of our time on the frontier. It is true that over a period I suppose we received an average of about five trucks a day; we simply had to accommodate our unloading parties as best we could to the supply vagaries.

'The railways,' said M. Bèle, 'have gone to pot. I am afraid you will have to make do.'

I soon found that undischarged trucks are the pet aversion of stationmasters; nothing annoys a stationmaster more. The man at Ascq had in fact quite a reputation for behaving badly about them. He was said on one occasion to have sent back a truck containing coal after it had been in his siding for two days because its new owners did not arrive to unload it immediately; whereupon it had been shuttlecocked back to him a few days later with an instruction from the railway authorities forbidding him on any account ever to do such a thing again; he was told never to return a truck to its starting-point until it had been unloaded. He waited another week, so the story went, and the truck was still standing unloaded in the siding, so one night, with the help of his porters, he unloaded it himself, stacked the coal in a nearby corner of the railway yard and sent back the truck empty – as he had been directed. According to the porter who told me this, the following winter had been particularly severe and they had been very glad of the coal in their office.

This stationmaster was the man who at one time had between a hundred and a hundred and ten trucks of small stones in his sidings for a week. Having unfortunately given him my telephone number, I was rung up by him four or five times each day, beseeching me to ask 'Monsieur le colonel' to do something about it. (Having once been in the French Army he had pathetic confidence in colonels.) But the colonel was helpless; all he could do was to pester me about the demurrage charges which he was now being questioned about by divisional headquarters. M. Bèle was the only person who was able to do anything about it. I look back on that week as the most unpleasant period of all my time in France.

In appearance the stationmaster was the complete nineteenth-century *petit bourgeois*; he might have stepped out of an early daguerreotype. In his youth he had been a sergeant in the cavalry and he still bore traces of it; he had a moustache *frisotté* with the curled ends hanging limply down at either end like a mandarin's, a fierce complexion, and a wisp of highly lubricated hair stuck on the front of his forehead with a permanent highlight in it. He affected a heavy gilt watch-chain which held together an egg-stained and buttonless waistcoat, and he always worked in shirtsleeves except when it was very cold; then he put on his old blue cavalry greatcoat now sadly studded with ordinary bone buttons. He was one of the best friends I made in France, and we agreed that if we were separated we would meet again after the war in the old station bistro at Ascq and drink to the great prosperous days when the station had been full of trucks of small stones.

He was a man of some humour, but much hampered and worried by all the Army forms I kept on giving him in receipt for the trucks we unloaded daily.

'These papers will be the death of me,' he used to say. 'I do not know what to do with them all.'

'Simply sign them and send them all off to your head office,' I said. 'They will know what to do with them.'

His railway station rapidly became legendary. When I even went as far back as GHQ at Arras to order stores, people used to say, 'It'll be for Ascq, I suppose?' Ascq was the last station but one before the frontier, a lonely, desolate little place normally managed by the stationmaster and two porters. When we arrived in October and stirred it into activity the stationmaster applied for another porter. But he did not get one until after Christmas when all our work was done.

Unloading at Ascq started at eight o'clock each morning. A party of infantry worked there until five in the afternoon with a break of an hour for lunch. In France everyone takes a break of two hours for lunch and the stationmaster used to say that I was a hard taskmaster to my men.

'*Pour les militaires, déjeuner bien, c'est travailler bien,*' he would say.

My obvious retort should have been, '*Pour tout le monde, déjeuner bien, c'est dormir bien;*' but I never made it.

The soldiers transferred the material in the railway trucks to RASC vehicles, who then distributed it to the pillbox sites where the RE were working. The co-ordination of all this in the early stages was not easy. I had to ensure that the various types of material, cement, sand, aggregate, etc., were all present at the station in the right proportions (a frequent source of trouble, because sometimes M. Bèle, the merchant, would concentrate to the exclusion of everything else for one week on sand, then for another on cement, etc.), and then to obtain details from the RE of the quantities required at each site, and finally to hope fervently that the RASC lorries would not lose the way.

In spite of all these troubles and my own limitations, pillboxes began to sprout up all over the frontier in a surprising manner, ugly monuments on an ugly land, rapidly making the frontier what everyone thought it had been for years – impregnable. It was, to me, significant that at the end of May 1940 the Germans did not attempt a frontal attack on these fortifications; I am sure that if the war had depended only on them, and things like them, there would have been no Dunkirk. The British Army, as a Frenchman once said, was only wrong because it was small; no other instance could be adduced.

The division had for its front a four-mile strip of frontier running roughly from Lesquin to Lille, along which, within a few months of our arrival, over a hundred pillboxes had been constructed by the engineer field companies. The reason for my attachment to one of these companies early in the war at St. Helens now became apparent. I was supplying them constantly with material.

Most of the stores for the construction of these pillboxes came by rail to Ascq, but just before Christmas the colonel, a man of many foibles and some public spirit, began an 'economy drive'.

'Being a soldier I cannot bear to see waste,' he said.

One of the features of this drive was to transport all stores by canal and not by rail. As he rightly pointed out, once the scheme was under way, exactly the same quantities could be delivered as by rail, only at a saving of about half the cost. It was certainly a sound scheme and, although it never got under way, it gave me an excellent opportunity to visit many out-of-the-way places.

The north-eastern corner of France possesses a fine network of canals which spread from Lille almost as far west as Paris and Abbeville. Such titles as '*La Bassée Canal*' or '*Le Canal du Nord*' which gained an odious celebrity among Englishmen in the last war were still, I observed, mentioned with familiarity by those who fought there.

I accordingly arranged with M. Bèle that we should send all the material by canal to La Bassée where it was to be collected and distributed by the RASC in the same manner that we had employed at Ascq. He was not very enthusiastic about it because, as he pointed out, it seemed uneconomical (and a great waste of his own time) to tamper with such a delicate thing as the machinery of rail delivery, particularly when it was working so smoothly.

'Your colonel ought to know by now,' he said, 'that the French railways take a long time to get started. Tell him that once they are started it is just as hard for them to stop. We shall have trouble. You see if we don't. Also – the bargees are a lousy lot. You will not get any good out of *them*.'

I had nightmares about the trucks in Ascq station after that. But, in spite of his predictions, the trucks stopped arriving at Ascq with the ease and fluency of the countermanding order he had given by telephone to the railway company. When I told him about the success he said he viewed it with '*plaisir et stupéfaction*'.

The canal trip, starting from the factories and quarries near Arras, took a day, and in order to encourage the captain of the barges it was decided that I should accompany the convoy on its maiden trip. I also wanted to get a barge-eye view of the country.

For me, canals have a certain repugnant charm, an air of belonging to the realist nineteenth-century French novelists of the chalk-and-cheese school. Being utilitarian and manmade they lead, unlike rivers, to everything that is mean, sordid, and immensely important. Those admirable canals running through pied green pastures in central England, of which Sir John Squire writes so charmingly in his travel book *Water Music*, are today unfortunately as exceptional as they are musical; the contemporary type of canal is to be found, like everything else, in Manchester and not in Venice.

Canals in northern France are true to type; they have a seaminess about them which is little short of enthralling. One instinctively feels, as one drifts on a grime-besmutted barge past the hulks of factories at Lens, between the gross mountains of cinder at La Bassée, and through the rotting yellow smell of Loos, that Zola was probably born on a barge.

I made my journey at the end of November when a suspicion of fog lent a fascinating murkiness. My only companion was the one-eyed captain who sat mournfully at the tiller of the leading barge, his legs dangling over the side, only stirring in order to spit neatly into the canal. It was hard to make him talk. He had made the trip alone so often before that he seemed to resent my presence.

'How long,' I asked, 'do you normally take to get to La Bassée?'

He thought for some time, then removed his pipe from the corner of his mouth and scratched his neck with the end of it.

'Until evening,' he said. It was not a proper answer but I saw he thought I was trying to trap him into a confession about the time he ought to take, so I asked no more questions and we drifted on in silence. The little motor plugged away beneath us as we crossed the grey landscape with its flat ocean-like fields falling away on either side, a prospect only relieved occasionally by a group of isolated buildings clustering round a pithead. We passed Lens with its chimneys and squat geometrical factories; the sun had set behind it throwing everything into relief, making the town seem blacker than it was. When we reached La Bassée it was dark. We moored the barges at the unloading yard which was normally used for storing coal. La Bassée may in fact best be summed up by identifying it with coal.

Later I used often to visit it to supervise the unloading of the barges and to arrange the distribution of the material. And I generally used to have lunch in the little bistro where the bargees fed and drank. Perhaps it was their patronage that gave to the bistro the spirit and atmosphere of the canal; it was almost as dirty inside as out. But when I first arrived for lunch the patron insisted that I, as an officer, must dine apart from the others and I was given lunch in her private sitting-room containing an upright piano and a chiffonier.

'Monsieur le Lieutenant could not possibly have lunch with the workmen and factory girls,' she said.

To please her I agreed, but on the following days I insisted on always dining in the main room. Towards midday the factory girls used to come in to lunch. I did my best to talk with them, but found it almost impossible; they would only snigger and squeal like schoolgirls. The patron was very ashamed of them.

'Of course,' she said, 'you must remember that they are a very poor class of girls. And they work in a very inferior sort of factory – a rubber factory,' she whispered.

It was their make-up that annoyed her most.

82

'*Beaucoup de fard – beaucoup de fantaisie,*' she said scornfully, nodding her head in distaste. And when I confessed that I personally found nothing wrong with them but that, on the contrary I would rather like to have an opportunity to talk to them she was astounded.

'*On ne parle pas avec ces gens,*' she said. '*Elles ne savent que rigoler.*'

CHAPTER EIGHT
Low Life in Lille

WHEN THE PURCHASING expeditions started the colonel insisted that Georges should accompany me to help establish good relations with the various firms. It was unwise, because Georges, although a businessman, was a stockbroker; and stockbrokers are quite different. Accustomed to sizing up propositions in a second, and to making lightning decisions, Georges treated time as if it was money. And the small businessmen of Lille, who had been quietly plying a trade in hardware or ironmongery for years, suddenly found themselves expected to make rapid decisions about contracts to which they would normally have given many weeks of careful thought. I told Georges that I considered his methods altogether too brusque and hasty, to which he replied that mine were too bovine – too English in fact.

'You remind me of Stanley Baldwin,' he said.

We therefore applied to the colonel for permission to separate. The colonel could not understand my complaints.

'But the fellow is a businessman,' he said.

He certainly would not have given permission had not Georges been equally keen to part. It was therefore agreed that I should continue to buy stores for the Engineers alone, while Georges was to help the doctor buy food for the mess; the doctor's French was very rusty and he was in need of help.

In spite of this disagreement, Georges and I generally found time to meet one another after a morning's work at the Café Jeanne which called itself an American bar, a title most bars assume in France when charging more than the normal prices.

The Café Jeanne was an atrocious institution. Centrally placed in Lille, it was really the heart of the British Army; around it revolved the lives of the officers of the whole B.E.F. Everyone, from general to second lieutenant knew it; it fleeced them all without discrimination, in an ingenuous manner that now seems incredible. Considering that it charged about twice as much as any other place, and that it was stocked almost exclusively with British officers and harlots, it is surprising that we ever went there. But something about it, some trick of the spangled lighting or the chromium-plated fittings, or perhaps merely the black man behind the bar endeared it to Georges, and he always insisted on having a drink there before lunch.

And this was strange, because Georges knew plenty of other good drinking-places in Lille; indeed, in this knowledge lay his greatest value to us. He had always managed, as he called it, 'to keep us one ahead of the British officer'. The great thing, as far as restaurants were concerned, was to keep ahead of the flock, because as soon as a place became known it immediately lost its native charm and became merely a home from home for Englishmen. For instance, a charming place like the Huîtrière soon lost its pre-1914 Café Royal atmosphere of easy-going inefficiency when the proprietor, suddenly realising that he could set himself up for life if he worked hard for a month or two, turned it into a sort of vulgar and efficient gold-mine. But he was no exception. Everyone in Lille, it seemed, from the most luxurious *bordel* down to the humblest confessor was determined to make what he could out of us, and the Café Jeanne during its short heyday must have set up a financial record for all time; one can think of no other restaurant in the world, with the possible exception of something in New York during the Peace Conference, that will ever surpass it.

As far as the Army was concerned Lille consisted entirely of cinemas, restaurants, bordels, and ENSA shows; and one of Stimpson's most realistic sets of paintings showed soldiers queuing up outside these places of entertainment. He had hung some of his paintings in the mess, including an excellent one of trucks being unloaded at Ascq and another good one of a French funeral procession. The padre objected to some of them.

'They are not true to life,' he said.

Stimpson also wrote a certain amount of poetry which he would sometimes recite to me in his bedroom. The colonel had once said that poetry was effeminate and Stimpson in retaliation had hung over his mantelpiece the celebrated Baudelaire dictum:

'Un homme bien-portant peut exister jusqu'a vingt-quatre heures sans manger, mais sans poésie – jamais.'

He had also set himself the gigantic task of writing an anti-military parody commencing:

Arma meretricesque cano...

'But,' he said scornfully, 'of course the people it's intended for won't be able to understand it, although it does sum them up so aptly.'

He was referring in the first line to a woman called Madame Ko-Ko whom Heddon had made friends with and who kept an American bar in the rue de Seclin. Heddon had once suggested that, in return for her hospitality, we should entertain her in the mess.

'I think it would do Stimpson a lot of good to meet a woman of experience and sensibility,' he said.

But the colonel would not hear of it.

'A mess is not a private house,' he said.

I occasionally used to accompany my friends to Madame Ko-Ko's soirees to act as interpreter. On my first visit Stimpson had been encouraged to come by Heddon on the ground that it was going to be 'a musical evening'; he had accordingly brought his clarinet with him. But the 'music' had only consisted in listening to dance music on the gramophone and to Madame Ko-Ko's peculiar conversation. It was this deception that had made Stimpson so bitter about her.

Madame Ko-Ko always provided champagne, but when no-one was looking she would empty a part of the bottle and fill it up with water. I got to know of this and she used to wink at me when she was doing it. She was a gross creature with a bosom like a dowager and a gift for bargee invective. She could defeat anyone in argument by sheer overwhelming personality; she had a trick like Mrs. Squeers, like all viragoes, of making you wilt when she looked at you. She had a fatal fascination for Heddon whom she always called Archibald.

'Archibald is a darling,' she used to say. 'He is the sweetest, the kindest, and the most generous of you all.'

I could well believe that he was the most generous.

Heddon always used to return from visiting her with some startling story of 'what he had heard at Ko-Ko's last night'.

He told us that there was one other officer who used to go there almost as much as he did himself, a major in the Guards called Fotheringhill. This man was a familiar figure throughout the division because of his black bushy moustache and magenta-coloured face; he was known to his workmates as 'the last of the Gents' on account of his obvious affinity with four-figure cheques and early Georgian silver.

'I have a new name for the last of the Gents,' said Heddon one morning at breakfast. 'I am going to call him the last of the Red Indians.'

We asked him why this was.

'Because last night at Ko-Ko's the place was raided by the Security Police, and old Fotheringhill was so frightened of having his name taken that he climbed out of a second-floor window, missed his footing and fell on the ground outside, letting out such a cry that even the police were frightened. The joke was that the police hadn't come to catch people and to take names. They only wanted to ask old Ko-Ko a few questions. When we brought him in he was furious.'

On one occasion Heddon succeeded in getting the colonel to go to Ko-Ko's. Madame Ko-Ko was delighted to have a real colonel under her roof again; she said it reminded her of her young days in the last war. She managed to recall some of the old conversational tricks she had picked up from British officers in those days and during her subsequent visits to England. At Heddon's instigation she tried some of them out on the colonel.

'I can see that your colonel is a real gentleman,' she whispered to me. 'Where were you educated, Monsieur le Colonel?' she said casually but obviously intending to be polite, as she poured him out some more champagne.

'On the Western Front, madame – from 1914 to 1918,' replied the colonel, but so seriously that we could not tell whether he was trying to make a joke or not.

'What an awful thing for anyone to say if he really meant it,' said the doctor to me afterwards. 'Why – you would almost take him for one of those journalists who fought in Spain.'

Madame Ko-Ko's house, in addition to many other photographs and coloured drawings on its walls, had two special postcards prominently displayed for everyone to see, and calculated, I supposed, to attract all patriots who visited her house. They were typical in their vulgarity of many of the cartoons of the time.

One of them depicted Hitler, his hands covered with blood, being admonished by two scholarly looking gentlemen wearing the clothes of an earlier age and carrying beneath their arms books bearing respectively the titles of their master-works – the 'Eroica' Symphony and *Wilhelm Meister.*

'Those are two good Germans punishing a bad one,' said Madame Ko-Ko observing our interest.

And the other postcard showed a young woman lying on the ground in a distressed condition; while over her, his eyes bulging with excitement, was Adolf Hitler again. On the back of the young woman was printed the word 'Poland'.

'And that,' said Madame Ko-Ko pointing at it, 'well, you can see what that is.'

What really interested me most about Madame Ko-Ko's possession of these postcards and the prominence she had given to them over all her more professional exhibits, was her motive; did she seriously imagine that she would get more clients in this way? Or was she really patriotic and completely in sympathy with them? It was hard to tell; she was such an old villain.

But the most patriotic person I met in Lille was a man called Manelle who sold sand.

'France is the greatest country,' he said. 'And England the second greatest.'

I made a special contract with him and we often used to have meals together in Lille. He was kindness itself; a tall, stooping old gentleman with a Van Dyck beard who used to give me excellent lobster lunches. After a while we became so friendly that he invited me to stay the weekend with him at his country house near Boulogne. I accepted gratefully and everyone in the mess, when they heard about it, said I was corrupt and selling contracts in return for food. Georges was particularly acrimonious. To annoy him I said that he was merely jealous of my good fortune.

'Jealous,' he said in that high-pitched tone which Frenchmen affect when they have been slighted in such a stupid way that it is amusing. 'Jealous of you staying with a sand merchant in Boulogne! Don't be funny.'

Life at Lesquin was full of these charming little differences. Shortly after this incident Georges left us for another division in the Maginot Line and he was replaced by a serious little schoolmaster with a spotted face called Béry.

CHAPTER NINE
Alsatian Journey

AFTER A VERY few years of existence the Maginot Line had become, in the eyes of its owners at any rate, a veritable Book of Ages; in fact, in the eyes of all peoples, except apparently the Germans, it stood for everything that was anti-German, at once a symbol and a facade for the strength of France. Being the best that money could buy, it was believed, American-fashion, to be as invincible as it was fabulous. That it stopped short half-way up the frontier should perhaps have given us some cause for suspicion; but, encouraged by the constant avowals of the French that they not only wanted, but even invited an attack to the north of the line, we remained as duped as we were fascinated; nothing, they cheerily said, could suit them better than a German attack through the Low Countries.

The Maginot Line is now only a legend; it is even fashionable in England, where old idols are so easily desecrated after they have been broken, to treat it with the derision and scorn which Jehovah is said to have constantly poured on his enemies, the poor old Philistines. But in spite of this revulsion of British feeling, it should be remembered that the line itself was never conquered; it only fell when all else had fallen. The Maginot Line still seems to me quite admirable; to all non-militant people in fact it must seem admirable; it is only the fire-eaters, whose lives are hourly spent in preparing just wars to obtain uneasy peaces, who could think otherwise. After all, it is usual when securing a house against burglars at night to put locks on the doors and windows in order to prevent their entry; it is unusual to scour the grounds in search of them each evening armed with a blunderbuss and a pickaxe – a policy which the critics of Mr. Chamberlain would have us follow at all times. Such a policy – which demands that you meet barbarity by barbarity – only becomes valid when hostilities have actually started; if practised before it would merely make peace as beastly as war. To talk about the 'Maginot mentality' as if it were akin to cretinism is a significant sign of the swing from decent living to jungle life which has now fully overtaken us; the 'Maginot mentality' is the only mentality for non-savage peoples.

There were some famous legends about the line in France during the early days of the war, many of them romantic, most of them untrue, and nearly all of them calculated to uphold the weak-hearted. Its interior for instance was likened variously, to the inside of a battleship, a grand hotel, and an American palais de danse, descriptions which I found did not prove to be accurate; although it is true that the maze of mean pipes, and the smell of cheap paint did possess a certain affinity with the first.

A less comfortable legend held that the line, as self-sufficient as it was invincible, could hold out for some years against a siege from all sides, frontal, flank, and rear, owing to the special nature of its food supplies. They contained, it was said, a nutritive substance invented by a clever but dishonest French sergeant, and appropriated in 1936 by the French Government in the nick of time, when the sergeant was in the very act of selling it to the Germans who had offered a better price.

These and other romances gave to the place an aura of mystery and vulgarity, and of course everyone in the British Army was immensely keen to visit it.

Their wishes were satisfied in the early weeks of 1940 when it was decided that a small sector in front of the line should be manned by our troops. This would relieve the French a little, as well as initiate the British into the mumbo-jumbo of modern war, an experience that many were craving after four months of inactivity on the Belgian frontier. Although without this craving myself, I had some good friends who lived near Metz, and I accordingly welcomed the news as gladly as my colleagues; in any case the line itself could not be uninteresting.

It was therefore a pleasant although not altogether unexpected surprise when the colonel proposed that I should take the place of a sick engineer officer, and visit the line towards the end of February. I was, he said, to accompany one of the engineer majors from the field companies on a visit that was to last four days. The British units manning the line normally made a stay of at least a month, so that our visit would be relatively short.

'It will, in fact,' laughed the colonel, 'be a sort of visit to the visitors.'

I gathered that I was to examine the stocks of barbed wire, hop-poles, pig-iron, and all the other engineer oddities now so much a part of my life; it would at least be a welcome diversion from purchasing them.

Before leaving I had the good fortune to meet a French sergeant in a Lille restaurant who was home on leave from the Maginot Line. For a drink or two he was prepared to tell me something about it, although I was careful not to disclose to him my reasons for asking.

'I'm not really allowed to tell you anything,' he said. 'It's all secret.'

'But naturally as your ally I am most interested to know something about your famous line,' I said, offering him another Pernod. 'You need not tell me anything secret. For instance, I do not ask you to tell me how many men there are in the line, or the names of the regiments that are there.'

'No,' he said, shaking his head and obviously mistaking my meaning, 'I definitely cannot tell you that. I am sorry. But it would be contravening the regulations if I did. I will, however, tell you what we do when we go into Metz on short leave, if you like.'

'Do,' I said. 'That would be most interesting.'

'Well,' he said, rubbing the stubble on his chin, 'of course you will never guess. I suppose you think we all want women when we leave the line, don't you?'

'Naturally,' I said.

'Well, you are wrong. In my case that is just what I do not want,' he said. 'I wait for my long leave for that. When I go into Metz I go straight to the Public Library.'

'And what do you do there?' I asked, fascinated.

'I read all the back numbers of *Figaro*. You see we only get the poor newspapers in the line and it is impossible to get any truth from them.'

This faith in *Figaro* so astounded me that, not to be outdone, I told a lie.

'I do exactly the same with *The Times*,' I confessed.

'Ah – but *The Times*,' he said. 'That is not the same as *Figaro*, is it?'

'Tell me,' I asked, 'have you shares in *Figaro* or is your father the editor? I am interested to know why you have such faith in a newspaper.'

'In these hard times,' said the sergeant sadly, 'one has to have faith in something, hasn't one?'

'But why not put it in your admirable church?' I said. 'Many men have taken solace from it.' I immediately began to feel uncomfortable in the role of evangelist.

'The Church,' he said, 'is no longer a force. The curés have become the buriers of the people – mere appendages. For my part I believe with all my heart in the Voice of the People, and in the Freedom of the Press. Honestly there is nothing like it.'

'Tell me more of the Maginot Line,' I said, seeing we were getting into deep water. 'What is the food like in the line?'

'The food is good,' he said, 'it is simple and well cooked, but there are too many carrots.'

'Why is that?' I asked.

'I do not really know. It may perhaps be due to the land around our part of the line. It was once owned by the Germans, you know, and ever since then carrots have been grown on it. It is typical of the Germans, is it not, to grow carrots everywhere? They have little taste.'

I saw that it was quite impossible to obtain any information about the line itself from him, and I came away with the strong suspicion that he had been pulling my leg.

But three days later I was able to form my own impressions. It took us a day to get to Alsace by road, a journey that was memorable for the extreme cold and the conversation of my companion, the engineer major, who had apparently lived and dreamed for the day when he would be able to visit the Maginot Line; we talked of nothing else.

'You will find,' he said, 'much to admire in the French system of fortification.'

He undoubtedly took me for a skilled fortifier and talked much of Vauban and the 'French system', contrasting it unfavourably with the 'English system' which he said had reached its perfection in the Far East where he had worked for several years. I had difficulty in appreciating the difference but, like the wedding guest, I could not choose but hear, for we were closeted together in the same truck and my companion, although a Boy Scout, was also a major.

We left Lesquin at nine o'clock on an icy February morning with the prospect before us of motoring two hundred miles to Metz. We were to spend the night there before going on to the Maginot Line itself, only a few miles to the east of the city.

An Army truck, certainly in so far as its occupants are concerned, is possibly the least suited of all vehicles to a continental climate; to drive in it through falling snow in the depth of winter or along a dusty road in full summer are both equally detestable experiences. Being open at the sides and covered for roof with a mere rag, its only real defence against the weather is the windscreen, a device that on most of these vehicles is limited to a bare minimum of glass. On this particular morning the temperature was well below freezing point and snow was still falling. In addition, our vehicle had a large hole in the floor-board near the clutch pedal, through which a gust of what appeared to be liquid air blew continuously upon the legs of whoever was driving; a flying stone had been responsible for this hole very soon after leaving Lesquin. I contrived to keep the upper part of my body warm by talking and gesticulating, but the rest soon became quite numb. Any conversation was therefore better than none, provided it was not entirely one-sided; and I took good care that, although I had little idea what I was talking about, I chatted continuously and fluently on the various topics which interested my companion.

Just after leaving Douai we ran into a snowdrift, and I had the unpleasant experience of getting out of the vehicle and walking about, feeling as if I consisted merely of a mouth and a pair of eyes suspended and isolated in the thin and nipping air. After a little while the circulation in my body began to return with that dull, throbbing pain familiar to all who have been injected by a dentist; but this time, instead of a mere portion of the mouth being affected, it was the whole body.

'Pretty chilly, isn't it?' said the major, stamping his feet.

This process of thawing and refreezing occurred several times before we reached Rheims, because we were forced on three occasions to make a detour to avoid snowdrifts. We arrived at Rheims at two o'clock; the major wanted to have lunch in the big hotel where he had arranged to meet an Air Force friend whose squadron was stationed just outside the city. This officer was waiting for us; he had had lunch but he consented to sit with us while we had ours.

The hotel, like the rest of Rheims, was full of RAF officers. Just as Lille, under the impact of the British, seemed to have become a sort of garrison town, so Rheims seemed now to be an RAF depot. The hotel itself was of the luxury variety usually patronized by British officers; in normal times its price would have been prohibitive to all except those of the calibre of Georges de Treuil. But, in order to accommodate itself to the new clientele, the management had cunningly reduced its charges, thereby making much more profit.

'Not at all a bad place,' said the RAF officer as I admired the Edwardian rosewood walls and the striped satin chairs. 'We like it. Have you been in the cocktail bar?'

We confessed that we had not.

'Damn good champagne cocktails they make,' he said. 'Extraordinary good value. Look – I'll order you a couple. Here, waiter,' he said signalling. 'Bring me two Angelo Specials. No, wait – on second thoughts make it three.'

The Angelo Specials proved to be as exotic as their name, and tongues were soon loosened.

'We really have a hell of a fine time here, you know,' said our new companion. 'Plenty of flying and plenty of drink. What could a man ask for more?'

'I suppose you come into contact with the Boche quite a bit,' said my major enviously.

'Yes, every now and then we go over and have a look at him,' said the RAF officer. 'But we don't really do anything you know. We just fly there for the trip, take a few pictures and then fly back. Lots of people here think we ought to do more. It doesn't worry me. It suits me as it is. I take life as I find it. But it does seem a bit odd perhaps not to do more,' he ended thoughtfully.

'Ah – but *drôle de guerre*, you know,' said the major, shaking his finger waggishly. 'You're lucky to have the opportunity to get over enemy territory at all. Look at us. We do nothing at all up at Lille except gaze at the Belgian sentries. It's a heart-breaking business. You at least are in touch with the Germans.'

'Yes, that's true,' admitted the RAF officer.

'Never mind,' said the major turning to me as if I was the envious one. 'We'll be in touch with them in a day or two, won't we?'

He was quite right, because that evening after arriving in Metz I heard, for the first time in my life, a shot fired in anger. While we were having dinner a heavy bang accompanied by a convulsion occurred somewhere outside.

'That,' said the waiter, 'is a Boche aeroplane being fired at. It happens very seldom, but when it does it frightens the chef who was in the Air Force in the last war. We have not had any fire like that for a fortnight. You are lucky.'

Our arrival in Metz seemed to be the beginning of the war to me. Metz itself, I found on looking out of my bedroom window the next morning, was shining beneath a watery sun, and doing its best to assume the garish colours given it by the characteristic French postcards, through whose medium I had had my first acquaintance with the city. But the Moselle on which it stands, the divine river that flows to its confluence with the Rhine in enemy country at Coblenz some hundreds of miles away, could muster nothing better that morning than a dark French blue against the turquoise Mediterranean variety ascribed to it in the postcards.

After breakfast we reported for orders at the infantry barracks in Metz where the British had set up a small office from which to administer their troops in the Maginot Line. We were greeted by a major in a Scotch regiment.

'Well, you chaps look to be in for a bit of action,' he said. 'We've just had reports that they're expecting trouble in your sector. You're lucky.'

I disapproved of these constant congratulations.

I inquired what sort of 'trouble' it might be.

'Two days ago,' he explained, 'the French heavy guns ranging into German territory shelled a German outpost by mistake. It is thought that some of the Germans were killed. There's almost certain to be a return packet from the Boche.'

'And what, may I ask,' said my major sarcastically, 'is the purpose of the French artillery if it is not directed towards killing Germans?'

'Ah,' said the Scot, 'that is just what you people don't understand when you come down here. You see there's a gentleman's agreement between the French and the Germans by which they don't shell one another. It has worked very well up to now. They each carry out all their ranging on open ground. Well – now the French have violated the agreement and all our information goes to show that the Boche is preparing to violate it in return. You should have some fun when you get up there. I envy you, I must say. Fed up with stickin' about in this damn city myself.'

I wanted to explore the damn city and I would willingly have changed occupations with him if it had been possible. He told us to report at a little village called Veckering, a part of the Maginot Line itself.

'They may not let you take your car up the whole way,' he said, 'because you may be under enemy observation.'

The major looked delighted.

Veckering turned out to be about fifteen miles north-east of Metz but there were so many road-blocks and detours to navigate that it took over an hour to reach it. At all the road-blocks we had to show our passes and prove our bona-fides, so that it soon became obvious that the Maginot Line was being taken far more seriously by its owners than the Lille frontier in the north – the frontier where the Belgian workers crossed and re-crossed daily with so little formality in order to work in the factories.

The weather had changed. Although snow still lay deeply on the ground, the sun was shining coldly on a landscape that in warmer days would nourish on its broad and undulating slopes the Alsatian grapes that give the lighter and more heady wines of France. Snow reveals landscapes for their structural beauty only; beneath it, the land charms or displeases by shape and form alone, and no embroidery of textured surface or generous bloom can prejudice the observer. The flat, unattractive, and sooty land around Lille was, for example, revealed beneath a layer of snow to be the possessor of a cold, impassioned beauty, quite unappreciated in its normal state.

But Alsace, whose main charm lies in its vegetation, seemed under these conditions characterless and trite, an undisciplined maze of various naked hills and valleys, shorn of their own beauty by the snow, but missing the hard stringent quality with which the snow had endowed the plains of Flanders.

A snow covering is at its best in a land of two extremes; in flat, vast inanes where a sort of majestic hopelessness is implied; and conversely, in a land of enormous mountain ranges of Himalayan or Alpine calibre, where majesty and hope seem identical.

We reached Veckering in time for lunch. All the civilians had been evacuated and most of the villages we passed through on our way from Metz were inhabited exclusively by soldiers. It was, for instance, peculiar and distracting to observe in the back gardens of the houses, clotheslines hung exclusively with male underwear; one instinctively missed the brighter colours always observed when arriving at any of the great termini of London – which so effectively relieve the monotony of the last few minutes of the journey. The shops in these villages were either closed or taken over by the military and turned into quartermasters' stores, their windows now stocked with bully-beef and other unpalatable foodstuffs. They were deserted villages beyond a doubt, if military occupation can be classified as desertion; they had a lifelessness about them as thrilling and as cheerless as a corpse.

These villages that cluster along the length of the Maginot Line are sometimes, like Veckering, a part of it themselves, actually incorporated in the Line, or, more often, they appear as an appendage just touching its border. Veckering was a minute hamlet with a population of not more than five hundred in normal times; it now accommodated a company of British engineers and a French tank battalion. It nestled at the foot of one of the so-called Maginot 'forts'.

A Maginot 'fort' is, I learnt later, the essence of the whole Line, its symbol and its chief component. The land had, in fact, been selected on account of its characteristic hills of suitable size and beehive shape, each of which was easily transformable into a 'fort'. A chain of these hills formed the backbone of the Line, the *'ligne de recueil'* as it was called, the ultimate resort into which the defenders would retreat when all else had failed, and where presumably they would fulfil the prophecies and subsist for several years on patent foods. In front of the *'ligne de recueil'*, stretching eastwards for miles, were of course many other lesser 'lignes' – of barbed wire, anti-tank ditches and pillboxes, through all of which the enemy would have to pass before reaching the big Maginot forts.

Each of these forts was manned by a special Maginot company of trained fortress soldiers, men who would not leave their own particular fort for the duration of the war to undertake any other work. And after visiting the inside of one of these forts and observing the highly technical devices with which it was furnished, I could readily appreciate the battleship analogy; the fortress soldiers would certainly require a training as specialised and as intricate as that of a naval engineer.

These disembowelled hills, each containing a warren of passages and corridors and each in reality nothing more than a manmade husk, still possessed their outward appearance. Apart from the cleverly camouflaged gun embrasures, only discernible from close observation, they must have appeared to the enemy no different from their more natural neighbours; but within them, so the French told us, were the most powerful guns in the world.

As we journeyed up to Veckering, over all the land around these forts hung the mysterious air of untried strength, of a Gulliver prone upon the ground, uncertain of his power if he should stir. And somewhere out east, not many miles away one felt, as one viewed these fortresses, was something of the same type, the Siegfried Line, the German variety of this vast expenditure of the taxpayers' money, following the line of the frontier just as faithfully as the Maginot, parallel in shape as in wastefulness.

The Siegfried Line was not visible from Veckering because between it and the village lay ten miles of no man's land, a country peopled only by the outposts of both sides, who lived like cats; because, as I learnt later, it is necessary to tread delicately in a land where friend and foe may often intermingle at night without knowing it. These were the people we were to visit and whose life we were to share.

CHAPTER TEN
Maginot Outpost

AS WE APPROACHED the village of Veckering a French sentry sprang out at a road-block and motioned us to slow down for the sixth time during our journey. It was too much for the major.

'Here are our identity cards,' he said wearily as if repeating a formula. 'We are visiting the British forces in the line. We are on duty. There is nobody in the back of the vehicle. We have no explosive on board.'

'It is not that, sir,' said the. sentry. 'But we have been warned to expect you. There is a special guide here who will take you to the English engineers. Will you please first step this way and sign the book?'

This vigilance was certainly a strange reversal of the French frontier methods near Lille, and I began to wonder if we should be blindfolded next. Major Cairns came out of the hut looking thoughtful.

'All this secrecy is a good thing, of course,' he said as he got into the driving seat. 'It means that the French have really woken up. They're not going to lose the Maginot Line in a hurry.'

'Naturally,' cut in our guide in the back of the truck, speaking in broken English. 'We have taken fifteen years to build it and it has cost us many millions of pounds. I dare say it is as valuable as the British Grand Fleet. We certainly don't intend to lose it.'

Within five minutes he had brought us to a small dwelling on the outskirts of the village, at the very foot of a Maginot fort. It bore on its roof the national slogan of the French Republic: '*Du-bon, Dubonnet*' – pathetically announcing that, although now a British army headquarters, it had in its time seen better days.

'Until you people came,' said the guide, 'it was the best bistro in the village.'

I felt reassured at the sight of this bistro with its comfortable words; although right on the German doorstep it seemed so essentially in France. The guide left us at the door, sadly, as Frenchmen do when they have performed a service for which they would normally expect a tip.

Inside the building all was excitement and activity. On the first door on the right was a notice in English, 'Security Office. Strictly private,' and on the next 'Do not disturb'. All the doors seemed to have a legend of some sort even if it was only 'Padre's room. Quiet, please' at the end of the passage. On tiptoe with military expectancy as we were, this last notice conjured up visions of soldiers being given their final benediction.

We met the padre himself at lunch. He was not as I had expected, a long, thin ascetic, careworn with perpetually saying goodbye to men for ever, and then later covering the last sod over their heads. He was a hearty, heavy man who obviously played the Rugby game and who was soon abhorring me because I refused a third 'Gin and It' before lunch.

'But no-one refuses here,' he said. 'Come along now. Don't be silly. Nothing like it.'

'It's awfully kind of you,' I said, 'but honestly I don't want another.' In this way I refused him three times.

Finally, in desperation, he poured me out a 'Gin and It' and thrust it into my hand, just as firmly as the Bishop had put 'The Sacrament of Life' into it at my confirmation ten years before. As politely as I could I put it down, repeating that I did not want it. This was too much for English good taste to bear and the padre spoke his mind.

'All right,' he said. 'Don't have it then. It's your concern, not mine.'

I felt as if I had been refused the last rites and I shrivelled into a corner where I read the *Daily Mirror* until lunch began. Lunch was a boisterous affair accompanied by much coming and going and clinking of glasses.

'We're always on the job here,' said the commanding officer. 'Not a moment's peace.'

This type of remark is generally a sure sign that no work is done at all, and I was surprised to find later that what he said was true.

'Ah – but I expect you enjoy it, don't you?' said my companion, Major Cairns.

'Oh – it's not such a bad life really, I suppose,' said an engineer captain. 'We kill a Jerry or two every now and again you know. You must come round the outposts with me after lunch and see how we live.'

After lunch, in response to his invitation, we rigged ourselves out in full paraphernalia with revolvers, gas masks, gas-capes, water bottles, whistles, etc., in order to meet the captain and to visit the front with him.

'Ah – good, I'm glad to see you've brought everything,' he said. 'But there is just one thing that is wrong. You shouldn't take a gas mask with you. None of the French do. They say they don't want to provoke the Germans into using gas. Silly, isn't it?'

It certainly seemed the reverse of the English ARP attitude towards gas. I threw off my mask gladly; it was a provocative thing, dependent for its existence only upon the expectancy of other people's ill will and as such typical of all armies, at once their necessity and their epitome.

We climbed into our little black vehicle and set off towards the outposts. The sun was shining on the Maginot Line as we left, giving its snow-covered hills and mounds a certain unnatural cheerfulness; even the gun embrasures seemed hospitable as we moved away from them towards the Siegfried Line.

The land we crossed on our journey east looked in nature what it was in fact, a seedbed for all that is suspicious, distrustful, and uncertain of itself. The villages, now entirely silent and lonely, seemed as self-conscious of their ephemerality in the cheap hastiness of their construction, as the ground around them was of its military past and future, in the pock-marks, scars, and ugly heaps of earth that adorned it. It was a land without much hope.

'There is one of our new predictors,' said the captain, pointing at a monster in camouflage colours looking like an enlarged tradesman's van, as it nestled into the side of a hill surrounded by fantastic wreaths of wire.

Some peculiar object of this kind unfolded itself at every turn of the road under the realistic description of our guide. So many and so varied were the devices that it seemed it would be impossible for any German to penetrate this maze of guns, mines, traps, and snares. They all tumbled and cascaded over one another, until at the front itself they seemed to solidify into a concentrated band, and we moved in fear of missing the secret paths and destroying ourselves on our own defences. We left the car in a wood and continued on foot.

'Where are we going?' I asked.

'We are visiting the Grünewald,' the captain replied, after we had left the car and were advancing on foot. 'Our most forward outposts in that wood ahead,' he pointed to a large wood that sprawled across the top of a hill towards which we were now walking. 'It's called the Grünewald. I believe it's really in Germany. It should be with a name like that. Lots of places round here have German names. This wood is the limit of the French advance last October. When the British troops took over the front in January the French unit they replaced had been here since October. Hallo, there goes a shell,' he said, pausing and looking up as a whistle like a train seemed to blow immediately overhead. I instinctively ducked. 'That's the French gunners having their artillery practice. They generally do it for about an hour every afternoon. Come along now. We must hurry and get into the wood before the Germans start replying; their shells generally land somewhere near here. As you can see there are quite a lot of craters in the field to the left over there. But they haven't shelled the Grünewald yet, though they must know it's full of our men.'

We hastened forward without delay after this piece of advice, climbing the hill that led to the large wood a few hundred yards ahead. I remarked to the captain that it was rather peculiar for the Germans not to shell the wood if they knew that it was full of our men.

'It *is* mysterious,' he said, 'but after a month here we have come to the conclusion that there must be some sort of secret agreement between Jerry and the French not to molest one another. As far as we know they have never shelled the Grünewald. But I expect you've heard about the mistake the other day when the French artillery on its ranging practice strafed the enemy positions in the wood on the other side of the valley. Everyone is now expecting some sort of retaliation, and as the wood they strafed is just opposite the Grünewald, we have a horrid feeling we'll be the ones to cop it.'

'That always happened in the last war,' said the major philosophically as if he had fought in it. 'The P.B.I. always had to pay for the mistakes of the gunners.'

'At any rate,' said the captain as we climbed the hill, 'I sincerely hope they don't retaliate for a day or two because in a few days' time the French will be taking over our positions, I hope.'

But, as if in reply and contradiction to his words, down in the valley behind us, where we had walked only a few minutes before, came the answering crash of a bursting shell; and out of the corner of my eye I saw a pillar of smoke and dust appear near the roadside, the sky above it full of moving clods of earth.

'Come on,' said the major. 'Let's run. Jerry's started his afternoon practice.' Within two minutes we had gained the edge of the Grünewald.

The Grünewald lay on the top of a hill from which it commanded the surrounding countryside; being on the highest point in the neighbourhood the ground behind us was now spread out in panoramic fashion, and ten miles away I thought I could just detect the village of Veckering which we had left in the Maginot Line. I remarked on the magnificent view.

'But when we reach the front edge of the wood,' said the captain, 'you will see something even finer. You will be able to see all the Jerry-occupied territory for miles around. But I bet you a beer you don't see a Jerry. He's a foxy devil.'

We turned and entered the wood. Although it was midwinter and many of the spinneys we had passed on the way up had been leafless, the Grünewald with its pinetrees seemed as dark and dense as an Alpine forest; inside one quickly missed the faint cheer from the watery rays of the setting sun outside.

We were immediately accosted by a British sentry and, in spite of our companion's presence, identity cards and papers were examined once again. Inside the wood it seemed as if an army had suddenly sprung to life; outside in the valley there had been no sign of life, we had been alone with the hills and the woods, observing only where the Army *had* been, unable to tell where it was. But here in the wood, as well as the trenches and dugouts and barbed wire were the defenders themselves. We passed them as we made our way forward; British Tommies working, eating, sleeping, shaving, and some reading the *Daily Mail*. They comprised a company of infantry, accompanied by smaller detachments of engineers. They took little notice of us. The captain stopped at one of the trenches in which a sergeant was playing cards, and asked him what sort of night he had had.

'Lots of Jerry patrols about last night, sir,' the sergeant replied. 'We heard them at the edge of the wood. No moon so you couldn't see a thing. But they sheered off when they made our cans rattle,' he laughed as he pointed to a barbed-wire fence some yards away; it was festooned with old tin cans which even now clanked in the wind.

'Did any of our patrols go out?' asked the captain.

'The Guards sent out a patrol, sir,' he replied, pointing to some Guardsmen who were shaving in another trench.

We walked forward to the front edge of the wood where some other Guards were cooking their evening meal on a Primus stove.

'Yes – we visited the big wood on the other side of the valley,' replied a second lieutenant in the Grenadier Guards to the captain's inquiry. 'If you come over here,' he said to us, 'I will show you where we went.'

I followed them to the far edge of the wood and looked out over an impressive landscape which stretched far away for miles on either side. On the extreme left was a distant church spire and, swinging round, one's gaze wandered over the enemy fields and spinneys, finally culminating where a river glimmered about ten miles away to the south. Straight in front, on the other side of the valley, and not more than six hundred yards away was the German wood, situated like our own upon the crest of a hill and stocked like our own with the densest trees. It required little imagination to suppose that, like our own, it contained observers standing motionless in the shade of its forward edge. It truly seemed an image, a mirrored image of the Grünewald.

'Stand back, sir,' said the Guards subaltern sharply as Major Cairns moved forward to get a better view. 'We must keep within the cover of the trees. If you go too far forward the sun will shine on you. Here we are in the shadows; to the observer over there we become a part of the wood. Sometimes,' he continued, pointing to the right-hand edge of the enemy wood, 'you can see a movement over in that corner. They are building some trenches in the very front. They generally do it by night. We visited it last night in the hope of catching them at work but there was no-one there. Look,' he said suddenly gripping my arm, 'inside the wood quite near the trench – can you see – there is a man. He is leaning against a tree. Here take my glasses.'

He handed me his field glasses and six hundred yards away, I could just make out a human figure. It was difficult, owing to the mist, to distinguish much about it, but its identity was clearly revealed by the whiteness of the flesh. The German appeared to be observing across the valley as we were, and I wondered if he had seen us. He made no movement.

'Quick,' said Major Cairns, turning to a Guardsman with a rifle. 'Pick him off. Quickly, man.'

'Please,' said the subaltern without moving, 'do no such thing. Our business is to obtain information. We want prisoners, not dead men. Besides, if we fire from here, it will only give our own position away. I am afraid I must ask you not to think of firing, sir. It will only mean an immediate reply from the Boche with mortar fire.'

'Yes,' said the captain. 'It would be fatal to fire at him. Last time that was done by the French they lost five men from Boche mortar fire as a result.'

Major Cairns sadly put down the rifle which he had taken from the Guardsman, and we all stood by the trees looking out over the valley.

In the no man's land midway between the two woods was a little village with a church spire, houses, and allotment gardens: its smokeless chimneys told that it was derelict.

'Both sides have been using that village for artillery practice,' said the subaltern, looking at his watch. 'About now the Germans often put a few shells into it. You can see some of the buildings damaged by shellfire. Sometimes our patrols go through it at night. It is said that two nights ago the organ in the church was being played. I'm going to buy some music in Metz and play it next time,' he said laughing. 'The Germans are too conceited about their musicianship.'

'Maybe,' said the captain. 'But I shouldn't trust them. You'll probably find they have put a bomb in the organ loft which goes off when you play "God Save the King".'

'Ah – but I shall play something by old Bach,' said the subaltern, 'so there will be no danger.'

I thought of my friend M. Busch in Evron and of his encounter with a German near Metz in the last war. If he had met one in an organ loft he would have undoubtedly suggested a duet.

'Do you see those railway trucks out there?' said our guide, pointing to a railway line near the village which ran out from beneath the Grünewald and disappeared into German territory opposite. On it were twenty derelict railway wagons, placed head to tail, standing as forlornly as everything else in the valley. 'The French Government have offered thirty francs for every one of those that can be brought in,' he said. 'There were thirty out there at the beginning of the war and, as we have only brought in three, it looks as if the Germans are more enterprising.'

There was something very sinister about the lonely trucks as they stood near the village with the sunlight falling upon them, each with a price on its head.

'But we have given up trying to get them in now,' said the subaltern. 'It is suspected that the German patrols have fitted booby traps to the ones at this end.'

'My God, what a fiendish devil Jerry is,' said Major Cairns involuntarily.

We stood for a few moments longer and then left the edge of the wood, taking a last look at the figure on the other side of the valley. I felt elated; after six months of war I had actually seen the enemy.

We made our way homewards to the now fairly regular accompaniment of French ranging shells; they went screaming overhead into Germany. Light was beginning to fail; it was four o'clock of a February afternoon and the men in the Grünewald were cooking their evening meal, or cleaning their weapons and preparing for a night patrol as we left.

'Where do you sleep?' I asked the Guards subaltern who had accompanied us to the edge of the wood.

'In a dugout here,' he said. 'Like to see it?'

He took me into a trench, a little larger than the rest. It gave onto a small underground chamber well strutted with timber and apparently dry. It was almost completely filled by a small bunk and on a chair an oil lamp was burning. Beside it lay an open copy of the *Golden Bough*.

'I'm studying savage customs, you see,' he said smiling as he took my hand and we said goodbye.

I could not help thinking of him on the way back, in his little cabin out on the edge of the world, reading about the totems of another civilisation while preparing those of his own.

The next morning Major Cairns and I went on a conducted tour of the nearby Maginot fort. To enter it we climbed the beehive shaped hill above the mess by a road that circled the fort; halfway up, about forty or fifty feet above the housetops of Veckering, we arrived at the main entrance, a heavy metal-studded door approached by a portcullis like the entrance to Bluebeard's cave; later inspection showed that this door was several feet thick and that it was operated by electricity. The beehive shape of the fort made it easy for an anti-tank ditch to be constructed encircling it. This ditch was at the same level as the main entrance, and the portcullis over which we crossed gave to the fort the air of a medieval moated castle.

We stood in front of the door on a raw, icy February morning waiting for it to open; we were well muffled, hands deep in our pockets, both stamping our feet to keep the circulation going. After a minute or two the door swung open, revealing a long straight passage inside, which disappeared twenty yards away where it swung out of view like a burrow. A small door just inside the entrance opened on to the passage and a French lieutenant appeared.

'Ah – you are the English officers who have come to see the fort,' he said shaking hands. 'I shall be pleased to act as your guide. But first you must have a drink in the mess.'

As we stepped inside, the great metal door, invisibly compelled, swung into position again. This was Bluebeard at his best.

We had been frozen while waiting outside, but I soon realised that the French, like most continental nations, never neglect interior heating. The inside of the Maginot was as warm and as fuggy as a bourgeois house in Lille. We took off our coats and scarves and left them in the mess.

The officers' mess, which was on a much lower floor, was reached by a lift at the end of the passage; I calculated as we dropped in the lift that the mess was well below the village of Veckering outside, because we must have dropped nearly a hundred feet. The passage leading from the lift to the mess was typical of its kind, the inside of the fort being a veritable warren of these passages. They were semi-circular in shape, about fifteen feet high, poorly lit, their walls covered with pipes running parallel to the passage like the interior of a warship. I observed tram-lines on the floor running down the centre of the passages and I asked the guide what they were for.

'All the Portage in the fort is done on electric trolleys which run on the tram-lines,' he said. 'Look – there is one of them;' and he pointed down one of the passages which we were passing. Coming towards us at about five miles an hour was a small trolley loaded with stores and driven by a French soldier who sat at the controls reading a newspaper. He rang a bell when he saw us, and smirked at me as he rumbled noisily past in his chariot.

'Are these men here permanently?' asked Major Cairns.

'Yes. We are all here permanently,' the Frenchman replied. 'We form special Maginot companies. We are never moved from here. Take my case for instance. I have been in this fort since the time of the Munich agreement. Once a man has volunteered for service in the line he becomes a part of it.'

We found one or two officers in the mess and together we toasted the healths of our respective countries in some excellent Rhine wine.

'We have good cellars here, you see,' one of them said. 'It is good to drink to the damnation of the Boche in his own wine, is it not? Let us only hope he tries to attack the line. It will be the death of him if he does.'

'Yes,' said our guide. 'I think you will agree when you have seen the rest of the fort that there is not much hope for the Germans if they attack *here*.'

When we left the fort two hours later I heartily agreed with him. Every known branch of warfare seemed to have been considered, down to the last detail. The anti-gas arrangements were typical.

'This is the pressure room for our anti-gas measures,' said the lieutenant taking us into a room containing several turbine engines. 'They are not working now. But we have a practice with them once a week. They are the pressure generators. They keep the pressure of the air inside the fort just a little greater than atmospheric so that poison gas cannot enter. Even if the Germans were to surround the fort and try to inject gas it could not stay for long. The air would be constantly cleansed and purified so that we could live for months in here – even though the gas was over all the country outside.'

'How long can you withstand a siege?' asked Major Cairns as we examined the stocks of preserved foods in the cellars.

'I am not allowed to say,' said the lieutenant smiling. 'As long as is necessary, I can assure you of that.'

The interior of the fort consisted of various floors or tiers, fully justifying the Grand Hotel analogy which I had heard in Lille at the beginning of the war; we visited all these floors by lifts, although several alternative methods by stairs existed. The men's dormitories were not unlike those in our own dreary barracks in England – except that they were also denied sunlight and fresh air, the air being conducted through the long pipes that lined the passages. This lack of light and air seemed in fact to be the only drawback to volunteering for service in the Line; but its occupants all seemed perfectly contented with their lot.

'During the day of course all the men go outside,' said the lieutenant as we peered out of the only type of window with which the fort was furnished – a gun embrasure – in reply to my observation that the lack of sunlight must be rather unpleasant. 'You can see the men out there now, working on the outer defences.' Along the anti-tank ditch, which would evidently be well covered by fire from our embrasure, we could see the French soldiers at work repairing the barbed wire and the ditch.

Inside our turret was a large gun of naval calibre.

'We practise with these guns once or twice a week,' said the lieutenant, whom I judged from his knowledge of the guns to be an artillery officer. 'We fire into Boche territory just to keep our hand in, you know. Here are the targets we fire on.' He pointed at a map on the wall which I recognised as depicting the country that stretched from Veckering eastward through the Grünewald and on into Germany. A mile or two inside enemy territory large crosses in red pencil had been made on the map.

'Those are our targets,' said the Frenchman.

'Do you ever shoot at *that*?' I asked, indicating the railway line in no man's land with the railway trucks on it, which we had seen the day before. 'I was told yesterday that the Germans use it for artillery practice. I wondered if you did too.'

'We did once,' he replied laughing. 'At the beginning of the war. But some of the shells landed a little too close to our own infantry in the Grünewald,' he pointed on the map to the edge of the wood from where we had seen the German soldier. 'We had trouble with the infantry colonel then. We fire well into German territory now, I can tell you.'

Before leaving the gun turret he showed us a device for showering grenades on to any Germans who might penetrate the anti-tank ditch outside and attempt to scale the wall up to the gun embrasure. It was a small trapdoor in the outer wall about nine inches in diameter with a lever at the side, functioning like the change-collecting devices in department stores in which a billet is popped into a small hole, whereupon a lever at the side is pulled and the billet mysteriously finds its way to the cashier at the other end of the building.

'In here,' he said, opening the trapdoor, 'we pop a grenade. We pull this handle here, and the grenade drops down a shute and explodes in the anti-tank ditch just outside. Boches won't stay long in the ditch with that going on.' The device reminded me of the medieval practice of pouring boiling oil on an assaulting enemy.

We finished our tour at the main control room, its walls hung with maps and range cards; we shook hands with the commandant of the fort and took our leave of the guide at the portcullis door.

'A pity you can't come and work with us permanently in the fort,' he said. 'You would love it.'

We walked down the hill towards the engineer mess, content that we had actually seen the famous line which people in England mistakenly thought we were living in. When we returned to Lille two days later neither of us could say that the 'Maginot mentality', in so far as it concerned the defenders at any rate, was either decadent or lazy. Both the British units in front and the defenders inside the line itself, seemed to be working hard, cheerfully, and confidently.

If the 'Maginot Mentality' stood for vague, weak policy it was not the defenders who gave it its reputation. Something far deeper than that, deeper even than the French Army, was responsible – the mass of political opinion that stretched far back behind the Maginot Line into France, reaching even to Paris itself.

CHAPTER ELEVEN
Paris

'PEOPLE IN GROUPS and clumps are always horrid,' said Stimpson, who was getting tired of mess life. 'They form hockey clubs and yacht clubs and armies and public schools and bridge sets; they become self-important and unimportant. They have no idea of how to live. The only life worth living is the life of self-sufficiency. Man, if he is to live reasonably, must live as nature made him, a single unit relying on no-one but himself. People do not become anchorites because they are worried about the desires of the flesh; if they are genuine, they do it to get away from the pettiness of the clubs and social sets in which they live. Only the barbarians in Africa ignore the clubs; only the barbarians in Africa are really civilised.'

'Is that an invitation to visit Paris again?' I asked, because the last time that Stimpson had inveighed against modern life in this manner we had been in a restaurant near the Madeleine, having dinner with the doctor. On that occasion Stimpson and I were in Paris on duty, the doctor on pleasure.

'It's all very well for you to run down public schools when you've been educated at the best school in the land,' the doctor had replied.

'Not at all,' said Stimpson, who was eating a plate of delicious lobster. 'I view my public school like Euston station – a place you have got to pass through to get somewhere else. It is only a few of the luxuries of life that are really necessary and a public school is not one of them. This city, Paris, is perhaps one of them,' he said, waving his fork at the four walls. 'It has, I am prepared to admit, a certain value. It corresponds to the exquisitely fashioned symbols of the African fetish makers; but that woman over there stuffing herself with fish is a sheer waste of time,' he said, pointing the fork rudely at a French lady eating alone at another table.

Stimpson and I had visited Paris several times before, on each occasion to purchase engineer stores which had fortunately been unobtainable elsewhere. The city had never been quite so lovely as during this last visit in the early spring of 1940, in an atmosphere of almost peacetime calm and satisfaction; only a few headlines in the Press and a few uniforms in the streets indicated that such a gross thing as war was possible.

To visit Paris on duty was not easy; the British authorities, who had correctly assumed that officers on purchasing duty would naturally do all their work in Paris if they got the chance, had decreed that it was only to be visited on duty in very special circumstances. One might, for instance, buy stores in Paris if they were unobtainable in the local cities of Lille and Arras. Otherwise, except to those on leave, Paris was forbidden.

In spite of this regulation we made one or two very enjoyable official trips in search of such technical devices as paint-sprayers, tie-twisters, reinforced concrete tie-wires, and other indispensable equipment demanded by the fastidious Royal Engineers for their pillboxes, and unobtainable elsewhere.

Our last visit towards the end of April was memorable both for the freshness of the city in spring, and for the reactions of the Parisians to Hitler's Scandinavian blitzkrieg, which was already a few weeks old. After the first fine enthusiasm characterised in the political 'Hitler-missed-the-bus' speeches, the people had settled down to what has since proved to be an even more characteristic attitude – wonder and dismay at this new and breath-taking form of warfare. They were amazed at the readiness of the Germans and the unreadiness of the Allies; some, it is true, were even inclined to congratulate themselves, putting it to the credit of the Allies that their failure in Norway at least invalidated the German charges about Allied intentions and preparations for a Scandinavian campaign – an ingenious argument. Causes, I was told by these people, are known by their results; thus, the winning side is guilty of provoking the war if the war is short, the losing side if it is long – a generalisation that was not without truth, because by the end of the month there was little doubt as to who was the winning side in Norway.

Some of the newspapers, elated in the early days, had quaintly and variously translated the Chamberlain phrase. '*Manquer l'autobus, en anglais, c'est à dire – bouleverser la voiture*' was the most adventurous attempt. But the conservative Press was more dignified. '*Le premier ministre ne compte pas sur une Victoire Hitlérienne*,' was their verdict.

On the evening after the great British action in Narvik, when seven German destroyers were sunk, we had dinner in a little restaurant in the rue de Bac, patronised by Stimpson in his pre-war painting days. It was full of the usual charming bourgeois crowd, all enjoying their food and talking at once. The proprietor's pretty daughter Marie remembered Stimpson and sat with us during the meal.

'Ah, Willie,' she said embracing him. 'How things have changed.'

'Ah, Marie,' said Stimpson gallantly, 'but not you, Marie.'

'Alas,' she said, 'in me, my old friend, you see a wretched girl. My mother's dead and my lover's a soldier. What could be worse?'

She seemed very unhappy, so we did our best to cheer her, talking of Paris in the old days, and of the orgies one could have had if one had only had the money. While we were talking some French youths in civilian clothes who had been drinking noisily at another table began to take notice of us. One of them came over.

'I congratulate you,' he said to Stimpson. 'You are indeed fortunate.'

'Yes, she is charming, isn't she?' said Stimpson, looking admiringly at Marie. 'We have known one another for a very long time, you know. We are very old friends, aren't we, darling?' he said taking Marie's hand.

'No, no,' said the Frenchman waving his arm in disgust. 'Not the woman – she is one of the oldest creatures in the place. I mean the British destroyers. In Narvik – you know. You are very fine fellows, all of you. Fine destroyers,' he continued patting us on the back. 'You will have a drink with me? Here, you chaps,' he said waving to his friends. 'Come over here. Here are the fellows who sank the German ships. Let us drink to them.'

'Don't be daft,' said one of his companions approaching and examining us closely. 'They're soldiers, not sailors. They don't sink ships.'

'No matter,' said the first man. 'They're fine chaps. English soldiers and sailors – all fine chaps. Fine ships you are,' he said, winking at me and raising his glass.

Their enthusiasm was general; the wonderful action in Narvik Bay had caught everyone's imagination and we were beamed upon wherever we went during those two days in Paris. Many people considered that it had pretty well settled the Germans' chances and one man even told me that he was expecting peace proposals from Germany as a result.

'Within two months,' he said, 'they will be trying to get out of it. You see if they aren't. The Boche may be a swine but he knows when he's beaten.' (Within two months the swine was in Paris.)

One has difficulty when looking back over those April days in focusing them correctly and in realising just to what extent the Parisian was duped; wherever one went, in the theatre, in the restaurants, even in the business offices, one found the same attitude, a distaste for war that manifested itself not in hatred (the Parisian was too civilised for that), but simply in humorous indifference; the war was a joke, a lark, a will-o'-the-wisp, something to be amused about, at all events, nothing to lose a night's sleep over. The Army, they seemed to say, was rather a peculiar form of adult occupation, but then, thank God, there were fortunately some people who seemed to like it; in any case it had won the last war – it surely could not lose this one! A businessman I visited fairly regularly thought that the war would finish without fighting, a strange echo of the optimistic pre-1914 days when it was even seriously considered that commerce had the power to stop hostilities. This man told me that Gamelin was the greatest general of all time.

'Not because he will win great victories,' he said, 'but because he will win a great peace. He is great because he will do anything but waste lives.'

Into these sublunary regions of strategy I could not follow him, so I asked him how he proposed to obtain a great peace without having a great victory.

'Because great victories are not necessary nowadays,' he replied. 'It is only swine like the Verdun generals of the last war who aim at them. But thank God, this war is not like the last. We are prepared this time.' It is strange in the light of after events to remember that this man was a fairly senior official in one of the larger Parisian steel firms.

'What is your plan for winning, then?' I asked.

'It is quite simple,' he replied. 'Because the Italians will come in soon on our side. Do not look so amused. I will tell you why. As you know, Mussolini has been telling their stupid youths that war is the greatest thing in the world – for so long now that they have really come to believe it. The idiots really want one. Well – who is stopping them? They are the hereditary enemies of the Germans. The Germans believe that war is a fine thing too. It only remains for the Italians to come in on our side and then they can have a war with the Germans until they are both blue in the face. While the Italians have no Maginot Line to shield them, we can wait behind theirs until it is all over. It is the same with the Russians. They will be fighting against the Germans soon too, I expect. And then, my young friend, the civilised countries like France and England will be saved of all the loss and bloodshed of the last war.'

'Yours,' said Stimpson, 'is the age-old plan – the dream of every statesman – of letting the others do the fighting and then pinching all the spoils for yourself. I thoroughly agree with you. I only hope if it is put into practice, that it will be as expedient as it is civilised.'

Most of our visits to Paris were confined to interviews with businessmen of this type, but on the last occasion we had been specially requested by our new interpreter, Bèry, to inquire at a government office about the regulations concerning the censorship of literary works about the Army. It was my first visit to such a place.

Government departments have been the subject for popular scorn since the beginning of history. No cheap newspaper, in a democracy at any rate, can be sure of its sales unless it has a daily article exposing some new incompetency in the Civil Service; it realises that, like the comic strips, abuse is always welcomed because it requires little mental effort to absorb it; unlike the comic strips, which are at least comic, this abuse article is generally completely boring. Its objects, in England, at any rate, treat it with good-humoured contempt. Secure in the superiority of their first-class honours degrees and rightly certain that they can run the country better than anyone else, they believe like the Greeks that government is the noblest function of mankind. Criticism fairly slips off their backs.

In France it is the same; the politician and the civil servant have been ridiculed even more than in England, the word '*politicien*' being almost synonymous with '*crapaud*' as a term of general abuse. But they are not similar in all respects; the buildings in France in which the administration is housed are for instance very different from ours. Unlike the government offices in Whitehall, which the newspapers tell us, so perfectly express the souls of their inhabitants, the French offices are not at all pretentious; in only a few of the government buildings in Paris is taste sacrificed to splendour, Most of them are ordinary pieces of genuine period architecture, making no attempt at Classical, Palladian, or Gothic magnificence. The office which housed the Deputy Assistant Censor was of this kind – a simple eighteenth-century building. At the main door we were stopped by a man in a cloth cap and a choker.

'What do you want?' he said, trying to block our entry.

'This man must be a hawker or a trades unionist,' said Stimpson to me. 'Let us ignore the fellow;' and he brushed past him.

'Here,' said the cloth cap who was evidently a commissionaire, pulling him back, 'you can't do that. Come here. What do you want?'

'We want to see M. Balarat, the Deputy Assistant Censor,' I replied. 'We have a special letter here for him.'

'M. Balarat is in conference. He cannot see anyone for the whole day.'

'Don't be absurd,' said Stimpson. 'A Frenchman can't be in conference the *whole* day. It's impossible.'

'Anyway,' said the commissionaire, 'those are my orders. Listen,' he said suddenly slanting his head. 'Can't you hear them up there?' He pointed at an open window on the third floor; I could hear a buzz of conversation, as of many Frenchmen arguing.

'There they are,' he said. 'All at it up there. They've got all the mayors and half the Press of Paris in that room.'

'What's it all about?' I asked.

'Nobody knows,' the man replied. 'But you see – I was right, wasn't I? Half the Press of Paris. And all the mayors. That's what all the noise is about. You'll have to come back another day.'

But Stimpson was determined to see M. Balarat. He had

promised Bèry that we would carry out the mission at all costs, and as this was our last afternoon in Paris, it would not be possible to do it another day.

'Here is my pass,' he said. 'I am going to wait outside the door of the meeting until M. Balarat comes out – even if I have to wait till midnight.'

'All right,' said the cloth cap. 'But don't blame me if he goes out by the back door.'

We decided to risk this, and after signing the visitors' book we went upstairs; the noise, which had at first been a faint buzz, got louder and louder as we ascended. On the first floor we were accosted by another man, this time wearing a beret; he demanded that we should sign yet another visitors' book.

'These people,' said Stimpson looking at him intently and speaking to me in English, 'are, I suppose, the French equivalent of those men in postmen's hats and brass buttons who stand at the doors in Whitehall. I'm not sure that they are an improvement.'

'But we have just signed the book downstairs,' I said to the man in the beret.

'That is no concern of mine,' he replied. 'The book you have just signed is for the ground floor. My book is for the first floor.'

'And there are three floors...' said Stimpson looking at me wearily as we signed again. But we had no more demands for signatures and we reached the third floor without mishap. By now the conference could be heard quite plainly.

A man whom I took to be a journalist was leaning against an upright of the conference door, peering gloomily at the scene inside the room. Through the door we could see about fifty people in various postures, some standing, some haranguing a small man in spectacles at a desk, and some sitting in chairs – but all, without exception, talking.

'Huh, they'll never settle anything,' said the man at the door in American. 'Gosh, they are a crazy crew.' He pushed his hat on the back of his head and scratched his forehead.

'What are they all arguing about?' asked Stimpson.

'God knows,' said the man. 'They don't.'

The little man at the desk in spectacles proved to be M. Balarat, and by dint of signalling and prominently revealing our uniforms we attracted his attention. As if glad of an excuse to get away from his mayors and journalists, he came over to us and asked us what we wanted. Stimpson explained that we had one or two questions about censorship on which our liaison officer wanted advice.

'Le Lieutenant Bèry says he is a friend of yours, M. Balarat,' Stimpson said. The little man was very harassed.

'I have so many friends that I cannot possibly remember them all,' he said irritably. 'I am a public man, you know. I am busy this morning. Tell M. Bèry that he must write me. Yes – I must have his request in writing. Everything must be in writing,' he said, waving his hands at the journalists. 'We must do these things officially. Good day. I cannot do more for you,' he said as he returned to his desk.

'At any rate Bèry can't say that we haven't done our best,' said Stimpson as we went downstairs.

It was annoying not to have obtained M. Balarat's help because, after getting the answers to Bèry's questions, I had hoped to ask him something about a court martial which was going to affect me personally.

I was to defend one of our NCOs who had given away military information by letter; he had tried to tell his wife the names of certain villages in northern France through which we had passed on our journey up to Lille at the beginning of the war. I hoped that the French authorities in Paris might have been able to tell me how far I could go in my proposition that certain of the villages mentioned in the letter were not in the Zone des Armées and therefore not indictable. The NCO was certain of conviction on some of the charges he had incurred, but if I could only secure that half of them were not indictable I would at least have been of some help to him at the court martial.

I was not very familiar with court martial procedure and I considered it a very great favour that the sergeant should have chosen me to defend him at his trial.

He was an interesting and unusual man, evidently given to sudden stupid and pointless actions, as was proved by this letter to his wife.

It had evidently been written in a great hurry. In it he had said something like this:

Dear Lu,

This letter is being taken by a friend going on leave who will post it immediately he gets off the boat in England. In this way it will avoid being censored. I have no time or space for saying loving things. Here is a list of all the towns we have passed through since we have been in France...

[Here had followed a bare list of French place-names taking up two sheets of paper.]

Don't tell anyone this or I'll be for the high jump. In a hurry.

Love, NOBBY.

But the friend who was to post the letter was unfortunately lily-livered, and when, at the French port of embarkation the usual formal demand to all leave personnel had been made at the barrier: 'Any more letters to post?', he had become frightened and had given up his friend's letter. The result was that Sergeant Sam Smollett was indeed for the 'high jump'.

With such incriminating evidence against us I could of course do little except plead extenuating circumstances, try to illustrate the soundness of the man's record, and hope that some of the places mentioned in the letter were harmless: M. Balarat could have helped on this last point.

Except in appearance Sergeant Samuel Smollett was not an ordinary soldier. He looked rather like an ox, a broad, thick-set figure, projecting and intransigent chin, and small, unwinking, rather pig-like eyes. He was well over six feet tall, and his bellicose utterances about what he would do to the French and Germans when the war started had more than once caused me uneasiness. His hobby was cock-fighting.

He was the transport NCO and had presumably been put in charge on account of his former association with the motor trade; a most unwise conclusion it had been to draw. His bulk was sufficient to exact a certain lip-service from his men, but they resented his position because he knew so little about vehicles, apart from how to sell them. He had fortunately behaved quite well throughout his time in France, his cock-fighting being considered an asset, and I was able to bring forward an exemplary record at his trial.

The doctor, who had always taken a morbid and rather pathological interest in Smollett, wanted to prove him insane at the court martial on the grounds that (i) Smollett had been dropped on the head when a baby and that he still 'looked at you in a silly way,' and (ii) Smollett, on being offered leave in February, had refused it. This second reason the doctor maintained was positive proof of his insanity.

I knew better. Smollett had told me that he would not dare to visit England again for some years. His only reason for joining the Army at the outbreak of war had been to get out of the country and away from all his creditors in the motor trade. Having a great sense of humour he thought the doctor's insanity idea a huge joke, and said he would gladly go through with it at the trial; its value as a present amusement seemed to mean more to him than its future slur. But the colonel unfortunately would not think of such a thing.

'We shall never hear the end of it,' he said, 'if it is known that we have a madman in the regiment.'

And so, a fortnight later when the trial was over, Sergeant Smollett came away with an unblemished record for sanity and the relatively lenient sentence of a month's detention. He was a philosophic fellow and he told me afterwards that apart from the prohibitions of smoking and talking the detention had been quite enjoyable because it had enabled him to 'think'. He was degraded to the rank of private, and I often used to see him afterwards sitting in a lorry reading Pelican Specials.

M. Balarat's refusal to co-operate did not seriously detract from the defence we put up at the court martial which at least helped to lessen the sentence.

After leaving M. Balarat's we strolled up the Champs-Élysées towards the Bois de Boulogne. Although we did not realise it, it was our last visit to Paris. A better afternoon could not have been chosen for such an occasion; it was a quiet April day, warm and cloudless, and the new leaves on the lime-trees scarcely moved as we passed the boulevardiers and observed the mass of colour ranging from the gold on the dome of the Invalides in the distance to the gay uniforms of the French cavalry officers as they sat out at the tables in front of the restaurants.

As an image of Paris to hold in one's mind afterwards it was nearly perfect, spoiled only by the photographs since published in England of German armoured vehicles passing up the Champs-Élysées. There was a timelessness about Paris that afternoon, a feeling, so very nearly contradicted two months later, that nothing in the world could ever destroy what had stood for so long. To the English patriot it is shameful that Paris was declared an open city; but the Parisians probably think differently. Even the newest buildings seemed permanent that afternoon; the marble Trocadero with its exterior bas-reliefs and lettering seemed to have sprung up to last for ever, as confident in the city as its older companions.

I saw Stimpson off at the Bois de Boulogne and then returned to the Madeleine to buy tickets for the evening performance of *Ondine*, the longest run in Paris, which was playing with Louis Jouvet at the Athenée. I knew that in so doing I was forfeiting a night's sleep, because I was due back in Lille at nine o'clock the next morning for an appointment. Stimpson had refused to accompany me to the theatre; he said he would far sooner miss *Ondine* and have a good night's sleep than see it and then sit in misery in an Army truck for six cold, dark hours while driving back to Lille when it was over. During the journey that night I began to see his point of view.

The Rhine legend of *Ondine* was new to me that evening, and I could not help thinking afterwards, as I drove out of Paris in the dark, of the peculiarly Teutonic nature of the myth. I wondered at its popularity with a French audience. It tells how an immortal maiden beneath the sea is loved by a mortal prince, to the chagrin of her father and other submarine folk. The legend is really another version of the Rhinegold story. *Ondine* seemed to attract Parisians in the same rather surprising way that Wagner did.

I left Paris at eleven-thirty. There was not a star in the sky and I soon began to regret my decision to drive back to Lille alone. It was so dark that I had the greatest difficulty in finding even the Porte de St Denis; I was not helped in this by various Frenchmen, to whom I gave lifts in the hope that they would direct me, when they merely conducted me to their own homes and then gave vague and inaccurate directions in return. In this way, shuttlecocking about the suburbs of Paris with Frenchmen on board, I wasted nearly an hour, and it was one o'clock before I finally passed the Porte de St Denis and found myself on the Senlis road.

The darkness in the sky was unfortunately and unaccountably reflected on the ground; the French seemed to have specially chosen this particular night to do their blackouts properly. There was not a gleam on the road to Senlis, and, after running into a ditch twice and nearly killing a woman once, I realised that I would fall asleep if I continued, so I determined to put up for the night and start again at dawn the following day.

This was much easier said than done, because by one o'clock everyone was in bed. In any case it was impossible in the dark to distinguish a hotel or a boarding-house. After a half-hour of stumbling about in the side streets of Senlis I managed to wake up a Dickens character of a woman who looked as though she would like to slaughter me, so large were her hands and so bull-like her neck; but her voice, as is often the case with such people, quite belied her appearance, a soft silvery tone of infinite kindness which asked me to have some hot chocolate and then offered me her daughter's bed, her daughter being away at school.

In spite of her kindness I slept with my wallet and papers under my pillow that night. While we talked and sipped our chocolate, her husband, an equally ferocious creature, appeared in his nightshirt, and began to ask questions about the British Army. I did not like to tell him to mind his own business, in case he told me to mind mine by getting out of his house at once. The expedient thing to do was to answer readily but untruthfully, and this I did to the best of my ability.

I set out at dawn the following morning, and, after a lonely journey in the early light, I arrived at Lille at eight o'clock, in good time for my appointment. The country I passed through was interesting because, after the Somme, the name of each town and village seemed an echo of a war, quiet places whose echo, did I but know it, was to change into a fanfare again within the next few weeks.

I settled my business in Lille and returned to my billet, the house of an old widow called Madame Wecquier who lived alone with her pretty daughter in Lesquin.

It was the 1st of May 1940. The phoney war was nearly over. After eight months it had become almost a permanency, so much a part of my life that WAR in the abstract stood for nothing more than motorcar rides into Lille and Arras to buy bricks and small stones. It had been amusing and interesting, and although I had better things to do in England if peace had been signed, I certainly did not want to change it for a more militant counterpart. I was to be rudely shocked ten days later.

CHAPTER TWELVE
The War Starts

I COULD WELL believe that Mlle. Wecquier, the daughter of the house, was immensely proud of her figure. Little Marie, the maid, once told me that she had had a special set of multifaced mirrors fitted in her bedroom by a Paris firm; she said that if I could only see Mlle. Wecquier really and truly ('as she really is' she whispered to me coyly) I would hold my breath. I replied in superior fashion that I had often seen women before, I told her that I had often drawn from models; among women I said there is a certain pitch of perfection beyond which no-one goes; when you have seen Venus you have seen all. But little Marie merely replied that I must wait, and that then perhaps one day if I was lucky I would see for myself. One fine morning in May I *did* see.

It must have been about six o'clock on the morning of May the 10th when my bedroom door was opened so violently that I woke; and my mind, still wandering in its own personal no man's land, had barely time to register the quick, fluttering movement of a form that passed the bed and alighted near the window. It was in this way that I was able to see Mlle. Wecquier for myself. She was wearing a silk nightdress and, charmingly silhouetted against the rays of the sun, her figure justified all that Marie had said of it. By now I was fully conscious in every sense, and I found myself sitting up and wondering. She obviously had something important to say.

'Lieutenant,' she said quite simply, 'we have been invaded.'

She paused for a moment to let this sink in. I kept on thinking that what she really meant was 'violated' and I wondered what I was expected to do. She looked so pretty.

'Invaded?' I said.

'Invaded,' she said. 'The Germans invaded Belgium and Holland at three o'clock this morning. They have just bombed Lille. Didn't you hear it? Mother and I were both woken up by it.'

'No.'

'Well, hurry up. The colonel wants you immediately.'

She seemed so calm about it that I remained in bed a minute or so after she had gone, wondering if I was still dreaming. Even so I was going down the stairs four minutes later; I have never dressed so quickly before or since.

As I rushed past old Madame Wecquier, on the stairs, I heard her repeating to herself like a parrot:

'The Germans have invaded Belgium – Belgium and Holland – the Germans have invaded Belgium – Belgium and Holland…'

I found most of the other officers in their dressing-gowns huddled round the wireless in the mess.

'I hear Lille's been bombed,' I said.

'It hasn't been touched,' said the colonel. 'Don't spread rumours. But thirty Boche planes passed over it and went on to bomb GHQ at Arras. I suppose you know that the Low Countries and Luxemburg have been invaded. We'll be off to Belgium before the day's out.'

We stayed and listened till seven o'clock when all the previous news was corroborated. There was a funny bit in it out of Ribbentrop's speech in which he said that if the Germans had not attacked Belgium the British would have done so. This made us laugh quite a lot because everyone knew that the British Army was incapable of *attacking* anybody. We had spent the whole winter doing *defence* schemes, thereby infuriating all our own firebrands who had never stopped wanting to 'have a go at Jerry'. A British attack on Belgium was not only laughable, it was impossible.

'Well,' said the doctor an hour later at breakfast, 'it's started. I only hope to God it's over quickly.'

But he was favourably impressed by the bombing of GHQ at Arras.

'Perhaps we won't get touched at all in the front line divisions,' he said. 'GHQ getting it hot like that will be a nasty shock for all the staff officers. No more cushy jobs this war.'

'Yes,' said Stimpson, 'it's going to be hell for all the scarlet majors at the base this time. Sassoon's out of date already. And then, when the Germans have finished bombing the brass-hats, they'll start on Whitehall. All we'll have to do is to stay here until the end of the war. That'll be when one of the rival governments has literally gone out of office.'

But there was too much work to do during the rest of the day to find time to be funny. Because we had been taken completely by surprise we had to spend the whole day making preparations instead of advancing into Belgium. It now became obvious that the British Army had not only been taken completely by surprise, it had been shamefully gulled by the bogus 'flap' which the enemy had evidently deliberately engineered on May the 5th, five days before. On May the 5th, in response to large troop movements in Germany we had collected bag and baggage and had gone up to the Belgium frontier where we had been ready to move at a moment's notice. The Germans had then started removing their troops, their practice on all previous 'flaps', and true to form, after a day or two's suitable wait on the frontier, we had followed suit and returned to our normal work, cursing the frequency with which the 'flaps' were occurring (we had had four during the last six months). Some people even thought that they were put-up jobs, a device by our own General Staff to give us something to do; as the doctor had said at the time, most people were fed up 'with waiting in the cold on the dreary old frontier'. The first time it had been exciting, but now it was merely irksome; we were bored stiff with frontiers; so far from being packed and waiting on the frontier ready to move at a moment's notice that morning, the British Army, to a man, was in bed.

During the morning I was sent into Lille to collect some 'vital' stores, and on the way home I took the opportunity of saying goodbye to my old friend Remier. I dropped in at his shop. He was still in bed; but when he heard that I had come he came downstairs in a dirty old nightshirt; it made his tall, stooping, pot-bellied frame look even more ridiculous. At first I thought he was drunk, but then I realised that it was only his indignation. His little goatee beard wagged furiously about the Germans.

'Damned Boches,' he said. 'I like their sauce. They're going to get hell; my God, they're going to get hell.' He was furious.

'Did you know,' he continued without letting me even say good morning, 'did you know that all the Boche planes that attacked Arras this morning were brought down? Yes – all of them. Now that shows you what our defences are like, doesn't it?' He rubbed his hands and nodded his head.

I congratulated him on this, and asked him if he proposed to evacuate his wife and family for fear of further raids. He was indignant.

'Leave Lille?' he said coming closer and wagging his finger at me, and looking more and more preposterous in his night-gown. 'Do you think we are going to let the Boche come where he likes? Why, my goodness – as if Lille wasn't the most important city in the north! Take it from me,' he said wagging his finger closer and closer at my nose so that I had to step back, 'take it from me – there won't be much bombing here. We have an air force, you know. If the Boche puts his ugly nose in here he's going to get it bitten off;' he opened and closed his mouth realistically.

Such confidence was inspiring, particularly as most Frenchmen thought like M. Remier. He offered me a drink before I left and lumbered down to the cellar to get something special for the occasion. Together we toasted the perdition and damnation of all things German in his best Courvoisier. He insisted on repeating this toast three times, so that I was a bit drunk when I arrived back at Lesquin, but in the general bustle of preparing to leave for Belgium it was unnoticed.

We were fully prepared to move by six o'clock that evening and we waited in long convoys on the frontier until it was dark; we congregated in little clumps, smoking and chatting near the vehicles. Everyone, except the French interpreters and the generals, was properly dressed for war, carrying gas-capes, water bottles, revolvers, shoulder-straps, veils, and tin hats. The Frenchmen could not be bothered to attach all this paraphernalia to their persons, and they still kept their service dress, their kepis, and their peace time slovenliness. The generals insisted on wearing their cloth caps with red bands round them. Stimpson was horrified, and pointed out that apart from the personal danger to the wearers, divisional headquarters would be advertised to spies; he said the generals were excessively vain.

Some German bombers came over while we were waiting and

our reaction seemed typical of the first day of war. We did nothing; we just stood glaring up at them hoping that someone would blow them to bits. The mere spectacle of our enemy for the first time had an emotional effect on some people, all the pent-up feeling of eight months of inactivity expressed itself.

'The brutes,' said someone fiercely. 'The bloody Boches. I only hope to God we smash 'em up.'

Just before dusk, the hour when we were due to cross the frontier, we went into the little douaniers' bistro near the yellow gates and heard the British wireless announce that Churchill had replaced Chamberlain as Prime Minister. It had a very inspiriting effect; most of us thought that it would give Hitler a dose of his own medicine. Only Bèry, our interpreter, was unenthusiastic.

'It means that the Allies weren't ready for the attack,' he said.

'Nonsense, you long-faced old froggie,' said the doctor. 'Don't you see what it means? It's a very clever gesture. It's a hint to the Boche to clear out of Belgium. In double-quick time too. You just see. We'll all be back having dinner again in Lille this evening.'

'Yes,' said the Frenchman, 'and I suppose Chamberlain will be back again being Prime Minister too.'

The proprietor of the bistro stood us all a round of drinks before we left, saying what fine fellows we were. And someone else, one of the French interpreters I think, said that at any rate we were not contemptible.

CHAPTER THIRTEEN
Belgian Blues

AFTER AN UNEVENTFUL journey we arrived at our destination at dawn the following day, a small village called Everburgh a few miles east of Brussels. 'Uneventful' should perhaps be qualified, because a staff officer was blown up on the way. He had been supervising the unloading of stores at a railway junction, a prosaic enough occupation for the first casualty of the war, but it gave an unchristian pleasure to Stimpson who had still got his head full of Sassoon's scarlet majors. Judging from what one had been led to expect, it was certainly not a nightmare ride.

Some of the towns through which we passed near Brussels had the facades of various houses lying in piles in the middle of the street. At one place we had to stop to clear away the debris before we could pass and a good lady wept her heart out to me; she told me that she was the owner of one of the piles of rubble. I did my best to cheer her up, describing what we would do to Hitler when we caught him. She gave us some coffee and confessed that she simply could not understand why the Germans should wish to attack Belgium of all places; besides, she said, she had some very good German friends. It made me realise that not only Englishmen are gulls about the Germans; it also made me see just how neutral Belgium must have been before the German attack.

Towards dawn we met a little man outside Brussels with a broken-down motorcycle; he was coming away from the city and his sidecar was bulging with chattels. He was working on the back wheel and, unlike most of his countrymen, he took no interest whatsoever in the spectacle of a line of British mechanised vehicles, except for a request which he made to my driver, almost without turning his head, for some puncture-mending material. He could not have been more than thirty, and certainly subject to military law. I asked him where he was going. He still went on busily mending his puncture.

'France,' he said.

He told me that he was a schoolmaster and that he hoped to find a new appointment in a Paris lycée. It seemed a very resolute attitude to adopt, but later I was sorry for him because he could hardly have been expected to foresee the fall of France. His case is an interesting parallel to that of a friend of mine who could not bear the thought of war and went to America in September 1939 to become a schoolmaster. He too must have been embarrassed by Hitler's habit of spreading his wars to remote parts of the world.

In the first light of the morning Brussels gave us a great welcome. People jumped on the running-boards, and threw sticks of chocolate in the car. They seemed to be putting a blind confidence in the French and British; perhaps our lines of mechanised vehicles contrasted favourably with the push-bikes with which their army seemed to be exclusively furnished. We passed a lot of these cyclist battalions on the way up and they had waved cheerily to us. In most cases their equipment comprised a rifle, a tin hat, and a spare pair of boots slung picturesquely round the neck.

We reached Everburgh, our divisional HQ near Louvain, in time for breakfast, and then began work immediately. We were told that the Germans were not expected on the line of the river Dyle for another forty-eight hours. We were going to defend this river, and the colonel impressed upon us the necessity of not wasting the precious time.

One of my first jobs was to find out what preparations had been made by the Belgians for demolishing the bridges in our sector of the front, and I visited the town hall to make inquiries. It was full of Belgians who had been arguing about evacuation for several hours. Feeling was beginning to run pretty high because most of them were trying to get petrol for their cars and there was only a limited amount available. In this atmosphere of almost continuous bickering nobody had any time for me.

'But my mother is eighty-four,' said one man at the bureau. 'She must be evacuated. I must have petrol to take her away.'

There was a sarcastic and uncharitable rival.

'How lucky for you it is that she can't drive,' he said icily.

It seemed impossible to find anyone who knew anything about the bridges but I managed to fight my way towards the man who was doling out the petrol coupons.

'Can you tell me where I can find the mayor?' I asked. It seemed the only solution.

'M. le Maire left first thing this morning,' he replied.

'Left? Do you mean he has...?'

'Yes. He's cleared off.'

'Well, perhaps you can help me. I want to know what preparations have been made by the Belgians for demolishing the bridges on the River Dyle. The British Army is taking over this town you know.'

'The only thing I can advise you to do is to go down to the bridges yourself. There is nobody here who could tell you. Perhaps the Belgian Army might know. But as you see we are very busy here.'

His attitude towards soldiering was, I suppose, very natural. He treated it as if it was not a proper adult occupation, but his own occupation, that of giving out little slips of paper, did not really seem much more advanced. Few of the other town halls that I visited were any more helpful.

I found out later that nothing had been done by the Belgians about any of the bridges. There were fifteen in our divisional sector, which all, therefore, had to be prepared by our own engineers; a terrific task. The biggest bridge was over the railway in Louvain and we were stupefied by the amount of explosive that had to be placed on it; three tons, it was calculated; a load that might quite well break the bridge under the weight of the explosive alone, without bothering to think about detonating it.

The problem of obtaining information about the state of the Belgian defences in the sector was simplified that afternoon because a Belgian officer was permanently attached to us. His English was atrocious, but of course he refused to speak French to anyone. He was supposed to possess the secrets of some vast mining scheme which was going to be sprung on the luckless Germans if they advanced; he and Bèry, our French liaison officer, went about together carrying little black diplomatic bags.

The doctor thought he was a spy. But what the doctor thought about spies was largely discounted on account of an episode earlier in the day with another putative Belgian spy.

During our first morning in the wood an inoffensive little paper-seller, who had been enterprising enough to get hold of some copies of the current *Daily Mail*, came round to the edge of the wood hoping to get some trade. He spoke tolerable English and he told me that he had lived for two years in Lincoln. Lincoln happened to be the doctor's birthplace, and I told him about the little Belgian.

The next day the Belgian returned for more trade. The doctor approached him, eyeing him very suspiciously all the time. The dialogue went something like this:

The doctor: You say you were in Lincoln?

Paper-seller: Yes.

The doctor: So you were, were you?

P.S. (surprised): Yes.

The doctor (abruptly): Where's Little Puddle Street? (or some such name).

P.S.: ????

The doctor (speaking slowly and advancing towards him): Come on now. You must know. Where is Little Puddle Street?

P.S.: Never heard of it.

The doctor (triumphantly): He's a spy. I knew it. (To the P.S.) You are not to move from here. I am going to have you examined.

P.S. (very indignant): I am not a spy. What makes you think I am anyway?

The doctor: Little Puddle Street is one of the most important streets in Lincoln. Everyone knows it. You can't have lived there.

P.S: I tell you I've lived two solid years in Lincoln and I've never even heard of your Little Puddle Street. And I ought to know the streets if anyone does. I was working for the New York *Daily News* there, the paper with the biggest circulation in the States.

The doctor (lamely): Oh, you mean Lincoln in America, do you?

My main job in those early days was to scrounge defence stores locally, a task calling for ingenuity and enough money to persuade the owners of the stores, with a glass of Vermouth, that the British Government would pay one day.

This menial task took on an increasing importance as the war progressed. As the German bombers systematically destroyed one railway junction after another, on each occasion further limiting the supply of material from France and England, a cry began to go up for local materials. The problem did not become really acute till the later stages of the retirement; but even at Louvain we were put in charge of all the Belgian Army stores and materials.

I had to be present at the official transfer of one of these stores dumps. A Belgian officer met me and handed me a sheet of paper.

'Here is a list of everything we have in the dump,' he said. 'It all belongs to you now. But I must warn you that there are ten tons of high explosive over in the corner there,' he pointed to a stack of black boxes. 'It is very dangerous concentrated like that; it really should be more widely dispersed. Why – you have enough there,' he estimated dramatically and incorrectly, as if it was something to be proud of, 'to blow up the whole of Brussels.'

He was obviously delighted to be leaving, and before he left he offered me a drink in the local bistro where I was introduced to twelve of his men who were sitting gloomily round a stove drinking black coffee.

'I will hand these men all over to you now,' he said. 'They will be under your command while you are using the dump. You understand that,' he said to the men. They did not seem particularly pleased to see me, but I was surprised when I returned six hours later to find eleven of them gone.

'What's happened? Where are they all?' I said to the only man who remained.

'They have gone to look for a better place to put the explosive,' he said.

'But – eleven of them? Why so many?'

'Well, you see, monsieur, they all had a great argument about where to put it. They all thought of different places. They are gone to make a choice.'

I walked over to the explosive dump and was surprised to find that all the explosive was still there, I turned round to ask the man why the eleven had not taken it away with them to the new dump.

But he was gone; he was cycling down the road for dear life.

It was the last I saw of my Belgians. After that we had to run the dump with our own men.

CHAPTER FOURTEEN
Brussels Believes in the British

WE SPENT THE first night in Everburgh living in the wood like gipsies. One night of this was enough for the less hardy members of the mess, and a movement was soon started to occupy various houses in the village which had been vacated by fleeing Belgians, so that on the second night I found myself sleeping in a real bed in a loft. This made me reflect on the falsity of the childish and romantic notions which Boy Scout stories of the last war had fostered in me. According to their standards it was indecent to be at war and not to be sleeping in a ditch.

The loft in which I slept belonged to a peasant who had refused to evacuate; he was a pig-headed man with quiet puzzled eyes; he was so silent and dauntless that it was almost impossible to get anything out of him. After some difficulty I gathered that he had refused to leave unless he could take his bêtes with him. There were some two hundred and fifty of these – unportable creatures, ranging from guinea-fowls to ostriches; so it appeared that he was fixed in Everburgh for the duration. I admired his noble attitude towards the beasts while at the same time feeling a certain sympathy for his wife who very naturally had only one desire, to get as far away from the British and Germans as possible.

She appealed to me one morning; sobbing violently, she asked me if I thought that the Germans would take the village; she said she would stay with her husband if I thought Everburgh would be safe; her husband had told her that he would refuse to see her again if she left him. It was an awkward decision for me to make, because the general had particularly requested all British officers to discourage the natives from using the roads; on the other hand, knowing as I did, that a battle or at least a severe bombardment might take place in Everburgh, I could hardly recommend her to stay. After consideration I advised her to go to some friends near Brussels, and I saw her leave later that morning, pushing a little barrow with a few belongings and a child on the top of it, while her husband stood at the door shouting curses after her. It was a pathetic scene and at the time I felt partly responsible for it; but a bombardment of the headquarters did take place the next day and I felt that my decision had probably been correct.

One of the results of this bombardment was that I was praised for something I had not done, or rather, for something that I had done quite unwittingly.

When the order for the selection of the billets had appeared on our arrival in Everburgh there had been the usual rush on the part of all the billeting officers to get the best billets for their own units. I thought I had forestalled most of them. I had foreseen the billeting order by about twelve hours, and had arranged with the caretaker of the White House, the best house in the district, that it should be reserved for our mess. But I had not foreseen his deceitfulness. Although he had promised me the house while having a drink with me in the bistro that evening, he apparently made a further agreement about it later with the general's billeting officer. I had previously been assured by this officer that I could have a free hand in the matter of the White House, because, as he said, he 'already had a good thing up his sleeve'. In reality he had persuaded the caretaker, presumably by giving him more than my gift of three Vermouth cassis, to earmark the house for himself; so that when the moment to install our mess arrived, the caretaker denied my first claim and said I was a liar.

In this way we lost the White House and had to go to a small semi-detached villa at the other end of the village, my colleagues bewailing my inefficiency. The bombardment was the sequel; it was this that brought me my celebrity.

The White House, because it was white and because it was on a hill, was far and away the most conspicuous house in the district. And two days later a stray German bomber, seeing a nice house to break up, dropped a bomb on it. Fortunately no-one was hurt, but the general and his staff moved out immediately, and I was praised by my colleagues who said I had been far-sighted. Stimpson said it was the general's fault for wearing a red hat.

This bombardment was not the only one that we had during our stay in Everburgh. The other one, which was more severe, occurred while I was shaving early one morning at my loft window with nothing on. (I always do this in the spring.)

It was a perfect spring morning and I was feeling that there was something to be said for the war after all, when suddenly out of the quietness came a faint vibration, a curious humming in the air. It gradually increased to a crescendo and as it did, it seemed to influence other material things around me; the house began to oscillate in sympathy, the pictures on the wall began to shake, the floor boards to quiver; I even began to oscillate myself. It was not until then that I realised that aeroplanes were swooping on the village.

Caught naked as I was, I felt rather ridiculous, and I tamely lay down on the floor which was now vibrating so furiously that I was bounced up and down on it with enormous indignity; while outside, shrieks and screams announced that bombs were being dropped.

Then suddenly, as suddenly as the attack had arrived, it departed; it was this suddenness of arrival and departure which impressed me most of all; I had never experienced an air raid before. All the weird sounds and ungovernable vibrations disappeared as remarkably as they had appeared, the air became quiet again, and I was left lying on the floor, covered in dust and shaving soap.

The suburbanity of our semi-detached villa was completely counterbalanced by the aristocratic food the doctor gave us in it. Throughout the whole retirement we lived almost exclusively on goose, chicken, foie-gras, champagne, and game of all sorts, supplemented by those luscious French butter sauces whose secret recipes the doctor had spent the last eight months learning. He regularly turned out meals on these lines at 1s. 4d. a day with cigars thrown in. How he did it no-one knew; no-one asked.

He also 'requisitioned' a luxurious motorcar which had been left behind by a fleeing Belgian. He was very proud of it because before he had always driven about in a sort of up-to-date mechanical dogcart which he despised; this dogcart had been the only thing he had been able to get out of the Army.

He took his new car into Brussels one day to buy engineer stores with me; it was only five miles away. People were still cheering madly in the streets whenever they saw a British officer, and the doctor was in his element, enormously affable, smoking a cigar, and bowing in every direction like Edward VII.

On this particular occasion I was searching for a timber merchant and it was only after some difficulty that we found one, an excited little man who was just about to leave for Paris. He was packing his car when we arrived and he had little time for us.

'I must put my wife in a quiet place,' he said, pointing to a terrified-looking woman sitting in the back, 'she is very nervous.'

It was immediately obvious that they were both very nervous, and as he could not wait, I offered to send him a list of everything I took from his store after his departure. He agreed to this and I was still checking over its contents when they drove off, their tiny car groaning under the varied load of trunks, bedding, picture-frames, flower vases and an enormous cage with a horrible fierce bird in it. This bird was so enraged at the new and hectic life it was leading that it kept on trying to peck its owners through the bars, but they were too preoccupied to notice this.

On the way out of the city we dropped in at a café to have a drink, and to hear the opinion of the Bruxellians on the war. To our surprise we were immediately mobbed. Inside we were surrounded by a wildly enthusiastic crowd; everyone started cheering, men patted us on the back and women tried to hold our hands. I was led, almost carried, to a seat, offered cigars, and soon swamped with drinks. Everyone started talking to me at once.

'The good old Tommies. Back again. They'll win the war.'

'They'll turn the stinking Boche out.'

'How is the battle going out in front? Have the English reached the German frontier yet?'

'Have you seen the bomb in the rue d'Alsace? It is an outrage. It must be avenged.'

'The English will avenge it. The good old Tommies.'

The doctor meanwhile was having a delightful time with a pretty girl who was being forced to kiss him. The doctor was behaving quite passively about it because all the forcing was being done by an altruistic young Belgian, who pointed out to the girl that the

Englishman deserved it after all; it was only his due; she should be only too glad to kiss a saviour of her country, he seemed to be saying. The girl finally yielded, whereupon the young man went one further and said that the doctor must take her away for the night; he could vouch for her voluptuousness, he said. It was hardly surprising that he could vouch for her because, I was told by the man sitting next to me, she was his wife. It seemed to me to be the absolute zenith of human gratitude and the doctor evidently thought so too, because he was on the point of accepting when I reminded him that we must get back to the war. He whispered back across the table to me that it might perhaps be impolite and therefore unwise not to accept our allies' hospitality. It was a very broad view to take but I convinced him that the narrower one, that he would almost certainly be shot as a deserter if he stayed away the night, was more important; and five minutes later, only after the greatest difficulty, we managed to tear ourselves away from all these kind people. Their hysteria was pathetic; they so appreciated what they hoped we were going to do for them.

We came out into the principal street of the city, a sort of Belgian Bond Street, and to my fuddled imagination, it seemed merely a transfer of dreams. The boulevard, with its lime-trees and its Bond Street figures, seemed as unreal and as far removed from the war as the café; up and down it walked smartly dressed women and well-tailored men, all forming part of the inherited atmosphere of civilisation that seems to invest all the great European capitals in springtime; the Temple gardens in London, the lime-trees in the Champs-Élysées, the covered walks in the Englischergarten in Munich, all are the same, all have something in common on a warm spring evening. As we came into the street, somewhere in the distance one could just hear a faint banging as if someone was beating a drum – the only indication that people were slaughtering one another out east.

One of Goya's most realistic drawings depicts refugees; he calls it, I think, 'The Children of War'. They trudge with a sort of grim hopelessness, a curious shine of almost barbaric vitality in their eyes. Ardizzone and others have since produced a modern pendant for the Hitler-wars, but their drawings are less frightful, there is less cruelty in them just as there is less vitality; if the bestiality has gone there is more hopelessness, their characters are people stripped of every shred of illusion, mere animals bearing sacks and fardels. Many of the people we passed on the Brussels-Louvain road that evening were doing their trek to the west for the second time within twenty-five years; they seemed to be doing it automatically, almost unconsciously, their heads bowed, their backs bent, all obeying the urge to escape from the Germans. Certain aspects of that traffic will always have an interest for me.

Firstly, the peasant's sense of what goods are vitally important: pots with withered plants in them, cousins to our own aspidistra; pictures in gilt frames, the counterparts to the English school of Highland cattle painting; quilts and cloths with strange l'Art Nouveau designs on them, such as are now so successfully peddled by Marks and Spencer's. There were birds and beasts and fishes of all descriptions, and on one pile I saw a little monkey sound asleep.

The few lucky ones who had managed to scrounge enough petrol travelled in their cars, and they came hooting their way along the road for dear life, passing everything they could see. One man had a donkey to pull his cart, and he sat on the top of a gigantic pile of gimcrackery looking just like the muleteer in the drawing from Don Quixote.

It is, I realise, callous and unfeeling to ridicule these stalwart people, but provided one had done what little one could to help them (and we gave them lifts whenever we could), I felt it was legitimate to observe and even to enjoy the humorous aspect, for there were so many tragic sides to the refugee, and at one crossroads the tragedy showed up only too clearly. Some refugees had been machine-gunned from the air and the ground still bore traces of it. It seemed unlikely that the Germans had done it deliberately, because there was such confusion between military and civilian traffic that it would have been almost impossible to distinguish any individual target. I felt that the refugees clearly travelled at their own risk and that they deserved more sympathy for having their country invaded than for having to turn out of their homes.

It looked for a moment as if we should have a sample of one of these attacks, because some German planes passed over and we stopped and lay down in a ditch, the approved official behaviour, while the doctor looked at me meaningly in the light of what we had seen at the last crossroads. One of the bombers was attacked by a British Spitfire which appeared from nowhere; it was hit and we watched the German pilot, who had immediately baled out, floating gently down to earth. We were just turning to go away when every machine-gun in the district seemed to open fire, and the figure suspended from the parachute gave a despairing little wriggle, hunched itself up into a ball, and then went quite limp, literally loaded with lead. The maxim 'The only good German is a dead one' had been admirably but brutally translated into fact.

When we arrived at the HQ we were greeted by Stimpson, who fittingly set off his love of the last-war poets of despair with an equal hatred of all the imperialistic ones of the preceding century.

'The Hun,' he said simply, 'is at the Gate.'

The doctor was not interested in Kipling.

'What do you mean, man? Don't talk such highbrow trash. What's happened?'

'I mean that we have just heard that our cavalry is in touch with the Boche and that he will be arriving in an hour or two. I also mean that Louvain has just had its first heavy bombardment. I believe there are some choice specimens of twentieth-century vandalism in the town. Or should I say sixteenth-century baroque? I can't remember (only a difference in style, in the treatment of pillars and columns, after all).'

We did not stop to bandy words with Stimpson, but went straight into the mess to find out the truth. Everybody was grouped round the wireless waiting for the six o'clock news. The adjutant told us that the bombardment of Louvain had been very severe, and that one of our engineer subalterns had spent the whole day in the centre of the city, sitting in a little hole down by the river near one of the important bridges. This bridge had been constantly bombed and the subaltern, who had on each occasion repaired the damaged electrical wires leading to the explosive, was being awarded an MC.

The news when it came was appalling. The announcer said that a great battle of strategic and perhaps even historic importance was about to take place just east of Brussels; he reminded his listeners that the British Army would be fighting very near Waterloo, the famous field where the greatest victory in its history had been gained. This was followed by the Commander-in-Chief's exhortation to us all to die like Englishmen.

I reflected on the enormous misapprehension under which I had laboured for so long. One had always read about wars; one had always thought that they were simple historical facts; as Max Beerbohm would say, one was rather foolish perhaps.

CHAPTER FIFTEEN
The Germans Arrive

ANY MISAPPREHENSION I had ever had about war was certainly removed during the following night. At three o'clock in the morning the war began in earnest in the shape, or rather sound, sight, and feel, of an artillery bombardment. I realised the next day that it had all been our own gunfire; but at the time, as I lay in my bed, to my childish imagination it seemed as if all the guns in the world were letting fly with every shell they had, from every quarter of the compass around me. If the house had quivered and quaked during the simple two-aeroplane stunt of the previous morning while I was shaving, in this welter of pandemonium and almost continuous flashlight it behaved like something out of a Walt Disney cartoon, a sort of india-rubber, infinitely elastic house, which seemed to jump up and down like a jack-in-the-box.

So noisy and unruly was the night that after breakfast the next day, the doctor and I had a chat in private about it. We agreed that the noise really had been excessive; the doctor said he would never have joined the war if he had known it was anything like this. We took very good care not to let anyone overhear our conversation because everyone else was saying what fun it had been. Bombardments were all the rage.

The only other person I met who strongly disapproved of the bombardment was a French liaison officer who had fought in the last war. His disapproval came from more patriotic motives; he could not bear to see such a waste of ammunition; accustomed to husbanding down to the last round he told me that he had winced at every round he had heard fired during the night. I told him that I had done the same – although I did not say why.

'I know your country is rich,' he said, 'but believe me, if you had all the ammunition in the world you wouldn't be able to go on for more than a fortnight at the rate you are going. But still,' he added, 'I suppose you'll learn.'

During the day the Germans started replying to our fire. They chose as their main targets the town hall and the public library, and soon showed that they had just as much ammunition to spare as we had. Louvain, as everyone knows, was once one of the most beautiful old university towns of Belgium. It was here that Goldsmith reports of its domestic peace and scholastic sleepiness, of the university principal who knew no Greek.

'You see me, young man,' the principal had said to Goldsmith's hero, 'I never learned Greek; and I don't find that I have ever missed it. I have had a doctor's cap and gown without Greek; I have ten thousand florins a year without Greek; I eat heartily without Greek; and, in short, as I don't know Greek, I do not believe there is any good in it.'

This was the Louvain that the Germans destroyed in 1914, and any good they did in the university by waking up the professors of Greek was more than outweighed by the harm they did to the university buildings. The fifteenth-century library and the town hall also suffered heavily. After the war much was rebuilt with the help of American gifts. And now, as we looked down on the town from a gun position on the big hill which commands it, I felt, almost for the first time, a cool, logical scorn and hatred for the lunatics who were preparing once again, assiduously, like clever monkeys, to pull down the same bricks and mortar; we could see columns of black smoke rising from the centre of the town as the Germans found their mark for the second time in one generation.

Picasso, when he portrayed that mixture of intransigent blockheadedness and half-stupid ferocity which characterises the German at war, drew an enraged bull; aesthetically it was faultless, but it lacked the element of Japanese cunning, of brain power misused. The perfect literary representation would incorporate the head of a *monkey* with the buttocks of a bull.

And I supposed, as I looked on the town, that when it was all over for the second time, the Belgians would laboriously rebuild it only for the New Culture or the Superman or the Yellow Peril or something equally stupid to come and knock it all down again.

The battle on the river and in Louvain was in full swing that morning, and grim stories continued to come back to the HQ throughout the day.

The doctor was placed after breakfast in the difficult and somewhat ironical position of having to examine a man for shell shock. The man, a private, had become imbued with one desire, one driving passion, never under any circumstances whatsoever to go anywhere near Louvain in his life again; and the colonel gave the doctor the problem of persuading him to return, on the ground that nothing could be more manly for a soldier than a bomb or two, accompanied perhaps by an occasional shell.

The doctor, who had of course a very strong fellow-feeling for this dissenter from good, healthy, sterling sets of values, displayed great cunning and a quite unsuspected persuasive power in dealing with him.

He succeeded and the man returned; the doctor had justified his military existence. But it is only fair to add that the soldier was found later in Louvain singing Halleluiahs, fully under the impression that he was an angel.

In spite of all these alarums and excursions in Louvain I found time to attend an examination of suspected spies in Everburgh that afternoon. A special section had been created in each division to deal with spies and their little twentieth-century cousins, the fifth-columnists. It was called the Field Security Police. After four days of war in a country already overrun by Hitler's civilian army the divisional F.S.P. were getting a bit rattled; they had been working night and day interviewing spies pretty continuously since they had arrived; and as they consisted of only one officer and ten NCOs, and had anything up to five hundred spies and bogus spies to interview each day, they were extremely glad to get helpers. I knew their officer and, with a view to helping him later, I attended one of his examinations and watched him in action in the courtyard of the local school. He sat at a little table in the middle with a revolver in front of him.

Opposite, herded into a corner by the NCOs, were about a hundred dejected-looking people, the suspects. I had never seen such a motley collection before in my life; the only thing common to them all was dirt, they were uniformly filthy, having just spent the night in the courtyard. Every walk of life seemed to be represented; there were priests, beggars, nuns, soldiers, shopkeepers; and every nationality; Belgians, Poles, Germans, Austrians, Czechs – even Indians.

I reflected how many CID officers would normally be employed in peacetime to interrogate such a number of alien criminals. Yet here today, in circumstances far more grave, was one officer with a handful of helpers, doing a day's work, only equalled I supposed, by the sum of all the work done by all the officers in Scotland Yard in a month.

The first suspect, a civilian, was brought up to the table. He was accompanied by a little woman who appeared to be the witness.

The captain consulted his notes.

'You were seen entering a house in Everburgh dressed as a Belgian soldier,' he said. 'You came out dressed as a civilian. You are a deserter. But I am not concerned with that. This lady says that you had a box with you at the time. It contained a portable wireless set.'

'That is a lie,' said the man.

'Do you admit you had a box with you?'

'Yes.'

'What was in it?'

'Food. I will tell you what it was if you like.' The man now tried to be funny. He appeared quite intelligent. 'Since it seems to interest you so much,' he continued. 'There was a cake my wife baked for me. Let me see – and there were two pieces of bread and butter.' He scratched his head, 'Yes – then there was a sausage.' He looked at the woman who was giving evidence against him, 'but that old sow ate the sausage.'

There was an absolute torrent of abuse from the woman at this. She gabbled her words so indignantly and so fast that I could not make out what she was saying. The captain was evidently quite used to dealing with jokers. After one look at the fellow's identity card he had decided what to do.

'Take him away. Hand him over to the French police,' he said.

This is a most extreme thing to do because the French police are not lenient with suspected spies; they treat them as guilty until they prove themselves innocent, giving them about a quarter of an hour in which to do it. Most of the other suspects, after an inspection of identity cards, were allowed to depart in peace – or rather in indignant rage; they all went off quietly, no-one pelting us with stones and pebbles, as the sergeant told me one Belgian had done on a previous occasion; they were all only too glad to get away.

The Field Security Police are not the only set of detectives and general legal advisers in the division; there is also the Provost Section. In peacetime they provide the 'red-caps' and any soldier will tell you what a nuisance they are when they come round on Friday evenings, telling you to do up your buttons and trying to catch you out tight.

In war they take on the additional job of providing firing parties for spies and their power extends over life and death; if the Field Security Police act as the CID the provost officer acts as the High Court judge; his power is prodigious. Our own divisional provost officer came to dinner one night, a Guards officer of the Teutonic variety, a man obviously ideally suited to his work.

'Do you really shoot spies?' asked Stimpson, assuming a proper air of awe.

'Of course,' said the provost officer.

'And do you do it entirely on your own? I mean the trial and all that sort of thing.'

'Of course.'

'But I suppose you take very good care that they really are spies, don't you? I mean – it's a sort of absolute power of attorney, isn't it?'

The provost officer nodded his head.

'It's absolute all right,' he said, grinning at the adjutant.

Stimpson told me afterwards that he thought it a very barbarous reply, but he agreed with me that we would both sleep much more easily hereafter.

There was one person who certainly did not sleep easily, Bèry, our liaison officer. He had told us that he was subject to nightmares, and judging by his behaviour at breakfast in Everburgh one morning, he had spoken the truth. He rushed in excitedly.

'Italy and America have declared war on Germany,' he said breathlessly.

'The Italians?' said the colonel. 'You're sure you don't mean they've declared war on us? Why the Italians?'

'Because there is a secret alliance between the French and the Italians,' said Bèry.

'But don't be absurd,' said the doctor. 'Old Mussolini and Hitler are almost blood-brothers. They're in league with one another. Much more likely that they have declared war on the French.'

'No,' said Bèry piously. 'They would never do such a thing. Have you forgotten that the French and Italians are Roman Catholics? They have religious ties.'

'Now you really are talking nonsense, Bèry,' said the doctor. 'You're about three hundred years out of date. Do you think we're fighting the war of the Protestant Succession? What leader today would give a damn for religion anyway? Why, Mussolini would become a Mussulman if there was any money in it!'

'Anyway I heard it on the wireless this morning,' said Bèry stubbornly, not to be ridiculed in this fashion.

'You must have been still dreaming. What news was it on anyway?'

'The Russian.'

Nobody took any more notice of Bèry at breakfast after that.

There were so many rumours about the various nations that had declared war on Germany during those first days that none of us had any business to be such a gull. At one time or another the Russians, the Americans, the Italians, and (quite inexplicably) the Finns, were all reported to have declared war on our enemy.

It was no doubt a part of the German grand strategy to spread these rumours about other people making war on them. They knew perfectly well that what people really hate about war is the unaccustomed exertion, that if people feel that someone else is doing the exerting for them they stop doing it themselves – a simple enough idea but it takes a German to think of it. Indeed it would be quite in keeping with German technique to have a special war department for national psychologies.

I must admit that in those early days, whenever I heard one of these nice stories doing the rounds of camp gossip I always used to congratulate myself and stop scavenging for engineer stores quite so earnestly.

And my affair with the local postman the day we arrived did not reflect very well on my own gullibility.

'Of course we're all right now,' he said to me as I passed him in the main street. 'Aren't we?'

'How do you mean?' I asked.

'Well, now that the Russians have overrun Poland and are on the road to Berlin the Boche is sure to withdraw some of his armies from Belgium.'

'Where did you hear that piece of news?' I said, delighted.

'Oh, everyone is talking about it,' he said. 'You'll see. We'll be in Berlin inside a month.'

He then offered me a drink in celebration. I refused because I was busy, but I wonder how many soldiers knocked off work for an hour to celebrate with him and his co-rumourists?

My other conversation of any note which was conducted in the main street of Everburgh was with a major of Belgian Guards who had just come back from the German frontier where he had taken part in the first fighting. He was passing back with the remnant of his company to reorganise behind our lines, and I met him just after I had heard the Commander-in-Chief's exhortation on the wireless, so that what he said depressed me even more. He was tall, good-looking, and obviously represented the cream of their fighting men, the equivalent, I supposed, of a regular officer in one of our own horsy regiments. He had a black scar across the shoulder of his coat which looked like a burn.

'You see,' he said smiling, 'the bullet was going so fast that it became hot. It missed me, but it made this burn.'

'And that was one of the first shots of all?' I asked.

'Yes,' he said, 'it was the very first shot that I heard.'

He told me how it had all started in the early hours of May the 10th.

'At midnight we were told that there might be an attack and that we were to get into our positions on the Albert Canal,' he said. 'Then a bit later two German officers whom we knew quite well came over the bridge to talk to us. They often used to come over like that and two of our officers spoke to them; everything was quite friendly.

They went away after a little, and at about two o'clock some German tanks arrived at the other side. Their officer came over to me and said that he wanted a safe passage through Belgium to attack the British and French. I was astounded. I said that of course he could not come. He said that it was a pity because there would be some fighting and he did not want to fight friends. I repeated that it was ridiculous for him even to think that I would allow him to pass. He went back to his tanks and I told our men to stand by to explode the bridge. The tanks went away for about half an hour and then suddenly we heard them coming back – much faster this time. When I saw that they were going to cross I gave the order to explode the bridge, but nothing happened because the wires had been cut. (I believe that they were cut while we were talking to the German officers.) Then the tanks started coming over. We knocked out a few but there were hundreds of them, and they soon overran our position; that's when I got this,' he finished, pointing to his shoulder again.

'What is your opinion of the Germans?' I asked. The question had the desired effect.

'Oh, you're one of these journalists, are you?' he said scathingly. I pointed out that I was still searching for a Belgian who really hated the Boche. Most of them, I told him, were lukewarm in their feelings.

'Well, you've found someone now,' he replied. 'I hate them, the swine.'

Perhaps he was a little biased having been shot at. I had no doubt whatsoever that I should hate them after they had sent a bullet or two after me. At present I still looked on the Germans as a misguided and immensely miserable people who just could *not* wake up from an intoxicating Nordic dream. I knew that very shortly I should have the hate fever in my own bones; but until then I still liked meeting people who really felt strongly about it, if only because it interested me to have a so-to-speak preview of myself in a mirror.

CHAPTER SIXTEEN
We 'Take up New Positions'

'WHERE DID YOU pinch that?'

'In one of the deserted farms. And I've found hundreds of tins of foie-gras in the cellars of the big house – and bottles and bottles of champagne. We'll have a dinner tonight even if we *are* on the other side of Brussels.'

This conversation with the doctor took place in the main street of Everburgh at four o'clock on the afternoon of May the 14th; it signalised, amongst other things, the retirement of the British Army. It came as the anticlimax to a day of surprises which had culminated in the order for our retirement. In spite of the general having ordered brand new ARP trenches outside his HQ that morning, in spite of the BBC's announcement at breakfast that we were definitely defeating the Germans, in spite of Old Moore and in spite of ourselves, we were going, as the doctor improperly put it, to 'retreat'. He had been reproved, because officially, at any rate, there is no such word in the British Army vocabulary; it savours apparently too much of Caporetto and Corunna, places where armies have had to move backwards quickly, at short notice and much against their will. A rather half-hearted attempt had been made to dismiss the retirement as a mere withdrawal, a part of a prearranged plan.

The doctor's announcement about the food was the only cheerful one I had heard during the day. He stood motionless in the street looking at a meat-safe he was carrying; inside it whimpering, was a live chicken.

'Nice one, isn't it?' he said.

'Yes, but you will never have room for that. The mess van is full already.'

'Wait and see,' he replied and, as if in proof, at that moment his new car drew up beside him; he got in and put the meat safe in amongst a lot of bottles in the back.

It was a hot, drowsy afternoon, a forerunner of summer; there was a curious stillness in the air, the stillness of a deserted village.

Only the rays of the sun seemed to be alive, beating down on the dry dust of the street; and the shops, stocked with goods, had their doors open, sometimes even their windows open as if inviting customers. But there was not a soul inside, not even the proprietors. We were the only people left in Everburgh.

We had only heard about the retreat two hours before, when we had seen a group of staff cars, with their red flags waving, drive down the main street of Everburgh in the direction of Brussels; and then later the colonel had told me to lead our own convoy of fifteen vehicles to a little village some miles west of the capital. It meant that Brussels was lost. We knew that the fighting had been very severe on the Dyle, but no-one had supposed it could have been quite as bad as this.

I was waiting for the convoy in the high street of Everburgh; the doctor was its first arrival. He asked me if I was coming in his car, which was full of food; he had come with the choicest pickings from the cellars and larders of our late and unwilling hosts. He had completely covered his new saloon car with an enormous fisherman's net in order to camouflage it, and to make it more uniform with the rest of the convoy. One of the results of doing this was to make it almost impossible to open any of the doors, so I decided that, as I had to lead the convoy, it would be wiser to travel in another vehicle.

When the other vehicles had arrived we took the main Louvain road to Brussels, and as we entered the city I was advised by a military policeman to instruct all the members of the convoy to hold their arms in readiness because a band of snipers had already caused considerable damage to earlier convoys; further attacks were still possible because they had not all been rounded up. He told me that the chief divisional staff officer had been killed in this way; this officer was a celebrated 'brass-hat', and he got little sympathy from Stimpson because he was said to have been wearing a cloth cap with a red band around it at the time.

It was quite unfair that, in Stimpson's eyes, to wear a red hat should be symbolical of the on-the-make staff officer, a symbol of self-advancement. It was even unfairer of him to say that 'to wear a red hat and to be killed in it was the perfect Gilbertian punishment'.

Brussels itself presented a very different spectacle from the memorable occasion three days before, when the doctor and I had been treated in it like the guests of a Persian shah – drink, cigars, and people's wives showering upon us. There were no cheering people this time, they all realised well enough that they were being left to the Germans once again. But they did not jeer or catcall. They just stood quietly and gloomily at the street corners watching the great sea of British vehicles flooding the streets, all struggling to get into their city and out of it, like rats escaping through a hole. There were no aeroplanes above the city; the Germans knew perfectly well that they were going to occupy it shortly and, apart from the busy, continuous, almost soundless turmoil in the streets, Brussels seemed dead. All other life had ceased.

If the city had changed from our last remembrance of it so had the roads leading from it. All semblance of that orderly journey into Belgium on the night of May the 10th was gone. That copybook advance over which the staff had spent at least nine months' preparation, whose mathematical precision had made us feel that we were members of a long and aristocratic cortege, was something belonging to another and more regulated world.

Today we were, one felt, simply competitors in a sporting race to the west. Like greyhounds released as the word for the retreat was given, there was a mad surge for the only two main roads leading to Brussels. Under such conditions there could be no free and easy motion, and we groaned on the roads, caught in the iron grip of motor transport constipation. Fumes thickened the air as the vehicles stood in their queues two, three, and sometimes four abreast, stretching out in one long line for miles with all the monotony of the curve that runs from Romney Marsh to Dungeness.

To make it more difficult there was the racing convoy leader, equivalent to the peacetime road-hog. He would spot what he thought was a chance of passing a whole line of rival convoys by opening up, for example, a fourth or even fifth line of traffic. His estimate would almost certainly be incorrect and the only result would be to stop all progress for about ten minutes while everyone sorted, unhitched and reoriented themselves.

It was during one of these stops that we missed the doctor. It was hopeless to stop and search for him in the concourse of guns, limbers, lorries, motorbikes, and red-cross vans. We could only hope that he would hitch himself to a passer-by.

Congestion reached its peak where a German bomb had landed. The German bombers, kept away at first by two British fighters, soon took advantage of us when the Spitfires went home in the evening to their aerodromes. Wherever a bomb hit the main road it was more or less certain that it would do some damage to a British vehicle. And after observing the unpleasant spectacle of other people being spiflicated, the mere advent of a bomber was enough to send people scuttling into the ditches; even if the aeroplane only passed over, no more harmful than a crow, vehicles would be stopped and everyone would go to cover. This of course aggravated the confusion because there was always a bomber hovering about somewhere overhead; and in consequence there was always a stoppage on the road beneath it. This communicated itself like a block in a water-pipe down the whole line of transport, so that vehicles miles away were affected. Where the bombers actually unloaded there was complete chaos and carnage for about three minutes. It was really very surprising how quickly people cleared up the mess and got going again.

Lastly, to add to our difficulties, there was the ubiquitous refugee who had not stopped traipsing the roads for four solid days and nights; this was his tail, with a ferocious wag in it. In his best moments he was a humourist and a comic character, an excited Latin arguing with the drivers of our vehicles because he and his dogcart had got in their way. In his worst moments he was a nuisance and a bore who ought to have stayed at home like a respectable peasant and tilled his fields politely and obsequiously for his German master.

The retreat went on like this for about five hours, a sequence of long, dull, patient waits at crossroads interspersed with sudden air attacks, each as swift, as intense, and as deadly as a tornado.

Towards nine o'clock, having covered twenty miles in about four and a half hours, we arrived at our destination, a sordid, grimy, but by now completely desirable, little Belgian village ten miles west of Brussels.

The colonel, who had gone on ahead, met us with the hardly surprising news that we were to repeat the Louvain defence from our new positions on this new river line a few miles to the west of Brussels. Why we had retired nobody could confidently say. The general belief was that the Dutch were to blame, the British Army having apparently fought stubbornly without yielding an inch; but one believed anything in those days.

In my official capacity as stores rag-and-bone man I took the first opportunity I found of inquiring about local material. There was only one entrepreneur in the district and he was most unhelpful. I asked him about the usual things... tin-tacks, timber, barbed wire, odd bits of lead piping, and the rest of it.

'Bah,' he said, 'about as much chance you have of getting such things as the British Army has of throwing the Boche back'; an observation in the worst of taste, not to mention premature. I pointed out that I would do good trade with him if he would only be civil.

'Well, you won't get anything here,' he said, pointing to some cheap tin trays hanging on the wall. 'That's all I've got.'

He typified, perhaps a little harshly, the attitude of most of the villagers: they refused to believe my idiomatic story about '*il faut reculer pour mieux sauter*,' or my bombastic story about Hitler licking Churchill's boots in one calendar month. They had all read the papers, they said, and were well versed in lies and their detection. They adopted a more sceptical attitude towards the patriotic lie than do our own people, who are prepared to believe that anything that has had the official sanction of the Archbishop of Canterbury is true in God's eyes even if not in Plato's. These canny Belgians, I felt, would hardly make good Old Testament characters. But it was a case of no bombast, no tin-tacks, and I put in some heavy canvassing that evening.

Perhaps the most difficult problem was that of billeting. Billeting procedure under normal conditions (i.e. with no Germans in the vicinity) is straightforward enough if you have the time to spare. Billets are normally paid for by signing an Army form which is handed over to the owner of the billet who signs it and in turn hands it over to the mayor; the mayor countersigns it and passes it on to the Département. It is then lost in a labyrinth of French bureaucratic channels for a few months, during which it goes to Paris where a police stamp is put on it. It emerges at last about twice as heavy as it started. The British Army on receiving this document then promises to pay the bearer at some unspecified future date, the sum of two francs per person per night. A small enough sum you may say, but the French peasant is not the one to laugh at it, he is a Shylock down to the last sou. We now found to our cost that there is little difference in this respect between the French peasant and the Belgian peasant.

The old idea of paying worked well enough in the placid pre-May days of Lille; people felt that the British Army had the Bank of England behind it, even if it did take about four months to pay. But in Belgium we were a shifting, fluid mass, here today, gone tomorrow; and investing money in a will-o'-the-wisp is poor policy. In short, the Belgian peasantry and small bourgeoisie suspected the Army forms we offered them in return for a quiet night's sleep, as a cavalier and extremely ingenious method of avoiding payment. After a while I was forced to visit the mayor to enlist his support. He pointed out how awkward it was for his people, with the German Army thrown in to make it more difficult.

'You never know, you see,' he said seriously, 'when the Boche will come.'

I agreed about this. It was a point.

'They will issue a moratorium and the Belgian Government will refuse to pay the debts of the British.'

'What do the Germans do about paying for billets?' I asked. I hoped to pick up a tip or two.

'Nothing,' said the Mayor, 'absolutely nothing. I was here in the last war. I know.'

'Well, our method is at least better than theirs,' I said hopefully. He shook his head sadly.

'I know it seems silly,' he said, 'but the people would much rather have it the German way. They know where they are then.'

'They like having no payment. Go on, you're fooling.'

'Well, it's not quite like that,' he replied. 'You see, the Germans take away all the food and then give them back enough to live on. That is the payment.'

He smiled philosophically; being mere English, I was incapable of understanding this continental logic, and he saw my plight.

'It is, I know, perhaps a little strange to you. But if the British could only be a little more successful...' he tailed off meaningly.

The old lady at whose house I wanted to have the mess refused to see me personally. A maid transacted all her business for her.

'Madame says she is sorry but she has no room,' she said. I had already been told in the village that the old lady was living alone with her two maids in this enormous house. Having already tried four other houses I found that, like the Germans, my patience was at last coming to an end. I accordingly resolved to behave like a German; the mayor, I suspected, was no fool; his advice would be worth following.

'I will see madame myself,' I said.

'Madame is *not* at home to visitors,' she replied.

'Madame is bloody well going to be at home to me,' I said, summoning all my histrionic skill, but inwardly quivering. 'Further, tell madame from me that if accommodation is not made available within a half-hour my soldiers will accommodate themselves. Tell her also that my soldiers are extremely hungry and tired, that they have been fighting in Brussels, and that they are on the look-out for food and drink – *and women.*'

The maid rushed back into the house like a shot rabbit; she probably had not been treated like this since the Germans had last been there. The ferocious picture I had painted of my stolid, meek, and inoffensive men amused me so much that I was still smiling when a minute later the chatelaine herself appeared at the door; but she probably thought it was the drunken smile of a barbarian about to sate himself. She tried, in that capable, dissembling fashion that women have, to appear gracious, unaffected, and hospitable, to give the impression that entertaining drunken soldiery was not only a pleasure, it was one of her most treasured social customs.

'Won't you come in?' she said. 'I had no idea you had been fighting,' a foolish (but accurate) observation as far as we were concerned. After that it was like the vicar's wife's At Home: food, drink, and comforts of every kind being lavished on us; all, I assumed, because she presupposed a tacit agreement that we would not touch the women. I was glad I had seen the mayor and learnt what a little Prussianism will do.

We had just arranged our billets in this new house when, to our intense delight, a black limousine with a fisherman's net completely draped over it drew up at the front door and the doctor got out, dirty, hot, and indignant.

'I've been machine-gunned by an aeroplane,' he said. 'I had to get under the car.'

We patted him on the back and said what a fine fellow he was, and noted that all the food was still there. There was an un-corked bottle of champagne, half-empty, on the back seat. The doctor easily explained it away.

'I was so frightened,' he said, 'after the aeroplane had gone away that I had to have a reviver. But we might as well finish it by celebrating.'

'Celebrating what?'

'My good luck in getting back with all the food of course.'

We had a dinner that evening of roast duck and sauce *au docteur*, three tins of foie-gras, some asparagus the doctor had picked up cheap on the way through Brussels, and an Army jam roll – all washed down with Heidsieck and Pommard'33; cigars and Napoleon brandy to round it off.

'No wonder Nappy always lived on the country,' said the doctor.

Just as we were finishing this meal a gallant NCO was brought in for commendation. He had waited behind in Louvain to blow up a mine when the advancing Germans were actually above it. We heard his tale from his own lips.

'It was getting dark,' he said, 'when they started to cross. I was about two hundred yards away and when they were above the mine I blew it. The German soldiers seemed to dance up into the air. Then I got on my bike and rode away like hell.' The colonel was delighted with this, as indeed were we all, and he promised to recommend the corporal for the Military Medal. The doctor gave him a bottle of champagne, but spoilt it by saying that he had so many he did not know what to do with them all.

We listened to the nine o'clock news to see how our retreat was viewed by the Government, or rather, to see how the Government thought it ought to be viewed. The announcer said that we had made 'a strategic withdrawal according to plan'. It appeared, according to him, that we had always intended to abandon Brussels, it was all part of our devilish scheme. Of course withdrawals and retirements are *vieux jeu* by now, they are two a penny today, and no-one would dream of raising his eyebrows if he heard them explained away in this jejune fashion; but we were fresh to it at the time and it seemed to us a little insincere.

'The bloody liars,' said the doctor.

'It's like Mons all over again,' said the quartermaster, an old soldier.

'That's a very defeatist remark,' said the colonel.

'I don't think Mons was a defeat, sir,' said the quartermaster. 'I think it was one of the greatest glories of British arms.'

It is all evidently a question of how you look at these things. A child will tell you how fortunate it was that we lost the American colonies, but old George the Third and his ministers nearly went off their heads at the time. It reminded me of my friend's assertion that the side that won a war was always the side that God was on, because God simply could not afford loss of prestige. It was at least comforting to think that whatever happened would be for the best, although, at the time, there seemed to be precious little cause for continuing that excellent philosophy, to regard this world as the best of all possible worlds.

In a frame of mind mellowed by these reflections and the doctor's Pommard I went upstairs to spend the first night of the great retreat on a feather bed.

CHAPTER SEVENTEEN
Booby-traps and Clarinets

MY BATMAN WAS tugging at my sleeve when I woke.

'The padre wants to see you, sir,' he said, 'something very important, he says it is.'

It was not Sunday and it could not be to ask me to play the hymns, so I expected the worst as the padre was shown in. It was just as I had thought, he had someone to bury and he wanted me to do the excavation and fill in the forms and documents. I was to help him in the main function of the cleric on active warfare – to give decent Christian burials. He was evidently an old hand at it.

'You must make out a list of the contents of the pockets in triplicate,' he said. 'And you should ensure that at least three of his fellow officers are present at the ceremony. The grave should be five feet deep and you should attach a bottle to the neck containing name, rank, and number. You will find the body outside; I will leave it here for you, draped with a rug. And by the way,' he said as he left, 'make sure that the grave is properly fenced or the cows will graze on it.'

I carried out these arrangements as best I could and attended the 'ceremony' myself that evening, reflecting the while on the perfunctory attitude which the padre adopted towards it. When death becomes a mass affair I suppose this is the only way to treat it.

The service was nearly marred by a parachute scare. Just before it was due to take place Stimpson was accosted by an excited little Belgian who was chattering madly about the German parachutists who had descended on The Hague the day before. He said that some were dressed as policemen, some as postmen, some as priests, and – what shocked him most – some 'were even dressed as nuns'.

'And you'd better look out,' he continued. 'A parachutist has just been dropped quite near here; he is dressed as a doctor and is carrying a small leather case which is really a sub-machine gun.'

'Yes, and I suppose he is wearing a trilby hat and a smart pinstriped suit,' said Stimpson sarcastically.

'You may laugh,' said the Belgian, 'but mark my words – he's somewhere about in this wood.'

He was quite right, because five minutes later, just as the padre arrived, we heard shots at the other side of the wood; but the padre, an old soldier, would not submit to the popular demand to postpone the service while its members absented themselves to shoot a bogus doctor. The service went on; but we heard later that the parachutist had been successfully shot in the wood. During his last moments, so the story went, he made efforts to direct the dressing of his wounds, saying he had been a doctor in peacetime.

'But that's nothing to do with what he was pretending to be at the end of a parachute,' said Stimpson.

The parachute scare was not the only one during that memorable second day of the retreat. There was a gas scare, an explosives scare, an aeroplane scare, and a booby-trap scare; retreating armies must be particularly susceptible to scares.

Ever since we had arrived in France there had been desultory mess chatter about gas. The British Army had been continually adapting itself during those dreary no-man's months to the various new gases which the scientists promised us the Germans would use. Our gas masks got longer and longer and heavier and heavier as contraption after contraption was added to the respirator.

So it was not surprising that the doctor should have reacted somewhat hastily when, coming out of the mess the next morning, after breakfast, he espied above the horizon in the direction of the enemy, an enormous yellow billowy cloud. It was moving steadily towards us and it was sufficient to make the doctor give one quick shriek of 'Gas,' and stampede round the mess looking for his gas mask, which of course he had left in his motorcar.

When we had all retrieved our gas masks from the various out-of-the-way places they had got into, we stood in the front drive in a body looking at the diabolical cloud, moving inexorably westwards, all ready at any moment to put our masks on.

We pointed it out to two Belgians who walked quite unconcerned down the drive, advising them to follow our example.

'What's all the worry?' one of them replied; 'it's only the petrol dumps that the Boche has set on fire.'

Even the colonel felt small as he took his mask off.

The aeroplane scare concerned me more directly. A German aeroplane had fallen in an allotment garden and, as it was relatively undamaged, it was thought proper to blow it up – on the scorched earth principle (it might belong to the Germans again one day). And I was entrusted with its inspection and demolition.

'It is almost undamaged,' said the major who gave me my orders. 'You will damage it.' It is only upon looking back now that I realise what a typical remark it was; one had become so used to accepting this sort of instruction that the curiosity of it went unnoticed at the time.

'And,' he added, 'you'd better be careful because there may be a time-bomb in it. The Germans are doing that now with all their aeroplanes; the pilot switches on a detonating circuit when he gets out of the thing.'

I found the aeroplane full of French children who were having a wonderful time climbing along the wings and swinging on the propeller. I hastily told them to go away, warning them against the danger. They went away only to reappear almost immediately accompanied by their parents; two of the parents accosted me and actually accused me of having encouraged the children to play on the aeroplane.

'Don't you know it's very dangerous?' said one of them, shaking her finger at me.

The injustice of this so incensed me that I said, looking at my watch, that they had two minutes to get clear of the aeroplane before it went up with an almighty bang. This had an immediate effect. As I opened the cockpit thirty seconds later the last peasant was disappearing round the corner some two hundred yards away. I inserted a guncotton charge and within five minutes the engine was lying in pieces on the ground.

Stimpson had the same sort of trouble with an infernal machine which mysteriously appeared on the following day in the back garden of a peasant's cottage. The peasant went down early in the morning to inspect his potato plot, and was horrified to find an obscene-looking cylinder sitting like a mushroom in the middle of the path. Our assistance was summoned by the local infantry, who had their headquarters dangerously near his back garden; as usual they thought it contained a new form of gas.

'Where is it?' said Stimpson when he arrived.

The old peasant pointed a skinny quivering finger out of the back window.

'My wife threw it over the back wall,' he quavered. 'She didn't want little Jacques to play with it.'

Cursing the woman for having probably put the time-fuse mechanism into motion, Stimpson gingerly laid the necessary guncotton to destroy the thing beside it, and retired to a safe distance, putting on his gas mask in case the threatened gas cloud followed the explosion. He had quite a little crowd of hangers-on by now, all eager to see the fun. They all stood about wearing their gas masks (if they had them) and putting their fingers to their ears in anticipation of the enormous bang Stimpson had promised them. After about two minutes Stimpson told me there was a barely audible pop and a little wisp of grey smoke hovered for a moment above the exploded cylinder and then vanished into thin air. Stimpson said that some of the spectators booed.

Inspection showed that the cylinder had contained nothing more harmful than oxygen, but to this day no-one knows how or why it got there.

If the explosives scare which took place a little later in the day was scarcely as exciting, it at least showed that it takes more than six days of warfare to awaken the British soldier to the realisation that he is fighting a proper enemy who really intends to kill him.

Just before dusk on this second day of the retreat the colonel had sent me to meet some explosive lorries and to conduct them to a safe place in a nearby wood; it was intended to use the explosive the following day for the bridges on the new river line. I was horrified when I arrived to find the lorries parked in the open outside the wood almost touching one another and containing in all about twenty tons of concentrated high explosive. Sitting on the front bumpers of these lorries, smoking, chatting, reading the *Daily Mirror* and eating sandwiches, were the drivers. Above them circled two German bombers on the lookout for targets.

I told the drivers that they had enough explosive between them to blow up the whole of Brussels – an inaccurate but very expressive criterion of explosive power. I also asked them to take a glance at the air above them.

Within three minutes there was a gap of about a quarter of a mile between each vehicle. I have never seen Army drivers move so quickly before or since. But, when I left, one of the drivers was reading his cinema journal – back in Tooting again.

The British soldier fights wonderfully when roused, but, if conditions are not completely active, his good nature is too much for him, and he likes to think of the enemy as a man like himself, of simple, generous tastes.

I had further proof of the inertness of our own men two nights later when I was orderly officer. I found the sentries near our headquarters smoking cigarettes, listening to the wireless, and chatting with local Belgians; one of them happened to be the Bren gunner and I asked him why he was not with his gun. He lamely replied that he thought 'it didn't matter so much at night because you couldn't see the aeroplanes anyway'.

The British soldier could not, at any rate, be accused of the current Belgian crime. With the announcement that Brussels was lost I am certain that many Belgians lost heart; and an order was issued to the British troops to arrest any Belgians observed entering houses dressed as soldiers and coming out as civilians. It was rapidly becoming one of the main worries of the Belgian High Command; they could find no way of stopping this novel form of desertion. It is, I suppose, one of the main drawbacks to fighting in your own country, that you are always liable to get worried about your wife and family; and you accordingly take a day's French leave (or English leave as the French call it) to visit them. If, as was the case with the Belgian Army, all the soldiers decide to do this on the same day, chaos results.

The British soldier had no such temptation. He merely diverted himself, if he was not actually in the front line, by pretending to himself that he was still at home listening to the wireless or watching the movies.

The next day brought yet another retirement. No reason was given officially, but it was generally supposed that the French and Belgians were entirely to blame. After breakfast, just as I was preparing for another day of store-scrounging, the adjutant rushed out of the mess with the depressing news that I was to find fresh billets on the Belgian frontier fifty odd miles away. We were certainly retiring quickly.

'A rearguard is to hold the river line until the main body is away,' he said. 'You have about half an hour to get packed and off. Don't waste any time; we shall be blowing the bridges in another hour.'

He showed me the route I was to follow, adding that there would be even greater confusion on the roads than in the retreat through Brussels; this he attributed to the suddenness of the order and to the impromptu nature of the arrangements.

Half an hour later we made off with great zest, and, by keeping to the side roads, were making good progress when we were suddenly stopped in a small village by a staff officer, who at great personal risk stepped into the middle of the road and stood waving his arms madly at us. I leaned out and inquired what it was all about. The red band round his arm gave him great authority although he was only a captain. He was so excited that it was some seconds before he could speak.

'A bridge has failed to go up,' he hissed in my ear. 'The engineers have made a muck of it. We must have an engineer officer. Who's an engineer officer? Quickly!'

I sadly confessed that I was the only engineer officer that I knew of in the district.

'The very boy,' he said. 'You'll do excellently. Now listen to me carefully;' he produced a map and pointed out a bridge on the river line I had just left, the river line that I had thought my colleagues were destroying. 'This is the place. I want you to return to it as quickly as possible – it'll have to be pretty quick too because the Boche is said to be arriving there any minute now – and, under cover of an infantry party who will protect you, I want you to get out along the bridge and blow it up. What's your name? Good luck, old boy. I must go now. All OK? Any queries?'

There were no queries, I had no doubt about it at all; neither had the doctor to whom I handed over the leading of the convoy.

'Never mind, old boy,' he said encouragingly. 'You'll come back all right.'

'Whoever said I shouldn't?' I said as I turned about, but I got less and less certain about it as we approached the bridge. We had to go against the traffic which was by now pouring back in one long stream, and it took an hour to get there, the nastiest hour I have ever spent in my life. I had a pretty shrewd idea of what it would all be like. The scene would be set; I could see it quite distinctly. There would be the bridge over the river with barricades at either end. There would be the British firing over the bridge, the Germans firing at the bridge, and me crawling along the bridge. And I had for one moment a brief glimpse of another, even less happy scene: a telegram being opened at home, in England:

'The MC for conspicuous... in the face of the enemy... posthumous.'

By the time we arrived I had evolved a scheme. I had never thought so hard before. I would have a long piece of cord tied on to my ankle so that if I was wounded on the bridge I could be hauled back to safety. Whatever happened I was determined not to bleed to death in the middle of the bridge; I had also determined to have a positive wall of sandbags to push along in front.

When we arrived at the headquarters of the infantry battalion which was to do the protection we could hear warlike sound down by the river; it seemed as if the Germans had already arrived. I found the adjutant in his office on the point of leaving.

'Hallo. What do you want?' he said.

'I've come to blow up the bridge at the end of the road,' I said. It sounded as if I was asking a favour.

'Which bridge is that?' he said. I showed him the map.

He frowned and rubbed his nose meditatively. His unconcern drove me wild.

'Oh, that,' he said. 'Let me see. I believe that's gone up already.' He thought again for about a minute.

'Yes,' he said, consulting his notebook and whistling. 'I think it has. Wait a minute. I'll go and ask the major.' He went out.

I prayed for that major and his decision while he was out of the room. Two minutes later he returned.

'Yes,' he said. 'Some of your chaps blew up that bridge ten minutes ago. Bad luck. Pity you weren't here a bit earlier.'

I whistled merrily on the journey back.

It was a repetition of the retirement through Brussels except that we had no convoy to lead and we could go faster. So we raced past everything. On the way we passed our old HQ and came upon Stimpson standing sadly in a gutter. He said he had remained behind to collect some explosive lorries but they were already three hours late, and he assumed they were lost. I offered him a lift.

'Do you mind if we stop in Tournai?' he asked.

'Sure. We might find some food there. Is that what you want?'

'No. As a matter of fact, I want to stop at a music shop. I want to buy a clarinet.'

'A clarinet? That will be very nice. But why do you choose Tournai as a clarinet centre?'

'Well,' he replied, 'one should be able to pick one up cheap because shopkeepers ought to be only too glad to get rid of stock before the Germans pinch it all. You see, I've just lost mine.'

We stopped in Tournai and Stimpson went off to search for his clarinet while the driver and I went into a bistro. Stimpson soon returned saying he could find nothing open.

'I'm going to inquire at the local gendarmerie,' he said. 'Care to come?'

'They'll probably lock you up as insane,' I said.

'I don't mind if they do. I am insane anyway. This war's driving me insane.'

There were three gendarmes in the office playing dominoes. They stood up when they saw two British officers, probably thinking we were about to declare the town under martial law.

'Good day,' said Stimpson.

'Good day, messieurs.'

'Are there any music shops in this town?'

'Music shops?' said one of them cocking his head.

'Yes. Music shops. I want to buy a musical instrument.'

They looked at one another. Perhaps we were the British secret service.

'One minute if you please, messieurs,' said one of them and he went into an adjoining room. He quickly returned.

'This way if you please. The chief would like to speak to you.'

The chief sat alone in his office. He had little black suspicious eyes.

'What is this I hear?' he said severely.

'I want to find a music shop. I want to buy a clarinet,' said Stimpson simply. I felt that there should have been more explanation.

'May I see your identity cards, please, gentlemen?'

These seemed to be in order. The chief ruminated, he looked us both up and down for a moment or two.

'A clarinet? A clarinet? What exactly is...'

'It's a sort of trumpet,' explained Stimpson quickly.

The chief was completely at a loss. He didn't know whether to lock us up as spies or madmen. He made one last attempt to get some sense out of us.

'But you are retreating,' he said. 'I was told that the British Army is retreating.'

It was the connection between clarinets and retreating armies that was worrying him. I felt we owed him an explanation.

'You see he wants to pick one up *bon-marché*,' I said.

We were shown out of the office quite politely. We were also given the name of a music dealer who was still open. As we went down the street the gendarmes watched us very closely. They obviously thought that we were suddenly going to undress and start firing our revolvers into the air.

We found the music shop shuttered and bolted. But through the shutters, we could see a brand-new, infinitely desirable clarinet with shining keys. We beat at the door and threw stones at the window without any reply; we were just leaving when the proprietor arrived, a fat Belgian scenting business.

'What can I do for you, gentlemen?' he said, unlocking the shop and rubbing his hands.

'I want to buy that clarinet,' said Stimpson pointing at it through the window. It was an unwise confession.

'Ah, you want that one do you?' said the Belgian. 'It is one of my best instruments. My best instrument,' he corrected himself. 'It is the best pick of all my stock.'

'Give you two hundred francs for it,' said Stimpson, evidently trying to retrieve his initial error by making a deliberately low bid.

The proprietor chuckled and went through the time-honoured formality of locking up the instrument and making signs to close the shop.

'You make good jokes,' he said. 'Do you know that that instrument is made by Boosey? It is one of your very best English makes. It is worth fifteen hundred francs if a franc, and you offer me two hundred!' He scoffed.

His estimate was probably not far off the true value of the clarinet, but at this point the town air raid siren blew for all it was worth. Tournai had already had one German air raid and this one had a most beneficial effect on the Belgian. Before the siren had even stopped blowing he had accepted Stimpson's second offer of seven hundred francs, pocketed the money, jammed his hat on his head, ushered us out of the shop, locked it, and disappeared in full flight down the street. It was a remarkable performance.

We were left in the middle of the street, Stimpson clutching his new clarinet, both wondering where in hell to go because the drone of the aeroplanes in the distance was becoming louder and louder. We had just reached the cellar of a nearby house when the first bombs began to fall. They were chiefly fire bombs and soon there was a merry sound of crackling and burning all round. Stimpson accompanied with the pathetically beautiful and sad melody from Mozart's Clarinet Quintet. It gave a fitting dignity to the raid in retrospect; at the time I felt it showed undue levity and even profanity. Poor little Wolfgang Amadeus had written the thing for civilised people.

In spite of all these troubles we arrived back at our new positions just after nightfall to find the doctor installed in the new mess which, in my absence, he had been entrusted with choosing. He gave us a splendid welcome, having long given me up for lost. With a complete disregard for all the lessons I had learned about choosing inconspicuous houses as messes, he had taken a luxurious place full of libraries and billiard tables, but situated on the top of a hill and painted a uniform white. I complained of this to him, and for answer he led me, without saying a word, to the well-stocked cellars and pointed out the compensation – unlimited champagne.

I spent that evening sitting in the library under a bust of Anatole France, trying to re-read *The Revolt of the Angels*, but the combination of the gramophone the doctor was playing, and the spasmodic ear-splitting noise of A.A. fire crackling outside made it impossible to concentrate on one of the funniest books in the world. The doctor was oblivious of the guns.

'The bloody war,' he said.

CHAPTER EIGHTEEN
Madame Ko-Ko at War

WE WERE NOW back again where we had started, or almost there, for the village of Watrelos, where the doctor had found our new mess, was on the Belgian frontier, very near the spot where we had crossed a week before on May the 10th, on our way up to Brussels.

The colonel arrived back for dinner that evening with the news that we were to hold the line of the frontier at all costs; it was, he said, a case of thus far and no further; to allow the Boche back into France would be the greatest disgrace in the world; this outlook found ardent support in Bèry, who was very caustic about the constant retirements.

'How can the French armies to the south possibly be expected to hold if the British keep retreating like this?' he asked.

Now, according to our intelligence reports, this was the very reverse of the truth, because it was the French who were constantly retreating, causing us to keep pace with them to avoid being outflanked. The major took Bèry to a map on the wall and pointed out the line of the French retreat.

'Observe,' he said frigidly, 'that the French have always been a little ahead of us in the face for the rear.'

The colonel felt that such disputes have a bad effect on morale and he asked them to stop arguing about it.

'If you must argue about the armies' movements, do it about our coming advance,' he said.

There was certainly little to encourage French or English that evening on the wireless. A prominent politician in London talked a lot of cold comfort about liberty and freedom, whereupon the doctor passed round the port observing that at any rate, the mess he had chosen was Liberty Hall. But there was nothing about the one topic that really interested us; the closing of the Sedan gap through which it appeared the German mechanised columns were still pouring. Where they were heading no-one really knew; some said for the Maginot Line, others said that they were going to attack the British Army in the rear, while the doctor thought that they would obviously be wanting to get to Paris. It was all most disquieting.

If Bèry was depressed about the course events were taking for France, another French interpreter I met the next day was almost crying his eyes out over them. He was a defeatist, with the novel idea that Hitler liked and respected the French.

'No tanks! No aeroplanes!' he said, shrugging his shoulders in despair. 'What's the use? We can't fight machines with our bare hands. There remains only one thing to do. The French Government must make peace.'

'How about us?' I said. 'What's going to happen to us if you make peace? Anyway, you've just signed a treaty with us saying that on no account will you make a separate peace.'

'That can't be helped,' he said. 'You will all have to go back to England. Perhaps you won't be quite so keen on having these wars if you have them on your own land for a change. And, in any case,' he added, warming to the idea, 'it would be much better if you made friends with the Germans instead of always having these wars with them. It does nobody any good. You must make friends with Germany; that's what we'll all have to do.'

'Make friends with Hitler,' said one of the British officers who had come into the mess and overheard his last remark. 'Not bloody likely.'

The interpreter did not bother to reply to this. When not under the nervous stress of thinking emotionally about Germans, English, and French, I could see he was a highly intelligent man. He had a magnificent, Hardy-like dome of a forehead and I afterwards learned that he was a university professor. He chattered on to me about tanks and aeroplanes and French culture.

'The Germans have always respected our culture,' he said. 'It is not likely that they will harm it now. They will certainly respect it if we make peace with them. Why! Did not Frederick the Great hire Voltaire to make him a gentleman?' he ended triumphantly.

When I heard later that evening that the Germans were in Arras, the interpreter's home, I felt a certain amount of sympathy for him. His last remark as I left was typical: it was about 'driving about in silly little motorcars and firing off silly little guns'.

'Hardly the occupation for a civilised man,' he said.

The following day was an aeroplane day; German bombers flew over us almost non-stop, treating the front line divisions with remarkable aloofness. They passed over in formation through a cloud of bursting anti-aircraft shells, majestic and untouched. I supposed that they were bombing France or England; but, because they were not dropping bombs on us, the doctor thought that they were merely doing it to impress.

'Of course,' he said, as we all got into our specially dug slit trenches outside the house for the third time within an hour, 'they haven't any bombs on board. They're simply showing off. I believe that the same lot of aeroplanes pass up and down the lines every time; I'm sure I recognise that one there. In any case all the bombs in Germany have already been used up on Rotterdam – according to the French news. You know, we really are being had for suckers – getting in these trenches every time.'

'Well,' said Stimpson, 'no-one's forcing you. You can stay drinking in the mess. Why bother to come out at all?'

In the afternoon there was another retreat, but this time a short one – of only a few miles – to the positions we had spent the whole winter in constructing just inside the French frontier. If we had to retreat from them one felt we might as well call the whole thing off and stop trying to be an army.

We had lost someone on every stage of the retreat so far, and this time it was Bèry; but he turned up again, indignant and ruffled, within three hours of our arrival.

'Hallo,' said the doctor. 'We thought you were finished.'

'Finished,' said Bèry. 'I should think I very nearly was finished. I'd like to finish some people.'

'What happened to you?'

'The Belgian gendarmes – the silly cows – they nearly finished me. Did you know how stupid a Belgian gendarme is? He is as stupid as...' he paused to think of the stupidest thing he could, 'as a *douanier*.' Now, this is no mean thing for a Frenchman to say. We all realised that he must have suffered.

'Tell us all about it,' said the doctor soothingly.

The little Frenchman was still badly ruffled. We sat him down, and gave him a drink.

'They locked me up,' he said, nodding his head significantly at each of us in turn.

'Locked you up, Bèry. But in heaven's name – why?'

'They said I was a spy. The pigs. I – a spy.' He almost spat the word out.

'But that is ridiculous, Bèry. Nobody could be more patriotic than you.'

'I know. Of course it was ridiculous. But I will tell you what happened. I stopped in a potty little village to ask the way at the gendarmerie. And, because they said I looked like some old photograph they had of a spy, they arrested me and locked me in a little cell.'

'How did you get away in the end?'

'Because the gendarmes ran away when they heard the Germans were coming. When I saw that they were going I beat on the door to be let out, and the last one to leave set me free. I think he realised that I couldn't be a spy because I wanted to get away so badly. It was horrible because I only just got away in time. As it was I was shot at.'

'How horrible,' said the doctor. At first I thought he was being sarcastic, but then I remembered he had been shot at himself only a few mornings before.

That evening, Heddon suggested that we should go into Lille to visit an old friend. The village of Bondues where we were now quartered was only a few miles from the city. The curious thing about our new positions on the old line that we had spent the winter in constructing was that no division appeared to be occupying the sector it had built. We were fighting from an area north of Lille, instead of in our old and familiar neighbourhood of Lesquin.

This did not prevent us from journeying into Lille that evening. Heddon wanted to pay his respects to Madame Ko-Ko.

Madame Ko-Ko was still there in the rue de Seclin but she was alone. The girls had left. The little American bar with its cheap red plush hangings and lewd decorations, had a pathetic air. It seemed out of touch somehow with the new life around it in a sort of no man's land, deserted by the English and not yet patronised by the Germans.

Madame Ko-Ko was asleep upstairs when we arrived. Heddon shouted for her and she came lumbering down, still dressing herself. Her fat coarse face beamed when she saw Heddon.

'My Archibald,' she cried, kissing him on both cheeks. 'My dear old Archibald. You old horse. And little Tony,' she said, turning to me and slapping me playfully and intimately.

'Well, how are you both? What a long time it seems that you've been gone. It's three weeks at least, isn't it? Where have you been all the time? Running away from the Germans I'll be bound, you naughty boys,' and she shook her finger at us. 'Come to Ko-Ko,' she said to Heddon, drawing up a couch and placing her hand on his thigh. 'Come to Ko-Ko and tell her all about it. You'll have a drink?' she said, business-like as usual.

'Of course we'd love to,' said Heddon. 'But tell me, where's Fifi? And Geneviève? And Rose? What's happened to them all?'

'Ah, it is very sad,' said Madame Ko-Ko, changing from mirth to gloom in a trice. 'They have gone. They left me this morning. They have deserted Madame Ko-Ko. When they heard about the bombs on the Belgian cities they went like rabbits. The dirty little bitches,' she finished aggressively.

She uncorked a bottle of champagne, winked at us, and poured us each out a glass.

'Just like old times,' she said, becoming quite merry again. 'Never mind. We don't mind, do we? We're old friends together. We can get on without the girls, can't we?'

'Not like it was when you were a girl – eh?' said Heddon smiling. 'Girls were girls then, weren't they? I bet you were a tough old tart.'

'Oh! what a rude man, isn't he?' said Ko-Ko, to me, while she playfully clutched him round the neck.

'What are you going to do if the British retire any more?' asked Heddon. 'Will you go away too, or will you stay here?'

Madame Ko-Ko had no doubts about what she was going to do.

'The Germans,' she said seriously, 'are very good customers. They are the best of all. I ought to know because I was here in the last war.'

'Ah, but the English are the best lovers,' said Heddon coquettishly.

'The English,' corrected Madame Ko-Ko, 'are the easiest to get money from. I tell you this because you are old friends,' she said graciously. 'It is the French who are the best lovers. Fancy not knowing that. I am a Frenchwoman,' she said proudly. 'But the Germans, they have their good points too. They are the most constant.'

'By constant, I suppose you mean the most regular.'

'Yes,' said Madame Ko-Ko, not seeing what Heddon was insinuating. 'They are certainly the most regular. You can rely on them. Why, do you know,' she said admiringly, 'there was one Prussian officer who used to come at the same time, on the same day of the week, every week for three years during the occupation. Can you believe it?'

'Yes,' said Heddon.

'You see,' said Madame Ko-Ko, ignoring him, 'it makes it so easy for us if people are like that. It means that the girls can have their day off at the proper time.'

'I suppose you were one of the girls in those days, weren't you?' said Heddon.

'And so I am now, aren't I?' she answered, winking artfully at me. 'Aren't I, Archibald? Come on now, say you love me just as much as Fifi,' she said, sitting her fourteen stone down on Heddon's knee, so that it made him wince.

'He is an old hog, isn't he? He really loves me quite a lot deep down in his heart I do declare, don't you, duckie?'

We had a rollicking evening after that, joking with Madame Ko-Ko who was really genuinely pleased to see us, and drinking pints of her watered champagne. Her only regret was the absence of the girls, for which she apologised several times, obviously feeling that it reflected on her professionally.

'But I have a great friend,' she said. 'She will always help a friend of Madame Ko-Ko's. She is a lady who lives in the rue de Béthune. She has some girls. You could go there; you would only have to mention my name.'

'What is she called?' said Heddon. I knew that there wasn't time to see these other attractions and I motioned to him to keep quiet.

'She is called Madame Polpop,' said Madame Ko-Ko, eager to put some business in the way of a friend. 'And she is a very dear soul, a very old friend. She has been in Lille almost as long as I have.' Madame Ko-Ko had always prided herself on her old-established position in the city.

'As a matter of fact Madame Polpop has been very sensible with her girls. She did not treat them so kindly as I did my girls. When her girls heard about the bombs on the Belgian cities and tried to go, she locked them up. So they are still there with her – earning good money too.'

'But,' she added, 'you must be very careful, because if you go with the girls you will have to be locked up too, and when you leave they may try to get away. You see I would never forgive myself if they were to get away just because friends of mine had not been careful. Madame Polpop is such an old friend, and besides,' she added thinking of a more cogent reason, 'she would think I had done it deliberately – for spite.'

I thanked Madame Ko-Ko courteously, but said that we were in a great hurry, that we had really only managed to tear ourselves away for a purely courtesy visit to see her, to see an old friend. Madame Ko-Ko was deeply touched.

'Dear boys,' she said, and insisted on kissing us both goodbye.

CHAPTER NINETEEN
Lille Revisited

THE NEXT DAY was May the 24th, a pathetic sort of Empire day; in the evening we listened to the King in a broadcast to the nation, and any doubts one had had about the seriousness of the situation were dispelled. There was no doubt about it. Things were hourly becoming what the French insisted on telling everyone they were *not* – catastrophic. The taking of Arras was said by a military spokesman in Paris to be serious but not catastrophic. As a member of an army that was now surrounded I felt it was a catastrophe of the first order.

We reflected that Ko-Ko need not have indicted her girls for running away from danger, because there were now German armoured columns between us and Paris, and it was unlikely that any refugees who had left within the last two days would get through. The great flood of refugees, gathering momentum and mass like a snowball as they moved westward, must have had a rude shock when they ran into the wall of Germans behind our lines. There remained little for them to do, except to turn about and tramp back the way they had come.

It appeared that the complete British and Belgian armies, together with a few French divisions, and apparently the collected refugees of all Belgium, were now crowded into a small pocket in the north of France. They all wanted, apparently, to do something different – the British to advance, the French to retire, the Belgians to capitulate, and the refugees, who were now meeting Germans wherever they went, not knowing quite what to want.

The two following days passed uneventfully. There seemed to be little activity on our front and optimism ran high. The popular opinion was that the Germans had at last found us in an impregnable position – that they were, to use a technical phrase, 'mounting' an attack, a period of necessary inaction; they were, however, going to get hell if they tried to advance again. We were determined to be optimistic.

It also became possible during those two static days to obtain, for the first time, some sketchy notion of where the various armies were. The British were evidently holding about thirty miles of front in the Lille area, the Belgians were north of us touching the sea, and the French were undoubtedly to our south – with several German armoured divisions in between. The beastly and efficient Boche was, of course, everywhere – south, east, west, and, for all we knew, entertaining some plan for going north. The popular method of solving all this trouble was to 'close the gap'; that is to say, to attack south and to meet the French armies somewhere about Cambrai. Opinions about the size of the 'gap' varied, some said it was five miles wide, some fifty.

Opinions also varied about the German plan. Perhaps the best pointer to it, however, was the barricade system which had been incorporated in every village which our Army was occupying. The barricades in Bondues faced in every direction, not simply towards the eastern entrance as they had throughout the earlier part of the retreat. It signified that an attack was also expected from the west. It also gave the lie to the French story that only 'forward elements' of German troops were in Arras.

On the morning of the 25th I had the good fortune to meet an anarchist. One of my stores errands took me to Roubaix, notoriously the most bolshevist part of France even before the war; it is quite in keeping with tradition that it should have been so, because the richest capitalists of the north of France lived there in their fine houses alongside the poor, the afflicted, and the penniless.

In the Grande Place I found a mob of what I took for malcontents outside the Mairie. I was delighted; I thought that I had at last stumbled upon the modern counterpart of those historic crowds which had clamoured in such fine fashion outside the Tuileries and the Bastille for their rulers' blood. I expected the mayor to be thrown out of the window with his throat cut at any moment.

It was a great disappointment to find that they were only demanding petrol coupons, much after the manner that Frenchmen en masse would demand anything. It was simply the congestion and national emotional bias of the crowd that appeared unruly.

But I was not entirely disappointed because it was here that I met my anarchist. With some difficulty I had made my way through the crowd to inquire at the bureau about timber; I was immediately handed over to the anarchist who was said to be a timber expert. He was a beefy fellow, well above the size of a Frenchman; he looked much more like a German. He told me that he had just heard the news about the fall of Arras.

'Just let me get hold of our Godforsaken government,' he said clenching his fists and obviously seeing red. 'Give them to me for one hour.' I shuddered. Such animosity was frightening even though I did not know, much less care for, the French Government. 'What in hell do we pay them for? Where are our tanks? Where are our aeroplanes? Where are they?' he shouted at me as if it was my fault.

'What political party do you belong to?' I asked, hoping to side-track him. It was like a red rag to a bull.

'Political party? Political party?' he shouted incredulously, and went off into a lot of unprintable stuff. When he calmed down I understood from him that he held no political faith.

'None,' he said emphatically. 'None. Not one of them is worth belonging to. A lot of grubbing swine.'

'How about the Germans?' I asked, interested in the purely academic point of whether he was a fifth-columnist or merely a defeatist. 'How do you find them?'

I was being superlatively tactless with him because he went off into another long diatribe.

'The Germans!' he cried. 'The Germans! *Sacrée Mère*! Give me a German. Just one – and with these hands,' – he produced a massive, gnarled, and grubby pair of hands – 'I'd slaughter them. Just you see if I don't when they arrive. Even if the spineless government doesn't give me any weapons I'll kill a Boche before they get me. Give me a club of wood.'

It seemed as if the delightful anomaly of anarchism being the best brand of government (from a patriotic point of view at any rate) held true.

His insistence on improvised weapons reminded me of Milton's Samson:

Then with what trivial weapon came to hand,

The jaw of a dead ass, his sword of bone,
Ten thousand foreskins slew, the Flower of Philistin.

I was certain that he could slay foreskins with his bare hands if necessary.

He seemed to think that I was partly responsible for all the trouble, because I belonged to a body so closely allied with the politicians. I did not doubt this for a minute; but, when he finally and grudgingly showed me a timber yard, I took great care not to get into a dark corner alone with him.

The crowds that had besieged the mairie in Roubaix were only a small section of the great civilian mass that still came rolling back from the east. The effect of the German ubiquitousness on these refugees was rapidly becoming evident. While visiting Seclin, a small village a few miles south-east of Lille, I fell in with some refugees who were coming in the wrong direction and, largely out of curiosity, I asked them why they had forsaken the Paris road. An old man replied to my question wistfully.

'The Boche,' he said. 'The Boche is everywhere.'

'Where do you intend to go to now?' I asked, perhaps rather unkindly. 'The Boche is over there too, you know,' I said, pointing east.

He looked at me very closely. He was an old man, unshaven and very tired.

'I am a Belgian,' he said slowly. 'I have been on the road for five days, and now I see that I cannot escape I am going to lie down in a barn or under a hedge and wait for the Boche to come. It is impossible to escape him.'

Most of the refugees on the road seemed equally forlorn. But there was even more despondency when Stimpson and I were passing through Lesquin the following day and dropped in at his old billet – owned by a man called Pascale.

Old Pascale was still there but he looked deathly. All the enthusiasm he used to show for the war was gone now that it affected him personally. He was pleased to see Stimpson, his old billetee, in a dim sheepish sort of way.

'What are you going to do? What is the British Army going to do?' he said desperately. 'We cannot have the Germans here again. You mustn't let them come. You must drive them back. You must, really you must.'

As he seemed to think that it was all the fault of the British Army we pointed out as politely as possible that the French High Command seemed to have made miscalculations too.

'But don't lose hope, M. Pascale,' I said. 'I expect we shall be starting an attack soon. We shall close the gap.'

'My business will be ruined,' said M. Pascale, who was a wicker-chair maker.

Stimpson tried to cheer him up – in a rather tactless way I thought.

'Never mind,' he said. 'I expect that even the Germans will have to sit down sometimes. Don't worry. You'll find a market all right.'

'How can you say such things, M. Stimpson?' said old Pascale shocked, obviously thinking of his beloved France and his wicker chairs.

But what really shocked him was the German block between Lille and Paris. He had tried to evacuate his family the day before, he told us; but he had been turned back near Seclin because of the Germans.

'The Boche is everywhere,' he said. 'It was not like this in the last war. We only had the Germans on one side then,' he seemed almost proud of this achievement. 'But now,' he said, 'they are everywhere.'

Stimpson pointed out that habit dies hard.

It was the same in Lille. Everyone was asking what was the next move. What would the British Army do? The suspicion that the Germans might soon return again to Lille after their twenty-two years' absence was beginning to form in the people's minds. All one could do was to reassure them by saying that the whole retirement was part of a grand scheme cunningly worked out by the French and British general staffs; but unfortunately people were beginning to lose confidence in the general staffs.

The best scene that day in Lille, theatrically speaking, was the clearing of a goods yard by hungry British troops. The yard in question contained enough food to supply the whole British Army for three months – so I was told by an enthusiastic soldier whom we met coming away from the yard on our way home from old Pascale's.

It appeared that the food had arrived before the German invasion of the Low Countries had begun and that the British authorities, frightened of making a free gift to the Germans, had now decided, so to speak, to throw the yard open. The distribution, or rather appropriation, had started in an orderly enough manner, an officer apportioning out the food as fairly as possible to all comers. But when the clearing got fairly under way it became like a jumble sale; we arrived when it was at its height.

Men fought their way in through the scrum and came out with a half-case of brandy or a tin of sardines after a quarter of an hour's struggle. Bottles got broken in the process and the floor was soon running with liquor; nobody took any notice of it as they staggered to and fro from their vehicles, trying to load them to bursting point.

The doctor was delighted when we returned with two bottles of gin and some pickled onions. Even then, because we had behaved, relatively speaking, in a refined fashion, we came away with much less than the other scavengers. Some people, the pushers, went away with their vehicles groaning under the load.

The sequel to all this occurred at 6.30 that evening. A German reconnaissance plane had evidently noted the unnatural activity in the goods yard during the afternoon; it must have been obvious that we were after food, soldiers taking part in a scene of far greater activity than, for example, the unloading of ordinary stores trucks would have created. In consequence at 6.30 five heavy high-explosive bombs were dropped on the railway yard completely destroying it.

The story goes, however, that at 6.15 the last British soldier was carrying away the last bottle of gin. The French railways were the only sufferers.

The doctor naturally received us with open arms, but there was a certain coolness on the part of the others towards Stimpson, as a result of something he had done, or rather not done, earlier in the day. He had overslept (if failing to get up at 5.30 can be called oversleeping); he had been due at that hour to visit a large wool factory in the forward area with the colonel and adjutant. They were to take explosive with them in order to demolish this factory before the Germans captured it; and it had been decided at the conference held the previous night that the work should be carried out in the early morning, before it was light, in order to avoid observation from the enemy front line.

When I came down to breakfast that morning I found the members of the demolition party, including the colonel and the adjutant, all safely returned from their early morning work and eating their breakfast. A few minutes later Stimpson came down, bleary eyed and still half asleep. He looked at us sheepishly.

'Hallo!' said the colonel cheerily. 'What happened to you?'

'I'm sorry, sir,' said Stimpson, 'but I'm afraid I overslept.'

'Well, that's bad luck. We had awfully good fun. If you look towards Roubaix you'll see something burning merrily. That's what we did to the wool factory. Pity you missed it.'

'Yes, sir, I'm frightfully sorry,' said Stimpson taking the opening. The colonel was fortunately one of those kind people who are always prepared to ascribe their own feelings and enthusiasms to others; this was particularly true with him about all matters concerning the war; a man of great personal courage himself, he was always ready to suppose that others were equally endowed.

During the retreat the colonel had done wonderful work in supervising (and often even executing) the demolitions on the various river lines himself; accompanied by the adjutant, he had often toured the rivers at the very last moment, when the enemy was almost on top of him, to ensure that no bridge should, by mishap, be left standing. It was therefore not surprising to learn afterwards in England that every bridge which our divisional engineers had prepared had been successfully demolished – nor was it surprising to learn that the colonel had received the D.S.O.

That afternoon I too was told to visit the firing line; the colonel wished me to inquire about the delivery of engineer stores to a certain infantry unit – it fortunately contained an officer who was an old friend of mine. I accordingly rang up the Brigade to which he belonged to warn them that I was coming; they told me where I was to meet the guide who would conduct me to the forward infantry positions in touch with the enemy.

When I arrived that afternoon I was told by the guide to leave my car about a mile behind the line so that it would be screened from enemy observation. As we advanced on foot I admired the high ground in front, across the valley, whereupon the guide warned me that it was full of lurking Germans; at one point he even instructed me to lie down and crawl, saying that we were passing a point often under enemy fire.

Guns and machine-guns fired intermittently, but it was quite impossible to determine which were enemy and which were our own. I was surprised to find that the guide could not distinguish between them any more successfully than I could; he treated them all with the greatest respect. I supposed that, like the doctor and Bèry, he had been shot at once before; and as we crawled from a ditch on one side of the road to a ditch on the other side, I reflected sadly that I should be equally experienced myself one day perhaps.

After the elaborate stalking rigmarole I had been put through on the way, I expected to find my friend in a trench at least. To my surprise, I was conducted to a small villa which my guide introduced as 'the mess'. Although apparently in the firing line it was happily screened from the enemy by a knoll of ground. I noted hastily and thankfully before entering, that it was sandbagged and encircled with trenches.

I was welcomed by a batman who told me that my subaltern friend would be shortly returning from a visit to some machine-gun posts. He said that I was expected to stay to tea, and that, by way of diversion while I was waiting, I could if I cared, watch a howitzer being fired in the back garden. If it was a question of diversions in gardens I would have preferred to have read *Alice through the Looking-glass,* but I did not want to hurt his feelings; and together we watched a little black gun emitting clouds of dirty smoke and destroying the vegetable patch it was placed upon. After being deafened by this for about five minutes I retreated into the house to find that my friend had returned. Together we drank our tea, reminding one another that our last tea-party had been held in more peaceful circumstances on a punt in the middle of the Cam. The batman stood in respectful attendance throughout the meal. My friend was the only member of the mess and he told me that all his meals were conducted in similar solitary state.

The domesticity of all this had a peculiar charm of its own, more than counterbalanced for me, however, by the strange noises and spasmodic shudders outside the house which never ceased. My friend ignored them all; being a Guardsman he talked about London.

CHAPTER TWENTY
Retreat to the Coast

DURING THE AFTERNOON of May the 27th we were warned that a conference of all officers would be held at 6.30 that evening at which the colonel, who had just received instructions from the general, would unfold an important plan.

There was some speculation about it at tea, the more impetuous members of the mess thinking that we were going to attack to the south.

'It's the only way to save the situation,' said the adjutant. 'The Boche can't hold if he's not regularly supplied. If we can only attack south and join the French he'll be stranded.'

The doctor had an ingenious plan to save Paris.

'The thing to do,' he said, 'is to pretend that we are going to attack towards Belgium. Then at the last moment, when we are all facing east, to turn right round and beat up the other Boches behind.'

'A nice idea,' said Stimpson, 'but you can hardly attack armoured units unless you are armoured yourself.'

Stimpson and Bèry between them favoured a sort of golden mean. They thought we would stay in our present positions fighting defensively in every direction, so as to form a pocket of resistance.

'And in the meantime,' said Bèry, 'the French armoured divisions will come up behind unawares, and give the Boche such an almighty kick in the pants.'

'The French armoured divisions,' said the doctor. 'Where are they? How many are they?'

'Ah,' said Bèry mysteriously. 'Who knows?'

The cellar in which we all congregated at 6.30 that evening had been specially strutted and shored to make it bomb-proof. In the flickering candlelight the long shadows cast by the pillars gave it the air of some old, ill-lit crypt; one almost expected the colonel, as he sat on a barrel, slightly raised at one end, to start intoning a Latin dirge. What he said was elegiac enough.

'Gentlemen,' he said, 'I have just returned from a conference with the general. What I am going to say will surprise you.' He paused, at a loss how to begin. 'You already know that the British and Belgian armies are almost surrounded. There remains, however, one small exit in the north. *We are going to evacuate France.*'

There was a stir among the attentive listeners. No-one had really expected anything quite as bad as this.

'Lord Gort has been ordered by Whitehall to withdraw the Army before it is too late,' the colonel continued. 'The French and Belgians may have let us down; we cannot be certain who is to blame for it. What is certain is that it is no fault of ours, and the general wishes me to convey to you his appreciation of the way the division has conducted itself throughout the fighting. The evacuation, gentlemen, is to take place from Calais and Dunkirk, the only two ports left in our hands.'

He gave time for the startling effect of this announcement to die down.

'We are going to attempt something essentially British; I venture to say that only the British would dare to attempt such a hare-brained scheme. Let us only hope that it will be as successful as it was when it was last practised – by Sir John Moore at Corunna.

'I can't tell you much about it,' he continued, 'because no plans have been made. We cannot even be certain that there will be boats at the coast to take us off. We have simply got to chance it. All I can tell you for certain is that we shall be fighting a hard rearguard action all the time. It is not yet even certain in what order the British divisions are approaching the coast. Divisional advance parties are to go ahead to prepare a reception for us in England,' – at this point he laughed – 'if we ever get there.'

'What's happening about equipment?' asked the adjutant.

'All equipment is to be left behind after it has been properly destroyed. Men will only carry their respirators on to the boats. There won't be room for anything else.'

He then went into technical details about the bridges we were to make on the retreat.

'The Germans are certain to destroy existing bridges by bombardment when they realise that we are retreating,' he said. 'The main task of the engineers will be to erect substitutes.'

'I knew it,' said the doctor, as we went out together. 'I had a feeling we were going back to England. What a scoop for any journalists on the spot,' he said enviously.

Amid all the bustle and commotion that followed I found time to leave my books in a wardrobe. They were the result of eight months' browsing in Parisian and Lillois backstreet libraries. It caused some heartburning to think that a German or French soldier might use them to light fires. They included what I liked to suppose were some original Guys drawings, but these I decided to take with me, thinking that if the worst happened I could always stuff them down my trousers; but I had to leave the rest. I laid a polite note on the top written in French and German asking the new owner to treat them with care, saying how I hoped he would enjoy reading them; and finally, asking him to come and stay with me at my address in London after the war (bringing the books with him of course).

An hour later the RSM and I set out in a small truck for Armentières, where the colonel had said we would find the other units of the divisional advance party; he said we would form part of a convoy bound for Boulogne or Dunkirk.

We had a collision with a cyclist in Lille. It was dusk and I was speeding, having been told to report at Armentières at absurdly short notice. The Frenchman was unhurt but indignant.

'Why don't you look where you're going?' he said, remounting his bicycle. 'Where do you think you're going to in such a hurry anyway? Paris?'

We assured him that it was not Paris but, like many of his countrymen, he would probably have had a nasty shock if we had told the truth.

Lille in the dusk looked as soiled and as sordid as I had ever seen it. The streets were full of refuse; they looked as though they had not been cleaned for days. A few people were hanging around at the corners, smoking cigarettes and looking forlorn. Only one or two bistros were open, and the Café Jeanne, once the smart and chic American bar, had had one of its plate glass windows vulgarly shattered; and its door was hanging drunkenly from the hinges.

Ko-Ko's place had a light burning, and I wondered vaguely what she was doing; I did not suppose I should ever see her again. If there had only been more time, I would certainly have stopped and had one last bottle of champagne and water with her.

The streets were almost clear of traffic, except for a few little black Army cars which scurried furtively about, preparing, presumably like ourselves, to abdicate. I reflected that the only difference between all this and its Brussels counterpart was that here the people had no notion that we were about to desert them. In a few days' time they would wake up in surprise to find they had new and grey-coated companions. Apart from a few patriots like M. Pascale, I imagined they would not mind much. Although our occupation would have probably been kinder than the German one, trade in champagne and prostitution would go on just the same.

We arrived at Armentières half an hour later and I reported at the Movement Control Office for instructions. It was full of officers, all talking at once, and all asking what they were to do and where they were to go.

The unfortunate major in charge looked like one of those comic characters in *Punch* cartoons, who are being besieged by tourist questioners, all asking for fatuous information. The only difference was that no information under such circumstances could be anything but highly relevant. Everyone was in deadly earnest, all wanting to get away from France as quickly as their legs or motorcars could carry them.

I joined the queue and when my turn came, I told him the unit I represented. He looked at his watch.

'It is now 8.30,' he said. 'You have six hours to wait here. Have you ever led a convoy before – under active conditions?'

This was one of my few military accomplishments.

'Yes,' I said proudly. 'Many times.'

'Right,' he said. 'You're just the man I'm looking for. At 2.30 tomorrow morning you're to lead a convoy of thirty vehicles to Dunkirk. You can't leave before because we are trying to avoid cluttering up the roads and your convoy is provided for in our timetable. But you *must* be careful to avoid going through Ypres and

Poperinghe at all costs. The only decent road passes through them but you must somehow manage to by-pass them.'

'Are the Germans there already?' I said, shocked.

'Never mind who is there,' he replied. 'Don't go through them – that's all. I should try to get some sleep now if I were you. You aren't going to get much for the next day or two.'

I was about to ask him what was going to happen to us when we arrived at Dunkirk but, having given me more than my fair share of time, he dismissed me with a wave of his hand, and started attending to another customer.

I went into one of the other rooms, where I found two officers drinking champagne in turns out of a bottle.

'Hallo,' said one of them looking up. 'Waiting for a convoy? Have a drink? There are bottles of this stuff in the cellar.' He uncorked a bottle and gave it to me.

'Where are you heading for when you leave?' he asked.

'Dunkirk,' I said.

'I expect I'll end up there too. I'm supposed to be going to Calais, but I should think the Germans are there by now.'

I began to suspect that it would not be long before the Germans were at Dunkirk at this rate. I told him that I was leaving early the next morning and, as he seemed so well informed, I asked him what he thought would happen at the ports.

'The major says the Navy will be there,' he said. 'But I believe the Germans have been bombing them pretty heavily the last few days. It's sure to be a ticklish business. Some people have had the luck to get a lift to England from the RAF,' he added.

The other officer who had been drinking steadily throughout this conversation came to life at this last remark.

'Yes, the dirty dogs,' he said.

Later I went to sleep.

I was woken at 1am by the RSM.

'Time to get ready,' he said.

It took about half an hour to collect the other members of our convoy; we found them sleeping in all manner of queer places and postures, some being already aboard the lorries we were to lead. As we were to travel in the front lorry I realised that we would have to abandon our own vehicle, but only after properly destroying it. It was an almost brand-new Humber, worth about a thousand pounds, and my squeamish nature objected to carrying out this piece of destruction. The RSM fortunately had a plan for dealing with it quickly. He suggested that we drained the oil and then ran the engine till it seized.

It was a sorry business. After about twenty minutes of this treatment the engine was suddenly seized with an attack of the most violent palpitations. (I had often wondered about the derivation of the technical term 'seize'.) They got worse and worse and, when the engine seemed to be on the point of jumping out of the chassis, it collapsed pitiably; it was almost red-hot. We finished it off by laying into all the more delicate parts with a sledgehammer and by cutting long gashes in the tyres. Never was destruction wrought with more distaste.

At two-thirty we set off in the pitch dark of a cloudy, moonless night. I had lost my torch so I had to read the map by the light of matches. (I was surprised to find at the end of the journey that I had used two boxes in this way.)

I sat with the driver of the leading lorry. He was a London taxicab driver he told me.

'Hope we don't get any traffic blocks on the way,' he said.

It was a forlorn hope, because almost immediately we found ourselves involved in trouble with a convoy of Belgian vehicles which were moving westwards at right angles to our own line of movement.

I descended and had some trouble in the dark in finding the Belgian officer in charge. One of his lorries had skidded at the crossroads, and the bulk of it was now lying across the road, with its front wheels in the ditch, making further progress impossible. We had to go round it by breaking into adjacent fields.

While this was going on the Belgian officer exchanged cigarettes with me.

'How near are the Germans?' I asked.

'About six miles. Over there,' he said pointing east. 'But we're all right here. My division will hold them up for several more hours.'

I reflected that it would have to be for several more *days*, not hours, if the British Army was to reach the sea intact.

'Where are you going?' he asked.

I was not sure if I ought to answer this question. I thought of the nearest town.

'Ypres,' I lied.

'My God, don't go near it,' he said. 'They're bombing it to hell. It's on fire. An inferno. Can you see a red glow over there?' He indicated the horizon to the north-east. A faint flush, as of a sunset, was just visible.

'What are you going to do there anyway?' he asked, curiously.

'I'm afraid I can't tell you,' I said.

'Oh, you English. You're all the same. All full of that,' he said. 'That's why there's no co-operation.'

This seemed to me unjust. I pointed out that if there was any place to maintain secrecy it was in his country.

'Belgium's full of fifth columnists,' I said. 'How do you propose to deal with them if you don't keep your mouth closed?'

He saw my point.

'Yes. Perhaps you're right,' he said apologetically.

'Is it true that the English are leaving France?' he asked, trying another line. He seemed rather too inquisitive to me.

'Wherever did you hear that absurd story?' I asked.

'Well, that's what some people are saying in my division. I hope it's not true, don't you?' he asked, eyeing me quizzically.

'So do I,' I said, feeling I was being superbly uncommunicative.

'Well, I must get along now,' he said. 'I passed a lot of your vehicles going north before dusk last night. Perhaps they're moving north to help us. I hope so.'

'So do I.'

The impasse was at last removed and we said goodbye. Progress was better after that; apart from an incident in a churchyard, when owing to the darkness I led the convoy in merry-go-round fashion, circling the church for five minutes, we kept going at a steady 5 mph for the rest of the night.

But at dawn we found complete congestion and stoppage again.

The roads were lined for miles with British vehicles. By four-thirty in the morning I was seriously wondering whether to disobey orders and to take the open road for Poperinghe; it invited us at every crossroads. After a short conference between the officers of our convoy held at one of these halts, we agreed to risk it. Dunkirk seemed such a distant but beckoning prospect that our dearest wish – to get there by fair means or foul – was the deciding factor.

The road to Poperinghe was strangely deserted and uneventful. Only once, when a fountain of earth suddenly shot up in a field close beside us, did we have any cause to regret our decision. I rubbed my eyes wondering if it was a hallucination caused by lack of sleep, but my driver had no doubts about its identity.

'Jerry's shelling the road, sir,' he said. 'I guess we'd best get off it!'

Overawed and feeling rather guilty, I told him to turn down a side turning and within a half-hour we found ourselves back again in the Grand Queue. Forty-five minutes of almost negligible progress convinced me again that the Poperinghe-Ypres road was worth the risk; we returned to it and once more were travelling towards those unfortunate and shell-beaten towns whose very names seem miserable.

Towards five-thirty the sun appeared above the horizon, illuminating the towers of Poperinghe, now plainly visible across the flat Flanders landscape. From somewhere out east came the sound of gunfire, so subdued that there seemed little cause for worry.

We entered a deserted town, I had half-expected to find it occupied by the Germans, but the side streets revealed nothing to our quick, apprehensive glances. Although Poperinghe had been partly destroyed in the Great War, its main street still had an almost Balzacian air. Perhaps because of the unreality given by the long shadows and because of the absence of people, or perhaps simply because my mind was still fuddled and half-bemused by the happenings of the last twenty-four hours, it would not have surprised me if, from one of the little narrow side streets, had emerged the figure of le Père Goriot. He would have been wearing a top-hat and a blue frock-coat – a walking repudiation of the life I was being made to lead.

My driver woke me from these heartening reflections; he had espied a grocer's shop, the front window full of eatables – cooked sausages, groceries of all kinds, and lumps of raw meat. He looked at me questioningly; and, because we had brought no food with us, I felt that scavenging was permissible. The front door had already been broken down, and the old excuse – that if we did not take the food the Germans would – was obviously the proper one.

The convoy stopped and we invaded the shop, coming out five minutes later like gorged locusts, leaving barren what had been fertile. We stripped it completely, making a good deal of commotion. I was surprised that no enraged shopkeeper came downstairs to remonstrate with us, or that no neighbour leaned down from his bedroom window to curse our noise. The town was dead; my suspicion that we were alone in it, in a sort of no man's town, so worked on me that I beat on the doors of other houses in the street. But I obtained no reply.

The road from Poperinghe to Ypres was equally uneventful, and I soon became convinced that we were truly travelling through no man's land. The most surprising feature was the complete absence of gunfire and sound; no man's land had always seemed to me so indissolubly linked with craters and bursting shells. I have since learned that we were simply lucky; our passage evidently coincided with a break in the German bombardment.

Once, just before we reached Ypres in the early dawn, a German reconnaissance plane passed overhead. It circled above us for a moment or two and then turned back towards the east. The Germans were reputed to have a remarkably quick liaison in such matters, and I wondered if it would be followed by a bombing attack.

While it was actually overhead I considered getting out one of the Bren guns to drive it off. It was perhaps fortunate that we did not do this because I heard later that a friend of mine had treated a German reconnaissance plane in a similar fashion, announcing that it was quite harmless and that such planes 'didn't carry any bombs anyway'. He accordingly peppered it with Bren-gun fire from the back of his truck, whereupon the German aeroplane, which was on the point of leaving, promptly turned about and dropped one bomb in reply. It landed neatly in the truck, killing my friend and two other soldiers, fully justifying the old maxim for young children, 'Don't play with angry animals'.

When we arrived at Ypres, fires were still burning in the centre of the town, but the Belgian officers' warning about continuous bombing was not borne out; apart from the crackling of timber not a sound was to be heard. All the aeroplanes had gone and the sky became clearer and bluer every moment, heralding a perfect summer day.

Some miles north of Ypres we crossed the frontier into France for what I hoped was the last time. We linked up again with the long train of British transport all moving imperceptibly north. The great queue of vehicles was still solid as far as the eye could see, and I wondered how many hours we had saved by coming through the forbidden towns.

As we approached the coast the clear blue of the sky on the horizon was darkened by an immense pillar of black smoke that stood up straight from the ground. Someone said it was Dunkirk.

CHAPTER TWENTY-ONE
Dunkirk

IT MUST HAVE been very nearly six o'clock on the morning of Monday the 27th of May when we passed over the hill that hides Dunkirk and saw the town in the distance; the pall of smoke above it came from burning oil tanks on the southern outskirts.

I was to have good cause to be thankful for those oil tanks later, but at the time I deplored the smoke and flame above them as a horrid sign, an omen that our reception and departure would not be quite the orderly affair that I, at any rate, had hoped for. I remembered peacetime Dunkirk as a pleasant place, full of hospitable hotels and shops for buying last-minute continental gifts. To hope that this visit would be quite the same was perhaps too optimistic; but I saw no reason why the whole thing should not be quiet and orderly, rounded off finally by the usual short sea trip to England. The British Navy, everyone knew, was all-powerful. It seemed quite reasonable to hope that an armada of destroyers would stand out to sea, and redress the balance on land by mercilessly shelling any Germans that came near. On catching my first glimpse of the sea that morning I certainly felt relieved; although a confirmed landsman, I felt that, as an Englishman, I was as good as home.

The main bridge over the Canal de Bergues just outside Dunkirk had been damaged by bombing, and during the wait to cross at a smaller one, I talked with some French bystanders. They realised quite well what was happening. I asked them how successfully the evacuation had gone on the previous day.

'The British ships came in to the docks but they got bombed to hell,' one of them replied. 'They all had to go out and wait till dark. I shouldn't think they'll come in at all today.'

This was a nasty shock to those of us who had hoped to get a bath and breakfast in the town and catch a boat after it at about ten o'clock. I mentioned this to the Frenchman.

'Breakfast,' he guffawed. 'You make me laugh. Do you really think that there are any hoteliers or tradespeople left in the town?

Listen to me,' he said confidentially, 'I have just come from near Boulogne. The Germans are there. This port, Dunkirk, is the only one left in British hands, the only one from which your army can get away, do you see? Do you think the Boche is going to leave it alone? Believe me, he isn't. He's going to blast it into a ruin. And don't these people know it?' He pointed at the long line of civilians passing us on the road; they were coming away from Dunkirk. We had become so accustomed to refugees that no-one had given a thought to the direction in which they were going.

'They're clearing out – leaving the place,' he said. 'By noon today there won't be a soul in Dunkirk except the British.' He looked up suddenly at the sky towards the north-east, cocking his ear. I could hear a drone in the distance. It got louder. Then suddenly, out of a cloud not more than three miles away, came the flashing wings of aeroplanes; I had never seen so many aeroplanes together in my life before. There must have been a hundred of them at least, flying perfectly aligned in serried ranks at about five thousand feet. They were coming straight towards us.

My first reaction was to suppose that they were just as likely to be British as German, a foolish supposition, promptly belied by the instinctive rush for cover on the part of everyone around me. The black crosses on the planes soon became distinguishable. People suspected, quite reasonably, that the bridge might be in for a second dose of the former treatment.

I found myself in a trice in a ditch at the side of the road with the Frenchman, not knowing whether to talk or to keep quiet.

'Don't look up,' shouted some know-all. I certainly had no intention of looking up.

Except for the thunderous noise that gradually filled the air there was complete silence on the ground after that first mad scuffle for cover; everyone had found a retreat, the betting was now closed, there was no time to change over position, to put one's money on another horse; all one could do was to remain motionless and hope for luck.

The bombers passed right over us blotting out the sun; and then, distinct from the mighty sound of the engines, came the scream of bombs. There was a crescendo as their noise became almost unbearable. Then a series of small earthquakes seemed to take place in succession all around us. We waited, crouching, for thirty seconds until the thunder began to fade. Then people gradually came out of cover and looked at one another.

'You see what I mean?' said the Frenchman.

I observed what I took to be an elderly Indian Army major getting up from the trench beside me.

'Damned degrading,' he said. His cheeks had quite lost their characteristic healthy colour.

The bridge had been fairly and squarely hit this time, and, except for a few wheels and odd pieces of metal that littered the approaches, the two lorries that had been parked near it had completely disappeared. It was the nearest approach to Maskeleyne and Devants that I had ever come across in reality, four tons of material had simply vanished into thin air in the space of thirty seconds.

The road around us had changed quite appreciably within that last thirty seconds too; it was now strewn with enormous clods of earth, bricks, and bits of vehicles. Whimpering noises came from the ditch on the other side of the road and we started looking for casualties. Another set of screams announced the fall of bombs on Dunkirk itself, half a mile away.

'Goodbye,' said the Frenchman turning to join the stream of refugees now emerging from the ditches and houses. 'And,' he added, almost mischievously, 'good luck.'

In the distance I could just hear the belated Dunkirk air-raid alarm.

As an introduction to Dunkirk so early in the day this seemed impressive but inauspicious. We managed to find another bridge and rather thoughtfully made our way over it into the town towards the office of the embarkation officer; it was rumoured that, without his sanction, it would be impossible to get a boat to England.

There were about fifty officers waiting in the passage outside his room.

'There are another fifty officers inside,' one of them told me. 'The embarkation officer is very busy. You might get an interview in about four hours if you get into the queue.'

I had already had my fill of queues but I prepared to under-go the agony again. I was just about to take my place when a colonel wearing the red armband of the staff came downstairs.

'There's no point in all you people hangin' about,' he said autocratically. 'You might just as well go away and wait in the town and come again this afternoon. The embarkation officer's got his hands full for the morning and you're only cluttering up the place.'

'Any chance of any ships getting in, sir?' asked someone hopefully.

'Ships!' said the colonel. 'Ships! Huh – you'll be lucky if you get a rowing-boat. There may be a fishing smack or two calling in after lunch, but the boys in here,' he indicated the office of the embarkation officer, 'will get first berths.'

When he had gone another officer and I agreed that forced elephantine heartiness under such conditions was quite deplorable. Being keen to get away, we just could not understand the joke; our interests had become completely parochial, a peculiarity that normally is evident only in other people.

'There are lots of cellars in the town,' the colonel continued cheerfully. 'I expect it'll actually be a case of "first come first served" when the boats arrive, but we can't say when that will be. The people nearest the docks should get away first.'

This last remark dispersed everyone at the double in the direction of the docks. Within half an hour, by subtle arrangement, I had my men quite comfortably installed in the cellars of a large house adjoining the docks. There was great competition for all the cellars near the quay, and I only obtained these by making a special agreement with an artillery subaltern who had got there first, and whom I had met once before in Lille.

The sun was shining very brightly when we came up from the cellars into the street in search of food. There was hardly a cloud in the sky and, apart from the pall of smoke which still hung above us, the first day of summer was unmarred. The horizon was a fine sharp line dividing the dark and light blue of sea and sky, stretching from Belgium in the east to Griz-Nez and Boulogne away to the south. We stood at the edge of the quay taking deep breaths of the cool air and looking out to sea for ships, but seeing none. The litter of portmanteaus, trunks, bags, and personal equipment of all kinds on the quay was the only indication that some extraordinary activity was taking place, although it looked no more heroic than the end of a perfect and expensive bank holiday at Margate. There was one pigskin bag with a zip fastener which I admired. Just as I was about to take it I remembered my own baggage; it would be hard enough to get that on board without adding to it.

We turned and headed towards the centre of the town and were immediately accosted by two drunken soldiers.

'Thesh wonderful champagne in thash housh,' said one of them pointing, swaying and hiccuping.

The artillery subaltern grinned at me. 'There are going to be some drunks before the day's out,' he said.

'If we're going to be bombed,' I said, 'I don't particularly want to get drunk, but if it's a question of having a quiet day and a drink before we leave, I'm not averse to a glass of champagne myself, if we can find it.'

It was a miserable hope because at this point the air-raid siren sounded.

'Before the bombers arrive,' said the subaltern admiringly. 'The French must be waking up.'

But the bombers were not far behind and we had to run for the cellars. We arrived just as the noise of the engines was beginning to drown all other sounds. If one had only had time to stop in the streets, an impregnable observer, the spectacle of people literally running for their lives would have been most educative. As it was we dived headlong down the steps.

In those days it was supposed that cellars were a very sure defence against bombs; no bomb, one felt, could penetrate a whole building, it was bound to explode in one of the upper floors. As there were three floors above us in this building we felt fairly secure, and I even stood on this occasion among the breathless crowd listening with an almost detached and scientific interest to the screams and thuds of the bombs as they landed around us.

When it was all over and we came up into the street again, the remains of an enormous building which, before the raid, had been standing foursquare opposite, gave me an unpleasant shock. A bomb had demolished the whole thing; all that remained was a pile of rubble about twenty fee high. Anyone who had taken refuge in its cellar must surely have been buried alive. I think it affected other people in much the same way because I noted the different air that people wore during subsequent bombardments, a sort of strained, apprehensive look. We all winced now at each bomb thud as if it had an almost personal message for us.

As the day wore on the air raids became monotonous. We had one every half-hour and during the morning the docks were badly hit. At the conclusion of each attack we came out, blinking in the strong sunlight, wondering what new change would meet our eyes.

It was not until after midday that I realised what folly it had been to risk staying near the harbour; if ships had come in it might have been justified, but the Germans seemed intent on destroying the docks and people were already leaving them. I suggested to the subaltern that we should choose a new and safer cellar on the outskirts of the town. He agreed, and between raids we made an inspection of all the suitable cellars farther away from the docks. Every one was full; the town was crammed with troops, all evidently obeying the staff officer's instructions to wait in the town for a ship. It would have been quite impossible to have crowded another sixty men in anywhere, so we returned to our cellar and told everybody to hope for the best.

It was a pity we could not have changed for another reason. By midday the cellar was becoming rather smelly, it held sixty men only with difficulty. Many of them did not bother to come up for air during the intervals, and it soon took on that musty, military smell, so much a part of an army. It was not improved by a well-intentioned soldier who had given some foie-gras to one of the stray dogs which had taken refuge with us; it promptly vomited in the corner on somebody's gas mask.

The cellar evidently belonged to a rich man; its foie-gras and champagne formed our staple food and drink. We did our best to dissuade the men from drinking too much champagne but our entreaties had little effect; the catcalls and babbling of the drunkards soon formed a curious and rather sinister accompaniment to the shrieks, whistles, and bangs that went on outside.

The raids generally lasted three or four minutes, a mass of composite and intermingled sound, ranging from the heavy throb of the aeroplane engines to the high-pitched scream of the bombs and the noise of falling bricks. Towards midday the Germans brought in dive-bombers; they dropped smaller bombs and their accuracy was fortunately impaired by the cloud of smoke above the town, but their terror value made them worth their weight in bombs.

The Frenchman's estimate that all the inhabitants of Dunkirk would have left the town was not strictly correct, because we had two women in the cellar with us. They sat huddled in a corner with shawls round their heads, not speaking a word, although several men tried to talk with them. They appeared to be a mother and daughter, and I had assumed, when we arrived, that they had some connection with the house. I had hoped that they would go when the bombing started, but they still stayed on; so I suggested to the older woman that they should leave.

'We are not going to leave the town,' she said determinedly.

'But why remain here when you are not doing any good?' I asked.

'This bombing cannot go on for long,' she replied. 'Besides, the Germans will bomb all the towns and villages anyway. We shall be as badly off wherever we go.'

She did not realise that the whole of the British Army was to be evacuated from Dunkirk and that the bombing would certainly continue for days (for all I knew for weeks and months). It would be unwise to tell her this but I was determined that they should go.

'You must go,' I said. 'It is absurd for women to stay in the town. And I can tell you that this bombing will not stop as you think. It will go on for days – until there is nothing left of the town. You must believe me.'

She seemed to take some notice of this assurance, probably because it came from an officer. She looked at me steadily for some moments.

'When you go, we will go,' she said finally. 'Not before.'

I had frightful visions of having to take the women on the boat when the time came. No amount of further cajoling could convince them of their folly, and, in all conscience, we could not possibly leave them in the cellar when we left. In any case there now seemed so little cause for even considering leaving that I did not pursue the matter.

By four in the afternoon our nerves were becoming a little frayed. One of the NCOs (wearing last-war ribbons) was crying quietly in a corner and several men began to make queer little animal noises – rather like homesick dogs. This was understandable because, as the raids repeated, they seemed to have a sort of cumulative effect on one's system; after a while the mere thought of a raid was far worse than its reality. One became accustomed, and perhaps even indifferent, to the raid itself as time went on; but the prospect or idea of it became less and less tolerable. Sometimes during the intervals one contemplated the next raid with a shudder and a repulsion quite belied by one's attitude, and even behaviour, during it a few minutes later. The two women remained perfectly calm and resigned throughout, a lesson to us all.

Some of the men who went up into the streets during the intervals did not return at the beginning of the next raid and we did not see them again. It was suggested that they had gone to the outskirts of the town in search of better cellars or, more sinister, that they *could* not return; one man I know was killed. I was in the open myself at the time with him; and, after that particular raid, I resolved never to be caught away from the cellar again. There was absolutely no excuse for being caught in the open because the regularity of the raids was typically Teutonic – one could almost tell the time by them.

On this occasion the gunner subaltern and I had visited the front of the docks with a few men. We had heard a rumour that a ship was in, and, on the advice of the colonel, we wanted to book space for our respective parties without delay. The rumour about the ship was, of course, quite unfounded. After twenty minutes' fruitless searching we started to walk back, thinking that we had just sufficient time to reach the cellar for the next raid. The raid came when there still remained another three hundred yards to go, and we were forced to take what cover existed among some empty beer-barrels on the quay.

It was during this raid that the man was killed and, struck by the ghastliness of the sight, I immediately resolved never to be caught in the open again. The barrels, from an ARP point of view, were far from ideal; we lay flat on the ground amongst them, listening to bricks and bits of corrugated iron flying about in the air above, praying, biting our finger-nails, and scratching the ground. One of the bombs that landed near made such a flash and vulgar commotion that I could well believe the testimony of one of the soldiers who said that, for one brief moment as it exploded, he imagined that he saw Satan himself alighting from it. I was interested to know what form he had taken, but he could supply no details.

It seemed to give this soldier fresh confidence afterwards, *vis-à-vis* religion, and he behaved in an appropriate fashion in the cellar. I suppose he thought that if Satan was on the side of the destroyer (the bomb) then Satan's counterpart must be on the side of the destroyee (himself).

As a matter of fact I had been surprised at the absence of religious rites in our cellar. Classical pictures of persons undergoing great physical or emotional stress in wartime always depict a small but devout body of believers on their knees, singing psalms and getting in everyone else's way. When we arrived back on this occasion and announced the death of our colleague the cellar certainly had an almost crypt-like atmosphere, an air of being about to be devotional; I was thankful that there were no cranks with us to exploit it.

'Do you think Churchill's a religious man, sir?' asked one of the men later, I could think of no answer to this peculiar and singularly imbecile question.

Towards four-thirty in the afternoon we heard shouts in the street outside; a cry for 'officers'. We ran up and saw the staff officer I had seen before, sitting on a pile of rubble in the street, talking to a naval officer. This was encouraging and we hoped for the best. Various other army officers appeared down the street picking their way through the debris, all answering the call.

'Gentlemen,' said the staff officer getting up, 'the Navy has decided that it will be impossible to carry out any evacuation from the harbour. The only chance you will therefore have is to wait on the beaches north of the town. I suggest that you collect all the men you can and go there immediately. The smoke is fortunately still blowing northwards, and if you are careful it should be possible to move there without aerial observation by the enemy. Under cover of the dark the Navy have agreed to take off as many men as they can from the beaches in small boats.'

Any hopes we had of an early evacuation were immediately dashed by this because thousands of men were hourly arriving at the port. I wondered how it would be possible to keep any sort of order at all while small parties of men were taken off in rowing-boats. No large ship, one imagined, could possibly approach the shore. One thing was certain – our wait in the dock area had been in vain. If I had only been more detached I might have appreciated the irony of the situation; it truly seemed a case of 'first come, last served'.

We had no difficulty in getting the men together; no-one wanted to stay a minute longer in the cellar now that the pointlessness of the wait was revealed. The two Frenchwomen accompanied us; they were particularly helpful, because they were able to direct me through the outskirts of the town, tortuous under the best conditions, but labyrinthine under these. We frequently had to bypass a street because it was cluttered up with bricks, telegraph wires, fallen-down shop fronts, and burning lorries. Over all hung the misty haze of burnt-out material, limiting visibility to ten or twenty yards. A long crocodile of men followed behind.

As we reached the outskirts of the town another air raid developed; we no longer had the covering which the smoke from the burning oil-tanks gave to the docks, and it now became possible to see a diving aeroplane as well as to hear it. Once again I felt that, had our minds not been clouded with petty doubts and fears, it would have been a most exhilarating performance. As it was, the instinct to shrink into the ground, to become a part of it, was too much for me. After a brief and fleeting glance at the diving aeroplane, I flattened myself out, face downwards, at the bottom of a bomb crater. (We all felt that the odds against a bomb landing in a bomb crater were prodigious.)

The German pilots must have observed the long line of men coming from the town because, after dropping their bombs, they turned about, and made a low-level machine-gunning attack on us as we crouched in our holes. The officially advocated behaviour of standing up and firing a Bren gun at the aeroplane, even when it is on top of you, was put into practice by two of our men who were both promptly riddled with bullets. The aeroplane was apparently undamaged but, as the authorities optimistically point out, 'you never can tell'. When the process was repeated later in the afternoon by another intrepid Bren gunner, he was told afterwards that he had hit the plane and that it had crashed two miles south of Dunkirk. The trouble about shooting at aeroplanes is that you can never see the results of your own handiwork.

When the raid was over we continued our erratic progress towards the beach, the two Frenchwomen still walking with me at the head. Behind us the town still continued to crackle, and to the sound of the burning was now added the staccato noise of ammunition exploding, while red and yellow flames leapt up above the house-tops giving the whole place a most diabolical appearance; we were heartily thankful to be away from it. Someone cheerily pointed out that, with the approach of evening, it was reasonable to hope for a cessation of the bombing.

As we turned the corner of the wood that gave on to the beaches I realised how difficult the evacuation would be, because the long beaches running north as far as the eye could see were now crowded with men. There were thousands of them; they had arrived after us and had evidently made no attempt to get into the town. Now they simply sat in groups at the high-water end of the beach, looking forlornly out towards the monotonous unbroken line of the horizon. Some were eating and some were sleeping, but the industrious ones, in preparation for the next raid, were already digging little pits with whatever improvised tools they possessed; here and there were readymade pits, bomb craters already full of soldiers; and down at the water's edge I saw the only hopeful sign – two naval officers talking with an army staff officer.

We made our way along the edge of the beach looking for a suitable waiting-place and I noticed an officer leading a bevy of men towards me; he asked me if I would include another thirty men in my party. As we had already shrunk from forty to twenty, I readily consented.

'Here they are,' he said to me. 'Will you please stand here so that they can see you?' he motioned me to a patch of sunlight. 'Now remember his face,' he said to the men. 'Take a good look at it and don't go away from it.' The chosen few looked at me sheepishly.

He went off, followed by his depleted band of bedraggled men, and I heard him repeating the formula further down the beach to another officer. 'Would you stand up, please, so that they can see you?... remember his face...' etc., etc.

It was a good sign, an indication that some sort of order at any rate was going to be kept on the beaches. What one really feared was a mob of people all out of control and all prepared to rush the first boat that came in; I knew the power of such instincts because by now I felt them at work in my own mind.

About two miles from the town we found our billet, a little hollow in the sand-dunes at the edge of the beach. Here we settled, another handful of men among the thousands around us, all waiting like ourselves for a boat or for the next raid.

An hour later, to the accompaniment of what we all hoped would be the last set of bangs and crashes in Dunkirk, the sun set brilliantly out in the sea. Never before could a sunset have been awaited with such longing and hope; like the cloud of smoke that had saved us in the town, it seemed that this sunset would save us on the beaches. We had watched its progress minutely; every detail peculiar to sunsets had impressed itself upon us; no sun worshipper, not even Turner himself, could ever have taken more pains in observing it than we took during that last half-hour.

'Thank God for that,' said someone as it finally disappeared. And then we settled down in our holes, pulled our overcoats a little tighter because it was getting cold, and all tried to forget that such things as aeroplanes had ever existed.

During the last two raids the Germans had, in spite of the numbers of men on the beaches, concentrated only upon the town; they had been using mainly fire-bombs and it was not until some of these were dropped on a nearby farmhouse, setting it ablaze, that we realised their full significance: a sergeant was the first to put the hateful thought into words.

'They're setting the place alight so that they can be guided in the dark,' he said suddenly. We had all realised this by now but no-one else had been quite so tactless as to point it out, and there was some sarcastic comment.

'We'd better get away from these houses, sir,' said the sergeant ignoring the men's remarks and pointing to the burning farm buildings.

He was quite right of course because within half an hour of the sunset we heard again in the distance the busy, droning sound that we had all been trying to forget. The town was now a magnificent target; it lit up the scene for miles around like a giant bonfire. Although it was fully a mile away, people's faces flickered in the glow as at a fireside. No sound came from the thousands of men on the beaches now that they realised what was about to happen; they had stopped talking and smoking cigarettes (one of the signs of confidence that the sunset had brought). They sat stolidly and silently listening to the growing noise.

As the aeroplanes passed overhead the sky became suddenly lit up from above by a brilliant mercury-like glare. The 'flare' was a new thing to most of us then; for all we knew that night it was the 'secret weapon'; it might explode in the air or it might even exude a new gas (and I had lost my gas mask); it hung there in the air with a naked-making effect that was terrifying; one felt completely revealed to the aeroplane for what one was – a British soldier stranded like a fish on a beach waiting for final extinction.

'Don't move. Keep absolutely still,' shouted someone imperatively as a half-movement, a tremor of fear, seemed to shake through the masses of men on the beaches. The speaker was perfectly justified because, under such circumstances, one has an instinctive and quite illogical desire to go somewhere else, it does not matter particularly where, anywhere will do so long as one can get away from one's present spot, which is obviously where the bomb is going to land.

His command seemed to steady us and we lay quiet and motionless watching our own shadows slowly lengthen on the beach while the flare, with infuriating delay, fluttered gently down to earth. It landed quite near and extinguished itself with a sort of hen-like clucking sound in the soft sand; it seemed an anti-climax.

But out of the silence that followed it came, with sickening gusto, the scream of bombs. They landed all around and in the shower of sand that came down with all the force of hail upon me I forgot where I was, and then for what must have been thirty seconds I lay dazed, my mind only half-working.

The RSM brought me to life by asking me if I had any food; I replied that I had none, whereupon he kindly offered to share his own 'iron ration' with me. An 'iron ration' looks, feels, and tastes like a brick. But I enjoyed it; it gave me something to stop my teeth from chattering. No-one was hurt close to us, the only bomb that had been near having landed on open beach, but further away people were scurrying to and fro searching in the sand.

'Some killed over there,' said the RSM jerking his thumb in their direction and putting another lump of chocolate into his mouth.

The air raids continued like this throughout the night. Although not so concentrated as they had been during the day, they gave us less respite; there was almost always an aeroplane overhead; its sound never ceased. The most picturesque but most fearful moment occurred when the whole sky overhead was momentarily lit up by a brilliant red and yellow flash, followed immediately by a sound that seemed to be the crack of doom, a sound that completely dwarfed anything that we had heard before; eardrums felt as if they would crack under the violent pressure waves. And then, out of the sky, things began to fall; first came heavy objects which landed beside us and buried themselves deep in the sand. Because there was no explosion we thought that they must be time-bombs and we crouched lower waiting for them to explode. Then lighter, smaller objects began to fall and it was not until the whole sky around us became luminous, full of little falling incandescent morsels which lit up the beach like a Japanese garden, shining and flickering like tinsel, that one's immediate and habitual suspicion about secret weapons was dispelled. Someone suddenly realised what it all meant and announced it cheerily; and then everyone cheered. The bombs in an aeroplane had exploded in mid-air; the French AA gunners had hit something at last and the various parts of the aeroplane had fallen, at intervals dependent on their respective gravities.

'But perhaps it was a British plane,' someone suddenly suggested.

There was a chorus of disapproval at this, the man being immediately and properly silenced; he had no right to question our optimism. 'The first nice noise of the day,' said the RSM.

CHAPTER TWENTY-TWO
The Beaches

'Les parfums du printemps le sable les ignore
Voici mourir le Mai dans les dunes du Nord.'

– from *La Nuit de Dunkerque*, by Aragon

THE DUNKIRK BEACHES are broad and shelving and the tide moves fast upon them. When we arrived just before dusk the water had been closer, but by midnight, when we reached the edge of the dunes, the sea had gone out. In front of us the little figures moving about with lanterns at the water's edge three hundred yards away, seemed to have become much smaller; in the deceptive light of the burning houses they sometimes disappeared altogether. But we seldom looked away from them, towards the darkness where the beaches disappeared on our right, or the brightness where they met Dunkirk on our left; we generally looked ahead. It was more encouraging.

The beaches stretched away on either side, their evenness only broken by the long queues of soldiers that had now formed up at intervals, every few hundred yards along the beach. Most of the men were sitting down, but sometimes one of them would stand up and look out to sea.

'How long do you think it'll take to get there, sir?' asked one of the men. I looked at my watch; it was just past midnight.

'A couple of hours,' I said. I might just as well have said a couple of days. I had not the remotest idea how long it would take. The evacuation depended upon too many incalculable factors for that – upon the number of boats lying out there in the bay – were there two, or were there two hundred? It depended upon the speed with which the boats operated; upon the speed with which the Luftwaffe operated, with which it destroyed the boats before they could reach the water's edge – and, I suddenly reflected, the speed with which the Luftwaffe destroyed us before we could reach the water's edge. A lot might happen before we took our places in the boats.

But my answer seemed to satisfy him and I heard him repeating it to the others. I felt pleased that I had given an answer at all – any answer is better than none in such circumstances. The day in Dunkirk had taught me that the great problem for an army in action is not, as I had always supposed, of whether the soldiers do as they are told or not, of whether they obey orders or not. It is much more the problem of whether they get any orders at all, of whether anyone is prepared to give them any or not. All the soldier craves is information and instruction; he eagerly does what he is told because he has lost all power of making up his own mind. For my own part, I can testify that it is extremely easy to forget everything except the urgent question of one's own survival; the question of giving orders is quite dwarfed by it. Hence my delight in having been able to say something.

It was for this reason that we fully appreciated the little major who suddenly took it into his head to run up and down the queue, talking nonsense interminably.

'Now, boys, don't get rattled,' he would say, when some particularly odious sound had startled us. 'It's all going to come all right. The Navy is coming. Keep quite still when the aeroplanes are overhead – and above all, keep your peckers up. Remember the Navy is coming.'

In retrospect it seems to me that he said all this to keep his *own* pecker up; but at the time he seemed a leader of men, a *'brave des braves,'* an Olympian, a god – although he was only five feet eight and wore spectacles.

Each time he came down the line – and he did so roughly every ten minutes – he had some new and optimistic piece of information to give. His visits were eagerly awaited.

'Yes – they're sending rowing-boats. Large ones. Very large ones – naval cutters. Room for about a hundred in each boat,' he said on one occasion. We could not gauge the inaccuracy of this statement at the time, of course. But another time, even as he spoke, fact gave the lie to what he said.

'Yes,' he said, as he crouched near us. 'The British fighters destroyed two hundred German bombers this afternoon. You didn't know that, did you?' All his questions were rhetorical so no-one bothered to reply. He suddenly cocked his ear towards the sky; a highly suspicious noise, as of a diving aeroplane, could be heard immediately above us. We all lay down instinctively.

'Don't be silly,' he said standing up. 'That's a Spitfire. Good old Spitfires – defending us as usual. Trust the Spitfires.' I thought he was going to take his hat off and wave to it.

The RSM estimated afterwards that the diving aeroplane fired a burst of about three hundred bullets at us at this point. They landed all around; but the little major, to his eternal credit, completely ignored them. Maybe he thought they were just the salutation of a Spitfire. Leadership may be defined as 'the ability and determination to tell lies in the face of the enemy'.

We all had one idea now, one impulse – we only wanted to reach the water's edge and be rowed away quietly into the night like King Arthur. This impulse could be seen in the men's eyes; it could be felt in their movements as slowly, too slowly, they crawled forward to take more advanced places in the queue. But unfortunately, as we advanced towards safety we also advanced towards danger, because the bombing was more intense near the sea. The German dive-bombers, coming down through the smoke and flame, could easily distinguish the groups at the water's edge, where the human arteries that straggled across the beaches thickened out into little bunches of crouching men – bunches that evidently formed excellent targets. We began to realise that our goal offered us everything to gain but also everything to lose.

The head of the queue received a near miss from a heavy bomb when we were half-way across the beach, and some of the soldiers immediately began debating amongst themselves about retiring to the relative safety of the sand-dunes. Already others were leaving the queue in front of us and running away towards the rear.

'You'll lose your places,' shouted the RSM 'It's not worth it.'

I was about to crawl along the line to advise our men not to abandon their hard-earned places when the RSM shouted, 'Lie down everybody. Don't move.' He was looking northward along the coast, and as I lay down my eyes followed his gaze.

A German aeroplane flying at about a hundred feet was coming towards us along the beach; in the yellow light it looked like a prehistoric bird out of a children's fairy tale. It was moving so fast that it seemed to reach us before its noise. Just before I ducked I saw the head of the pilot silhouetted against the sky behind, and I noticed the thin, black line of the wings. Four little patches of yellow, symmetrically placed on either side of the cockpit, suddenly flashed out towards us from the wings. The pause before the bullets arrived seemed very long; during it I remembered that if the focus of fire of all four machine-guns coincides with the target, large bombers are said to disintegrate like chaff. The aeroplane was flying straight towards us and I wondered where the focus would be.

A violent disturbance took place in the sand twenty or thirty yards in front of me, and the aeroplane disappeared in the direction of the Dunkirk flames, leaving behind only its noise, and a cloud of sand above the beach where the bullets had landed. It had all happened so quickly that the RSM still appeared to be in the middle of his warning sentence; he was still warning us not to move when a cry further up the beach announced that one of the men had been hit.

'Has anyone got a field dressing?' someone called.

We ran over. Fortunately the bullet had hit him in the leg; it had gone right through below the knee and blood was coming out on both sides. We made a tourniquet and bandaged the wound. Most of the bullets had landed wide of the queue, and this man, probably the victim of a ricochet, was the only casualty.

'We'd better get him back,' said the RSM.

'No,' said the wounded man firmly. 'I can't feel it. I'm staying here. I'm not losing my place.'

But he had little say in the matter because two medical orderlies ran over to us, examined his wound, and then escorted him away towards the sea where bomb splashes were still appearing. Sometimes, as a result of the bombing, the group at the head of the queue would break up in confusion – only to re-assemble immediately.

We were nearer now and I could see what was keeping them together. A rowing-boat manned by two sailors had approached the beach, and soldiers, up to their waists in water, were scrambling into it. At the head of the queue, in charge of the loading, was a naval officer. The boat, laden with men hanging on to one another like swarming bees, would disappear into the darkness – only to return empty a quarter of an hour later for its next consignment. This consisted of another twenty men who had been selected in the meantime by the naval officer – a selection that always gave rise to much jealousy among the candidates. The naval officer, in order to avoid a rush, segregated the selected men each time; and they stood up to their knees in water, a few yards away from the others. After doing this he would turn and face the sea, ready to signal to the rowing-boat when it returned, so that it might easily identify the queue it was serving.

As soon as his back was turned the little group of selected men would begin to grow larger; gradually at first – perhaps two or three men from the head of the queue would slip away unnoticed into the sea and join it; then another two or three men would follow suit, then perhaps a bunch of five, then more – until finally the group in the sea seemed almost to have doubled in size. From our position at one of the bends in the straggling queue I could see all this happening about fifty yards away. On one occasion the officer turned abruptly towards the beach and caught two men red-handed as they slipped away from the queue and joined the men in the sea,

'If another man comes out of turn I'll shoot him,' I heard him announce. A growl went up from the men at this. Whether out of sympathy with what he said or whether in open rebellion I could not say; one's attitude depended, I supposed, on whether one had already been selected or not.

The naval officer had now been at his post, the most important and the most dangerous on the beach, for at least two hours, continually preventing the one thing that would have ruined all our chances – a rush for the boats. Once I saw a man suddenly rush past him out of turn. Immediately a determined shout went up from the other men who were in front of him in the queue.

'Get out. Get back, you bastard. Have him back. Have him back, the swine.'

There was no mistaking their tone. The man failed to reach the boat which was now putting out to sea. He shrank back, immediately forgotten and unobserved, into the queue. This incident, perhaps because it was forgotten so quickly, perfectly illustrated our singleness of mind. In our urgency we forgot things as quickly as animals, we had the memories of monkeys.

I looked at my watch again. Another hour had passed and we now seemed to be making better progress.

'Getting used to the noises, sir?' said the RSM, as he lay by my side; he was doing his best to be light-hearted.

'I think so,' I said doubtfully. It was true that the past twenty-four hours had made us so familiar with bomb-screams that it was now quite possible to estimate their nearness. We now no longer lay down at the sound of a bomb falling on Dunkirk a mile away; we instinctively knew how close it was.

'How many men have gone back to the dunes, do you think?' I asked, looking over my shoulder.

'Only two or three,' he replied. 'They're nearly all here. We'll get them off all right.' I admired his calm; it was pleasant to talk to someone who was so confident.

The sand was damp below high-water mark and I soon noticed that my clothes were wet. It showed just how close to the ground I had been keeping, an attitude that was now evidently as damping as it was degrading. Some men, in their attempts to lie low, had dug little hollows for themselves; they used their rifles, their boots and sometimes simply their hands to dig. Like bees they seldom benefited from their labour because the queue moved on. Whereupon, as indefatigable as bees, they merely renewed their efforts on a fresh piece of sand. They seemed to be perpetually scraping little holes for other people to occupy.

'Burning mighty pretty,' said one of the men to me suddenly; he was looking south towards Dunkirk. The centre of the town was on fire; yellow flames, twice as high as the houses, licked up into the cloud above – a combination of yellow and black that seemed to throw off a rainbow effect, as if other colours were generated by it. Along the dunes behind us the yellow flames sometimes gave place to a dull, glowing red, where a pile of embers now marked the site of a house.

In the excitement of the queue we had ignored these fascinating colours. It was only now that I noticed the effects they produced on the sand. Looking northwards along the beaches, the sand, like a white dress in a variety show, reproduced whatever colour shone upon it. Near the burning houses it flickered red and yellow; where incendiary bombs had fallen it glowed green; and in the light of a parachute flare it had turned violet. Only the men on the beaches did not change; whatever the neighbouring colour they remained black.

'Only another hour now,' shouted the RSM to the men behind; their spirits were picking up and conversation had begun again.

At this point, when for the first time there really seemed a chance of getting away before morning, a disaster occurred in which we had no part. Out in the bay the destroyer which was serving our queue, whose boats were picking up our men and whose officers were superintending our evacuation, received a direct hit from a bomb and sank. This was announced by a tremendous flash out at sea. At the time, of course, it conveyed nothing to us. But after a wait of half an hour without the regular visits of the rowing-boats we began to realise that something was wrong. One of the men in the queue announced it for us:

'No boats. Where are the boats? What's wrong? Why aren't we going on?'

The naval officer, who had been waiting patiently at the water's edge, heard this hysterical cry and quickly took control. He turned towards our queue which still stretched back to the sand-dunes, and cupped his hands to his mouth.

'Listen, everybody,' he shouted. 'I think the destroyer's been sunk. But I've just been told that big boats are now going into Dunkirk harbour. The tide's turned and they'll soon be able to get up to the mole and take people off. I advise you all to go to the mole. It's no use waiting here unless you join another queue.'

These words affected people in different ways. Those who had been on the point of leaving the queue before, took advantage of them to run off in the direction of the sand-dunes and Dunkirk; we did not follow them because we had already spent the day in Dunkirk and we had no intention of ever visiting it again. Some, the more optimistic, ran down to the water's edge and peered out into the bay; while others, like ourselves, who found only cold comfort in his advice, broke up into little discussion groups.

'I'm for staying here and trying to pick up another boat,' said the RSM. 'New boats will keep coming in now – we ought to be able to signal to one of them. But I'm dammed if I'm going to join another queue.'

I thought that new boats would, as the naval officer had forecast, go to Dunkirk harbour, but I did not say so. I looked at my watch; it was nearly four o'clock. We had been on the beach nearly five hours. Bangs, crashes, and aeroplane noises were still going on all around us; and overhead was a parachute flare. It was a difficult decision. But one of the men voiced the general feeling.

'Hell,' he said, turning to the RSM 'I'm with you. We've been on this bloody beach four hours. I'm not leaving now.'

And so it was settled. Those who wanted to go back to Dunkirk could; the remainder stayed with us, and took their chance. About thirty men stayed; and together, now unobstructed by the queue, we went down to the sea.

There were several bomb craters at the water's edge, now filling up like children's seaside excavations as the tide came in. Perhaps because we were now no longer at the head of a queue, or perhaps just because we were lucky, we seemed to avoid the bombs in our new position. At the other queue heads, where boats were still arriving, we could see and hear them exploding.

After half an hour of standing up to our knees in water someone spotted a rowing-boat about fifty yards out in the bay.

'There's a boat there,' he cried. 'It's only half full. It's rowing away.' We shouted at it without success.

'I'm going after it,' said a soldier. He threw off his coat and boots and began swimming out to sea. He must have been a good swimmer because five minutes later we saw the half-laden boat returning in our direction.

'There they are,' I heard someone cry from the boat and I recognised the swimmer's voice. There was a man in charge at the helm.

'Room for ten,' he said. 'Quickly. Who's coming?'

'We've got thirty here,' I said. 'Can you come back?'

'The trawler's full,' he said, pointing over his shoulder. 'This is our last journey. Hurry.'

'Please,' I said. 'Please try to make one more trip. There will be another twenty men here waiting for you if you do.'

While we were arguing ten of my men had got into his boat. Another ten were trying to climb in too.

'Here, blast you,' said the man at the helm. 'Can't you keep your men in order? Get off. Keep off,' he said, savagely hitting out with an oar at one of them. 'Do you want to sink us?' The boat was certainly overloaded now. At the other end, another uninvited soldier who had climbed in by means of the painter was grappling with one of the oarsmen. The RSM was doing his best to keep the others in order. I apologised for our eagerness and once more entreated the helmsman to return.

'I'll see,' he said gruffly. 'Let go. We must go now. Wait here.' His last words held promise. He pushed the boat off with his oar; it disappeared into the night and we found ourselves waiting once again alone on the beach, unconsciously advancing in our anxiety further and further into the sea, so that at one point I suddenly realised with a start that the water was already up to my waist.

Twenty minutes later we were delighted to see the boat returning; the man had kept his promise. There were two oarsmen in it; we quickly took our places beside them and they began to pull away from the beaches. The helmsman seemed quite unconcerned by it all. I was pleased to see that he had forgotten his former grievance.

'I expect you'll be glad to get away,' he said. I tried to thank him for returning to fetch us.

'That's OK,' he said. 'My mate and me run a trawler. We don't take no notice of them naval fellows.' He jerked his thumb in the direction of the harbour presumably referring to the Royal Navy. In a dim way I realised that the Navy had saved us after all; he had only returned out of some obscure desire to spite them.

After five minutes a small trawler appeared out of the darkness. A man was standing on the deck with a signalling lamp.

'Here we are, Jim,' shouted our helmsman. He turned to us. 'Now out you get,' he said, 'there'll be just about room for you – and no more. We aren't taking any more.'

We scrambled up a gangway and found the decks of the trawler already crowded with soldiers. Some were leaning over the sides, looking at the beach three-quarters of a mile away, but most of them lay asleep on the decks. Apart from an occasional bang from the guns of nearby ships it seemed very quiet after the beaches.

'Come down to the engine room,' said the helmsman. 'You can dry your clothes down there – and meet my mate.'

We descended a steep ladder into the engine-room, and, in an atmosphere of sweat, steam, and oil, I undressed completely and hung my things over an improvised clothesline. The mate was standing in front of the engines in a dirty singlet and dungarees, a cigarette hanging from his lips. He grinned when he saw me.

'Hallo, Bill,' he said to the helmsman.

'They're all aboard,' said Bill. 'Let's get going. There's no more room.'

'Can't go,' said the mate – he jerked his finger in the direction of Dunkirk. 'Jim's just got a message from them by signal lamp. We've got to go into the harbour to pick up more. The destroyers can't go in yet. They draw too much. These blokes,' he pointed at us, 'are going to a destroyer.'

'Cor blast 'em,' said Bill. 'Who the hell do they think they are – ordering us about? Bloody Navy!'

'Oh, come off it, Bill,' said his mate. 'We come 'ere to help, don't we? We're under their orders, aren't we?'

Bill seemed to see the sense of this and he went on deck, only to reappear immediately.

'Jim says destroyer's coming alongside now,' he said. 'All the soldiers to go off now. Come on, you boys,' he said to the few soldiers drying their clothes like myself in the engine-room. 'Up on deck. You're going to meet the bloody Navy.'

I hastily bundled together my dripping clothes and went on deck again; wondering when we should ever reach the final stage of our journey; as I arrived on deck the trawler gave a lurch, announcing that another vessel had come alongside. It was the destroyer, just visible in the reflected light from the beaches; I could see the clean lines of its decks gleaming ten or fifteen feet above. Together with the other soldiers I climbed up a gangway on to the destroyer, naked but still tightly clasping my wet clothes. The transfer had taken place so quickly that I had not even been able to say goodbye to my new friends on the trawler.

The ships parted and I found myself looking down onto Bill; he was standing, legs apart, on the deck of the trawler, staring up at us as he slowly receded into the darkness. An officer with a megaphone stood beside me. He raised it to his lips.

'*Vivacious* calling,' he shouted. 'Are you sure you're OK to go into Dunkirk harbour, Trawler Master?'

'Yes,' replied Bill. 'All OK. All OK, *Vivacious*.'

I marvelled at his politeness to a member of the Royal Navy.

The trawler gradually disappeared into the night. I tried to find out its name from one of the sailors, but he could not help me.

'Hundreds of them small craft here tonight,' he said. 'You can't tell which is which.'

We stood shivering on the deck until someone shouted, 'Everyone below'; they evidently wanted the decks cleared. We shuffled off towards a hatch, which led us down to the seamen's quarters, a long dormitory full of pipes, tables, and hammocks. Thirty or forty men were sitting at the tables, eating cake and drinking tea; they looked as tired, as dirty, and as happy as we were. They talked and laughed as they ate. They wore a variety of clothes: vests, pyjamas, singlets, battle-dress, grey trousers – all dirty and all sweaty. Some people had got into the hammocks and one soldier, his head lolling drunkenly out, was already asleep.

Room was immediately made at a table for the newcomers and we were offered food and drink. The cake and tea tasted excellent.

'How long before we leave?' asked one of the soldiers eagerly.

'Oh, you're all right now,' said a sailor, seeing his anxiety. 'No need to worry now. You're in the Navy now. You'll be OK.'

He summed up an attitude. To most of us the destroyer was as good as home; the half-mile of water that now separated us from the beaches might have been as wide as the English Channel or the North

Sea. Although we were only in Dunkirk Bay we seemed to have left France completely. I suspected that the anxious soldier had had a very bad time on the beach, because he refused to be reassured.

'How about torpedoes?' he asked.

'We don't worry about torpedoes,' replied the sailor. 'Submarines don't trouble us in this war. Only the aeroplanes sometimes. But we'll be in England before dawn – before they can get at us. Why – when I was in Plymouth in February, when the *Exeter* came back...'

I had meanwhile climbed into a hammock where, lulled and comforted by this news about submarines, I fell asleep. It could not have been more than a few minutes before I was woken by someone shouting:

'There's an Army officer here – an officer come off the beach. He's wanted in the wardroom.'

I turned over, hoping I would not be observed. But someone must have pointed me out, because he came straight over to my hammock and touched his hat.

'Commander's compliments, sir, and will you go along to the wardroom? The officers are there.'

I got out, collected my clothes, tied my shirt around my waist and followed him.

Everyone was drinking in the wardroom. About twenty officers, as dirty and as strangely dressed as the men I had just left, were all talking at once. There was only one naval officer among them.

'... and then the roof fell in,' one of them kept on saying. '... it fell in and I lost all my kit. You see it caught fire.' No-one seemed to be listening to him; they all had their own stories to tell.

The air was full of smoke. I sat down in a chair, wishing it had been a hammock. The naval officer came over, shook my hand and put a huge glass of gin into it. He noticed the shirt around my waist.

'Here, come to my cabin,' he said. 'I'll lend you some clothes. Put those wet ones outside the door to be dried.'

He led me to his cabin where he gave me some flannel trousers. He saw I was tired and offered me his bed to sleep on. The last thing I remember was the photograph of his wife on his dressing table: she was wearing her presentation dress, and she would not keep still, because the AA fire on the deck made everything vibrate.

I was woken by men cheering on deck. The ship now seemed to be stationary so I went into the wardroom. It was empty and the clock over the mantelpiece said seven o'clock. I ran up the gangway on to the deck to find the sun shining brightly on shipping at rest in a harbour. Across the water was Dover Castle. Our ship was moored against the quay and soldiers were already going down the gangways and mixing with English civilians.

As they left they picked up their clothes from a pile on the deck; the clothes had been dried in the engine-room. I found everything except my trousers, but I soon gave up searching for them because, judging from the appearance of the other scarecrows walking down the gangway, I would not be out of place in my grey flannels; I forgot entirely that they did not belong to me. Five minutes later I went down the gangway on to the quay.

In this way it ended. People told me afterwards that I was fortunate to have undergone such a great experience. A girl at a dance said I ought to feel proud of having been at Dunkirk; and a politician once patted me on the back and congratulated me. Thousands had certainly enjoyed it, while tens of thousands had heartily detested it. Some looked upon it as an Olympian experience, while others considered it a vulgar brawl. Many were indifferent; some I know would just as soon have been reading a novel under a tree, and the London stage, holding one of its mirrors up to nature, saw only two things at Dunkirk:

'The *noise*, my dear! And the *people*!...'

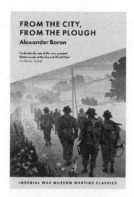

ISBN 9781912423071

£8.99

'Alexander Baron's *From the City, From the Plough* is undoubtedly one of the very greatest British novels of the Second World War and provides the most honest and authentic account of front line life for an infantryman in North West Europe.'

ANTONY BEEVOR

ISBN 9781912423163

£8.99

'Few other novels of the war describe the grinding claustrophobia, violence and lethal danger of being in a tank crew with the stark vividness of Peter Elstob... a forgotten classic that deserves to be read and read.'

JAMES HOLLAND

ISBN 9781912423095

£8.99

'Takes you straight back to Blitzed London... boasts everything a great whodunit should have, and more.'

ANDREW ROBERTS

ISBN 9781912423378
£8.99

'A highly unusual war novel with several
confluent narratives; moving, interesting
and of great literary value.'
LOUIS de BERNIÈRES

ISBN 9781912423156
£8.99

'When a man has been a soldier and
seen action, he writes of war with true
understanding, and with authority. When
that man writes with with, elegance and
imagination, as Fred Majdalany does in
Patrol, he produces a military masterpiece.'
ALLAN MALLINSON

ISBN 9781912423088
£8.99

'A tremendous rediscovery of a
brilliant novel. Extremely well-written,
its effects are both sophisticated
and visceral. Remarkable.'
WILLIAM BOYD

ISBN 9781912423101
£8.99

'Much more than a novel'

RODERICK BAILEY

'I loved this book, and felt I was really there'

LOUIS de BERNIÈRES

'One of the greatest adventure stories of the Second World War'

ANDREW ROBERTS

ISBN 9781912423279
£8.99

'A hidden masterpiece, crackling with authenticity'

PATRICK BISHOP

'Supposedly fiction, but these pages live – and so, for a brief inspiring hour, do the young men who lived in them.'

FREDERICK FORSYTH

ISBN 9781912423262
£8.99

'Witty, warm and hugely endearing... a lovely novel'

AJ PEARCE

'Evokes the highs and lows, joys and agonies of being a Land Girl'

JULIE SUMMERS